Into the Fracking Fields

By Steven W. Simon

Fourth Edition, February 2023

979-8-3484-8166-7

www.boundharepress.com

For Mom, Dad, and Elyse.

Part 1

1

The trees had yet to bud, though the air felt as if they should any day now. The evening sun was descending. An aged minivan roared with rusted exhaust pipes, followed it west, slowed, and disappeared down a desolate side street. A church stood, paint peeling from its white steeple and wood façade. The brick faded at its base. 'Last home-cooked meal before Fields,' in black block letters were stuck upon a tipped over sign laying among the weeds and dirt near the street. Behind the sign was an abandoned diner that anchored a strip of stores—each with dusty windows and adorned with signs announcing lease opportunities, a phone number. Some of the windows were shattered, open to the elements, and a few were boarded up. Each shuttered save for a liquor store at the west end with its flashing neon welcome.

A dented white pickup truck was parked in front of the forgotten diner with wheels set upon the weeds that peeked through the cracked pavement and loose gravel. The doors were swung open to expose the speakers that provided a soundtrack for two teenage boys as they sat on the downturned gate of the bed and faced the quiet of Main Street.

"C'mon," Carmen started as he made circles with his BMX bike around the truck, the little bits of gravel crunched under the tires, "you got a thirty pack." He was black with thick hair that sat rounded about his head two inches high. Chubby, rosy cheeks and lips full in that oddity of growth between elementary and middle school whereas the rest of his body was thin. He wore a black hoodie with the zipper pulled up, faded blue jeans, and aged Adidas.

"Screw you," Dorian responded briskly without looking from the pickup truck. His hair was identical to his younger brother's, deep midnight, firm yet forgiving. They sipped on cans of Natural Ice from the case that sat between them on the bed while the Oldies radio station played Guns 'n Roses at a reasonable volume.

"We'll share it, Johnnie, it's just one," Alice bargained with her own older brother, with whom she shared the same freckled features. Her auburn hair bounced, pulled tight in a ponytail between her shoulder blades. The pale pink t-shirt loose to hide her changes. Jeans snipped just above her knees with kitchen shears. Scuffed sandals, failing Velcro against the pedals as she maneuvered her blue bike counter to Carmen.

Johnnie chugged his beer then tossed the empty can behind him, and it bounced a few times before settling on the metal bed frame. He took another from the box, flipped the tab, and took a sip. Carmen scowled at the perceived slight, but with the sound of engines, he turned his attention to Main Street. His friends set their feet on the pavement and steadied the bicycles. Johnnie held his beer, while Dorian slid his can behind his back.

Three patrol cars zoomed down Main Street from the west and moved fast into the parking lot across the street from the dilapidated strip. Another two moved in from the east. Heavy on the breaks and the cars created a perimeter, with three cars centered in the lot and two cars near both entrances.

Two officers exited from each car with purpose, each Caucasian with a short beard and in navy-blue with a badge over Kevlar. Armed with handguns, tasers, and handcuffs, they took up positions near the edge of a curb along the station platform that faced the train tracks. Their shotguns held firmly with both hands, they stood and waited. Near the aged brick station with dusty windows lined with paper signs yellowed at the corners, the padlocked restrooms, and the aura of abandonment. They stood and readied for action, as it was all they knew. Across Main Street, the teenagers watched from the truck bed, the younger from idle bicycles, and the ground murmured. Rocked the pickup truck and nudged the police cars. Carmen and Alice applied the brakes and set their feet on the pavement. Any other reaction to the tremor was imperceptible.

The Texas Eagle's horns blared east of the station, and the large wheels of each car impressed upon the steel track. An Amtrak in silver metal interspersed with blue and red. Aptly named for originating in Chicago, south through Illinois, Alabama, then west through Mississippi to its namesake and then continuing to Los Angeles. The Eagle had, many years ago, tracked south through

Arkansas and west the length of Texas. Now the track lay idle through The Fields. Abandoned, it comingled with weeds, parts that jutted at odd angles, with its rotted wood and scarred oxidizing metal.

Slower still, and The Eagle jolted forward, its soul needed to make a statement. The brakes hissed, squealed, and subsided as the train came to rest at the platform. Several tense seconds elapsed, then a dozen more. Finally, the officers heard the hydraulics release and watched the gray doors slide open and clunk into position.

An officer appeared in the door from the dark recess. Dark skin drawn taught with pursed, serious lips and focused eyes under an officer's cap. His large, muscular frame overlaid with a uniform pressed and olive-green. He stepped down from the train car and took up position to the side of the door, his shotgun held firmly and ready.

"Down the stairs," the officer commanded, "to your left and the first one stops at the last officer. Single File!"

The men emerged single file from the darkened interior and into the sunlight. They were young, and while each varied in size and race, they all wore white shirts with "D.O.C."

and "CAMP A" printed with matching white pants. Their hands were set about their groins and secured with white zip handcuffs. Their left wrists were adorned with a bright red bracelet, a half-inch in width, pulled taut which blinked intermittently with a small green LED light. The bracelets had their names in digital next to a set of numbers and then scrolled with more information. They were curious about the new surroundings and all noticed the teenagers and kids on bicycles across Main Street.

The men formed a line facing the navy-blue clad officers, and last out of the car was an officer in olive-green that matched his colleague. He was equally large, yet less threatening with pale skin and a gut that covered his belt and hid the top of his pants. He stood for a moment at the base of the stairs with his shotgun, then turned and disappeared into the train. His colleague followed shortly.

With a clunk the train doors closed. With a jolt, the Texas Eagle lurched out of the station, and the men dressed in white stood and faced the officers in navy-blue. They were docile as the senior officer motioned for his men to take several steps back from the curb as if he was uncomfortable with the proximity.

The quiet remained as the train's engine receded. A car drove down Main Street. Then two went the other way. The charter bus's size made it known in the distance. It became known, recognizable on Main Street and then pulled into the train station parking lot. Sleek white under a coat of dirt that ran the length near the wheel wells. With seating for 55, the vehicle was long, and heightened by storage bays between the axles. "New Madrid Energy," written in a commanding font and completed with a blue flame atop a half-circle of orange in logo, prominently displayed along each side.

The driver directed the bus to an empty stretch of parking lot nearest the street. The door opened with a pneumatic hiss, which clarified the muffled sounds into song.

"Welcome to Missouri, gentlemen!" Nate screamed after turning off the stereo. He was thin, almost sickly, yet he was spry and alert. His cheeks were sunken, as age and experience had shrunken him. His head was covered by stringy, oily reddish-gray hair that appeared wet, slicked-back and reached his shoulders. A sparse goatee covered his chin. Eyes a deep brown. Arms, unhidden by a black tank top, were thin but conditioned with blue veins protruding. He stood from the captain's chair, and it rose slightly. From the dashboard, he grasped a black tablet and his green wristband blinked green as he limped his way down to the pavement. He wore blue jeans that led to a white sneaker on his left foot. On his right, a different sneaker, off-white that connected to a prosthetic just visible at his ankle. The senior officer approached him and conversed softly, then spoke into his walkie-talkie upon his shoulder.

"Let's get this over with," the officer yelled to everyone, at a decibel that included the teenagers and kids on bicycles across the street. He walked to an open space in front of the bus. "Stand here! get in line!" And the men obliged.

"Gentlemen," Nate started as loud as he could while pacing the line of men, the twang in his voice known. "Gentlemen, it is a privilege to be standing here righ' now, as we all know what the alternative is."

"Gentlemen," he continued but now read from the tablet text, "you are about to transition from the custody of the Federal Department of Corrections, from here on known as D.O.C., to the custody of New Madrid Energy, Incorporated, from here on known as NME. However, you will remain under the jurisdiction of D.O.C., and are bound by their rules. D.O.C. regulations supersede those of NME. You agree to abide by all rules set by either party and any deviation *will* terminate your relationship here. If terminated, your previous sentence will be reinstated, and you will be transferred to a prison facility. If you do not accept these terms, you have the option to return with an officer before boarding to be placed at a prison facility. Your acceptance of these terms will be documented upon boarding. Do you understand?"

The men nodded.

"Alrigh' boys, boarding is as follows," Nate continued while looking at the tablet. "Enter the bus as you are directed and take the seat furthest back starting on yer left."

The senior officer took up position at the bus door, while the other officers forcefully prodded the men into a queue with the butts of their shotguns. The men had arranged themselves by race, perhaps subconsciously, which afforded them some semblance of safety. A Hispanic man stepped toward the senior officer, and once he clipped the hand ties from the man's wrists he walked to the door, boarded. The second boarded, then the third, until they had all boarded. The driver turned to climb the bus stairs, lithe despite the limp. "Let's get this caravan rollin'!"

The muffled music resumed from the bus as the officers returned to their vehicles. Two squad cars were positioned in front of the behemoth vehicle and the remaining behind and the blue and red lights bounced off the white sides and tinted windows

Quick into gear, and the bus churned into drive. The senior officer sped out of the parking lot and with a quick siren chirp the patrol car bounded over a curb and set off down Main Street. The kids on bikes took off after, and the caravan whistled past dimmed commercial buildings. Gas stations with rusted pumps and handwritten signage. Convenience stores. A strip of fast-food establishments with active drive-thrus. The sparse traffic pulled to the side of the road as the procession passed. Horns blew, middle fingers rose out of windows with matching vulgarity and anger from the drivers and passengers alike.

There were two options at the highway entrance: to the left was north, which was unimpeded. The bus took the second option to the right under a sign allowing only authorized vehicles. A notice of severe tire damage. A notice of monitoring and then another authorized vehicle sign. The senior patrol car pulled off to the side and the other cars joined him. The bus continued and stopped in front of the imposing metal gate that spanned the width of the road. Bright red lights flashed on either side of the gate, and beyond that, a chain link fence crowned with razor wire. The driver leaned out of the bus window and entered a set of numbers on the keypad that jutted out from a concrete pylon.

The gate clunked into action and rolled open from left to right as Carmen and Alice tossed their bikes on the grass embankment. The charter's headlights switched on in the purplish gray of pre-dusk aura and illuminated rusted tire spikes that receded into the pavement beyond the barrier. The kids caught their breath as they pressed their faces into the cold metal of the chain link fence. The bus shifted into gear and pushed over the border and as the metal gate closed, the patrol cars dispersed north and east. Carmen ran his hands over the fence as he walked west, with Alice several feet behind him. Their eyes were set on the southern horizon, the bus as it grew smaller between vehicles pushed against the highway concrete sides and into the quiet unknown. The kids followed the fence down an embankment as it dipped, and the untended grass and weeds rose to their hips. They stepped over faded whiskey bottles, crunched Coors cans, and pushed bullet shells into the earth. Twenty-twos and forty-fives. Carmen ran his hands over the fence, until he didn't. Hidden behind the green and white flora the fence was missing. He knelt, disappeared into the brush, and stared at a three-foot square section of empty air cut from the metal. Alice squatted, carefully extended her arm through the gap, and it disappeared into the tall grass on the other side.

"There's a way in," Carmen exclaimed.

2

The felt marker made a dull thud as Ms. Woodward pressed it against the whiteboard at the front of the classroom. Dated posters crumbled at the edges lined the back wall. The empty desks outnumbered the occupied, yet each was etched with graffiti which touted rebellion. Death. Love in uncouth language.

She was determined in the way only a young teacher could be; when the realities of her charge, her location, and her limitations had yet to fully register in her mind. Before the percentages of success, or, more accurately, failure, had reached the point of calculation. In this determination, she scripted "Career Day" on the board as her Brazilian-inspired bracelets clicked together. Her svelte figure in soft caramel skin under a patterned summer dress. Her black curls that bounced from vigilant preparation. Her long lashes and inviting eyes. She turned around, looked to the doorway, and counted the parents and/or guardians who had shown up as they stood along the wall. Three. To her class she counted even though she knew: seven. She felt the calculation register and quickly shuddered it away. It was not time yet, and she turned to the students.

"Class," she said with a smile and pearly whites, "welcome to Career Day!"

The students responded with sixth grade antipathy, accordingly. Alice sat in the middle row and reclined in her seat, uninterested. Carmen sat next to her and rested his chin on his folded arms.

"First up," she continued and went to sit down at her chair behind her desk, "we have Mr. Miller, Michael's dad."

Mr. Miller smiled uncomfortably as he walked to the front of the classroom to half-hearted applause. He wore a Budweiser t-shirt with a slight rip in the armpit and khaki pants over thin limbs. Michael remained aloof and put his eyes on anything but his father. He was thin and bony like him, as if they could tip over with a sudden breeze. He had inherited his height as well and was several inches taller than his nearest classmate.

"Hey kids," he started with a forced smile of crooked stained teeth. He took a quick sip from a water bottle filled with unknown liquid. "How many of you have pets?" Several students lifted their arms slightly. "Well I work at the pet food factory."

The audience waited for more words, but none came. Michael ran his tongue over his teeth in an illusory attempt to feel the color, a habit he had acquired upon learning the concept of self and envy.

"How about you tell us what you do there," Ms. Woodward implored sweetly.

"I make sure all the equipment and stuff is working so your puppies and kitties have food to eat," he tried to come off as cute but instead relayed creepiness.

"Like what?" she asked.

He paused and scratched the back of his neck with dirty fingernails before answering. "Like the conveyor belts and the machines," and he stared at the students and then looked for additional feedback from Ms. Woodward.

"Does anyone have any questions?" she directed to her pupils, to which she received no response. "Thank you, Mr. Miller." He nodded a slight acknowledgement and returned to his spot on the wall near the doorway. "Next up is someone you all know, Susan's mom, Mrs. Johnson."

Mrs. Johnson took her place in front of the whiteboard to louder but still indifferent applause, . She was full-figured with dyed blonde hair that ran down past her shoulders. Bright red lipstick and shadowy eyeliner. She wore a flowered blouse with navy blue pants. "Well," she started with a reassuring vocal tone, "as you all were in my class last year, you know that I am an elementary school teacher. Let's see," and she put her finger in front of her lips, "I decided I wanted to be a teacher in college at Arkansas State, go Red Wolves. I love teaching, and my favorite subject to teach is mathematics, but as you know I have a passion for art."

She felt the indifference deeper than their current teacher as only a year ago, the children before her were studious, avid for knowledge and innocent play. Before the doubts and realizations accompanied by puberty and access to information from elder peers that brought on realization which touched on the fate. The fate of being born to poverty in a border town to The Fields—not within the walls for FEMA aid and relocation, and not far enough from them to be shielded from its effects.

"So," she continued with a forced smile, "does anyone have any questions?" Michael wrote crass poetry with thin, bony fingers in the margins of a history textbook while the others stared with the intention of passing the time in silence. "About being a teacher?" No movement. "Math? Art?"

"Thank you, Mrs. Johnson," Ms. Woodward said sweetly, knowing that no question was coming. "Next, we have Alice's dad, Mr. Wilson." Robbie pushed himself from the wall and nodded politely to Mrs. Johnson as they crossed paths. Alice slumped lower in her chair to hide from any future embarrassment, which she already felt as her father wore his Walmart vest to Career Day.

"Um, hello," he stared and cleared his throat. He surveyed the room, his daughter hiding in plain sight, Carmen's eyes barely open and his face hidden behind his forearms. The boy writing. The others set in indifference. He looked to the other parents, Mrs. Johnson smiled politely, and Mr. Miller took a sip from his water bottle, pushed the door open and abruptly left. "I'm Alice's dad," then paused for the door to clang shut. "I'm a shift supervisor, and I work at Walmart. I do most everything. Stocking items, doing inventory. Sometimes, I'll help with scheduling. Uh, the registers, sometimes I'm a cashier. Oh, I make sure all the money's there at the end of the shift."

Throughout his soliloquy he had been staring at the back wall, beyond the students. Yet at this point he had run out of things to say. He turned to Ms. Woodward, who whispered, "Ask a question."

"Um," turning back to the students, "does anyone want to know what it's like to work at Walmart?" Those that had been listening responded with indifference. "Well, thank you Mr. Wilson," Ms. Woodward said sincerely yet knew it was the end of *Career Day*.

"Robbie," he responded to her. "You can call me Robbie."

"Okay," she said awkwardly. "Thank you. Robbie."

He started to walk to the wall but stopped mid-stride and stared at his shoes. Ms. Woodward had followed his lead and stood from her chair to replace him at the front of the class but froze in place when he didn't continue.

"I was there that day," he said to his feet. "I was there."

"Where?" asked Michael.

"The Fields."

"Bullshit," he retorted, "you got all your limbs and you ain't dead or crazy or a drunk."

"Michael! Language!"

"I'm sorry."

"I ain't lying," and Robbie walked slowly back to the front of the classroom, in front of the whiteboard with "Career Day" in black felt marker. The outburst had grabbed the attention from the entire room, each student now rapt and drawn forward.

"Was a hauler, drove the Sand Kings, the blenders, the pipes," and as he spoke, he unbuttoned his vest. "Worked with Carmen's dad, he was a derrickman," and he set his vest down on an empty desk. "Great job," as he unbuttoned his shirt, starting near his neck.

"This is stupid," Michael muttered to himself.

"What's that, Mr. Miller?" Ms. Woodward asked sternly towards Michael's desk.

"Nothing, ma'am," and he shrunk down into his chair, hoping to be hidden by the small wooden desk in front of him.

"Um," Robbie continued as he unbuttoned, "great job, got paid real well and felt really good and got food on the table." He took off his shirt and set it on the desk with his vest which left him with a white undershirt. "Like I said," and he lifted the undershirt and showed his bare chest and stomach. A deep scar of mangled tissue ran from the right side of his stomach, up through his chest and ended just below his shoulder. The left side of his chest was splotchy with burn scars of textured red and white. Once he felt the students had seen enough, he lowered his shirt. "The past is the past, I ain't a hauler no more. But I'm alive, and I know school sucks sometimes, but each an' every one of you should study hard and try to be whatever you want."

"Except like Michael's dad, stupid dog food," Alice chided.

Michael started to respond but saw the anger in Robbie's eyes that caused Alice to wilt and quiet herself. She was embarrassed, embarrassed that he had just taken off his shirt in front of her classmates. Yet mostly, she was angry, angry that her father had just told her class more about The Fields than he had ever told her. Without prompting, even. She felt she deserved to know, from him or from anyone else.

3

The sparse lawn blushed with pale green amidst the dirt brown hue that covered most of the plot. A row of bushes lined the living room windows, giving some semblance of privacy in the summer months. Now in spring, the twigs gave no protection from passers-by, and the brown couch and further back the television were visible from the street.

The house was a small structure, boxed with the larger window centered, and to the left, a wooden door and a smaller window. The garage door was broken, angled and stuck, the white paint peeled back and rolled from the edges to the center. In the driveway nearest the house, were olive-green plastic garbage cans, a black trash bag of unknown contents, and a haphazard pile of cut wood. Down further, an aged lawnmower, a pile of rakes, and other garden tools that gathered rust and mingled with a small trampoline and an assortment of toy balls.

A truck approached and slowed as its right wheels went up on to the curb. White, with an oblong metal cylinder behind its cab. The driver stepped out and walked in front of 'Marty's Water' written on the side as he pulled on the fireman's hose attached at the back. Over the yard. Past the bushes and to the side of the house where the water tank sat bolted into a cement base. He reached into his back pocket, pulled out a phone and cradled the thick case in his open hand. Press. Swipe. Press. The lock unclasped at the opening and swung down. He climbed the two metal grated stairs and placed the hose, turning it until it was tight against the intake. Press, press, and the water rushed from the truck and began to fill the tank.

In the kitchen the orange powder appeared brilliant pressed against the pale beige of the elbow macaroni and glistened with the thin layer of remaining water from the boil. Alice's mom tapped the side of the white paper pouch and the remaining powder fell into the pot. She scooped a tablespoon of butter from the yellow tub, then poured the remainder of 2% reduced-fat milk directly from the carton. She stirred with a wooden spoon as the steam released and rose to the grease splattered fan above the stove.

She was a brunette of small curls with streaks of gray. A thick figure, yet not obese. Her cheeks were eternally flushed, which contrasted with her soft tones and were accentuated by the bright pink T-shirt with 'Saved by grace and coffee' in white print.

She pulled the oven open, and the chicken nuggets sizzled and crackled as she placed the metal baking sheet on the burners. In the patient moments of cooling, she sat down and sipped a tall glass of lemonade. It too had originated as powder. It too required a wooden spoon. The kitchen table was covered with a blue plastic tablecloth, which hid the many dings and dents that had accumulated—from curious children and the generic man's despair when reality outweighed options and emotions superseded reason. The chairs swayed slightly as the screws had gradually loosened from the years. Burgundy cabinets with brass knobs that, with every sunrise that faded their veneer, seemed more and more to match the beige refrigerator.

The front door opened, then shut. Backpacks heavy with books hit the wood floor, and the television came to life from the living room. She pressed her palm against the table to help her stand, then pulled two lime-green plates from a cabinet. She scooped the macaroni onto each, slid the spatula under the baked nuggets and apportioned each. A thick squirt of ketchup in between, two metal forks and she delivered the meals to the living room and set the plates on the maple-colored coffee table.

"Drinks?"

"Chocolate milk," answered Alice while watching the television.

"No milk. Lemonade?"

"Fine."

"I want a beer," Johnnie said, and looked up slyly from his phone to gauge his mother's reaction. "Lemonade."

Several blocks west within the neighborhood sat a house of identical size and design with two thick, aged oaks rooted in the front lawn. The exterior was covered by ash-gray siding which kept better than painted wood. The window planters were primed for Spring blooms. The garage door was ajar. Operable. The water tank identical to that of its neighbor, its neighbor's neighbor.

In the kitchen, the hot dogs sizzled in the dim yellow light muted by the tinted glass of the microwave. Juices ran down their length and puddled on the plate with small oily circles of fat. Janice Smith dumped the potato chips from the crinkled bag and they settled on the plates, eggshell white with blue ribbons that lined the rims. She slid her long pink polished nails between a hot dog bun. She found the slit and placed it alongside the potato chips on one of the plates, then repeated for the second. The microwave chimed, and each bubbling hot dog was inserted into a bun. The first took ketchup and was cut in half, the latter two whole with ketchup and mustard.

There was exhaustion on her face, yet her eyes remained alert and her movements taut. A dark complexion offset by magenta lipstick. Her hair was cropped close to her scalp but hidden by a wig of sleek ebony hair, eternally straight and settled just above her shoulders. She wore powder-blue scrubs, and a nametag was clipped to the breast pocket.

She glided with a quick turn to the table with the plates and set them gently, each in front of a wooden chair. Then plastic cups filled three-quarters with white milk and finally a folded paper for each.

"Get off a me!" Carmen screamed at his older brother who held him in a headlock as they entered the kitchen.

"Stop bein' a bi..." Dorian started, then stopped at the sight of his mother. "Stop bein' a wuss!"

Janice shot them a look of condemnation, which caused Dorian to release Carmen at once. The boys set their backpacks to the side of their respective chairs. They took turns washing their hands with liquid dish soap and each dried with a frayed towel that hung from the refrigerator door handle.

Without question or hesitation, the boys sat down at the table with their mother and their hands reached out and their heads bowed. "Bless us, oh Lord," Janice started, "and these thy gifts which we are about to receive from thy bounty through Christ our Lord. Amen."

"Amen," the boys echoed.

4

Dust had settled on the steel links of the chain, cobwebs formed within the oval spaces and spread downward to the dangled padlock. 'Gymnasium' in white letters pressed to the cracked brick above the doors and 'DO NOT ENTER' on bright red placards affixed to each thick wooden door. Gray plastic tables were lined down the center of the hallway; the first originated a few feet from the gym entrance. Each had wheels and the ability to be folded and pushed to the wall. Six circular seats ran the length of each side and were occupied sporadically by sixth graders nearest the gym. Then seventh and cumulated with the eighth graders. In all, less than 80 students occupied the lunchroom hallway.

Ms. Woodward stood with her back against the faded blue lockers nearest the sixth-grade table. She wore an opaque blouse which exposed just a hint of cleavage, khaki pants, and ecru pumps. Her seventh-grade counterpart stood watch over his students, and further down, the eighth-grade teacher.

A low, guttural rumble coursed through the hallway, underneath the conversations of pre-teenage concern and unwarranted argument. Ms. Woodward felt it first through her shoulder blades, then down her back and the cumulation that vibrated her rear. With it the combination padlocks—some blue, most black, and a few pink—chimed as they bounced against the gray metal of the locking mechanisms. She kept her body pressed against the cold surface and used the vibration for a free massage.

"The Frog People are too real," Michael responded to Alice at the sixth-grade table. He ignored the tremor, they all did, and took a bite of his bologna sandwich.

She considered the level of rage in conjunction with her retort. Surrounded by reused paper lunch bags crinkled with faded names printed in black marker. By handed-down steel lunch pails, dented and covered with stickers dissolved at the edges from years of soaks in the sink. Union proud. Semi-nude and suggestive ladies posed. New Madrid

Energy with the blue and orange flame logo. Peanut butter and jelly between white bread. Brown-spotted bananas. Crumbled potato chips in zippered sandwich bags. No-name juice boxes adorned with generic cartoon characters. Faux-chocolate treats sealed in plastic.

"That's so stupid. You're so stupid."

"Shut up."

"You shut up, and who said you could sit here anyways?"

"What do you have for lunch?" Carmen asked Michael, attempting to change the subject.

"They live in the woods called 'Radiation Woods' cause that's where the plant is."

"Who told you that?" Alice asked.

"My dad."

"Your dad?"

"Yeah. He seen them."

"Your dad's stupid."

"Screw you!"

Alice again studied her options as Ms. Woodward shot an intense look toward her. She resigned to her PB&J and dug fruit pieces out of gelatin with a plastic spoon. She took in the muffled conversations from other tables and tried to discern the topics.

"No one likes you," she said quietly, leaning in.

"What'd your dad say?" Carmen asked Michael, partly out of boredom and partly of curiosity.

"Don't matter, you'd just make fun of me anyways."

"C'mon man, I wanna know."

Michael looked up from his sandwich and sought validation in Carmen's eyes and in his expression, then did the same for Alice. Satisfied, he took a sip of juice and leaned in.

"So, um, only some of 'em have the things on their throats," Michael started. He raised his hand to his throat, his thumb outstretched, and it looked as if he was choking himself. "That's why they call 'em 'Frog People,' but they got the things anywhere."

"You mean tumors?" Carmen asked.

"Yeah, yeah, the tumors. They got 'em cause they didn't leave when they were supposed to. So they stayed cause they were stubborn, and they got the tumors, and they hide from the workers who are putting up the building around the towers, but sometimes they come out and they are all angry..."

"Cause of the tumors?" Carmen humored.

"Your dad told you this?" Alice asked incredulously.

"Uh-huh."

"And how does he know? He ain't been there."

"Oh he knows. He knows a lot of stuff."

Drunk idiot, Alice thought. "Tumor means you got cancer and you gonna die," she said aloud. "How are they all runnin' around attacking people?"

"They live off the land, they eat these special plants that grow down there so they don't get sick."

"Michael you're so dumb," Alice said.

"I ain't dumb, Alice."

"You believe that shit?"

"Yeah, cause it's true."

"Let's go find out," Carmen said.

"What?" Michael asked.

"Let's go see if it's true."

"Ain't no gettin' in there."

"We got a way."

Alice kicked Carmen under the table and cautioned him with her eyes and pursed lips.

"You got a way?" Michael asked with intrigue about his face.

"Nah," Carmen said as he looked down at the table, "ain't no way. I was just kidding."

"Aren't you afraid of the 'Frog People' Michael?" Alice asked. "Won't they eat you?"

"They don't eat people they jus' bite you and make you sick."

"Still," Carmen said, "that shit is scary too."

"Besides," Alice said, "even if we could get in there we'd get arrested."

"Or get killed fallin' into a hole," Carmen added.

"Or get the tumors," Michael said.

"It's stupid," Alice said to convince not only them but herself. "It's a stupid idea. And I told you not to sit with us."

5

Carmen sat up on the top bunk. The bedroom was dark, save for the flickering blue from the television out the door in the living room. The room was quiet, save for the ticking of the table clock upon the dresser that his mother had insisted was a family heirloom. He coughed, cleared his throat, and backed his body to the step ladder and started down. Dorian snored unevenly in a t-shirt and boxer shorts with one leg exposed over the comforter on the bottom bunk. Carmen watched him for a moment, then hopped to the carpeted floor.

He turned on the bathroom light switch and his eyes flushed with the brightness, then adjusted. He lifted the toilet seat, relieved himself and flushed the toilet. His nostrils had become accustomed to the chemical odor released within the water and made no reaction. As he went to turn off the light, he paused with his arm raised and a finger against the switch, then released. In these moments, in the dead of night, he found himself reflective. Even more now as his twelfth birthday approached. He stared in the mirror and remembered how real death is in the instant that directly precedes sleep. In that uneasy gap between the past and present. He stared at his dark skin and thick ebony hair and wondered why and what it meant. His t-shirt and boxers and why the second-hand store? Why not Walmart where Alice's dad works? The *whys* of interrupted sleep in the deep of night of an uncertain mind that needs not be fully formed.

He pulled the cold-water handle on the sink and the pumps chugged, gaining momentum before the water fell from the tap. He cupped under the stream quickly and splashed the water upon his cheeks. There was a delay from when he pushed the handle down and the pumps quieted.

His mother had fallen asleep on the sofa in pink scrubs and her head was awkward against the arm. He stood in silent stare and then turned to the television. A pale man crisped with tan touted the benefits of some cooking device. His receding hairline was pulled taut into a ponytail that reached his shoulders and he wore a white chef's apron that said, "blue ribbon master chef." A middle-aged white woman with a permanent smile of astonishment followed him behind a long counter. She repeated the amazing feats as she pushed her busty chest forward, knowing full well the best angle to stand for the camera. Carmen watched the man open the small oven door and reveal glistening roasts and roasted potatoes and steak and pepper kabobs and his stomach growled involuntarily. He turned his attention to his mother, knelt beside her near her head and compared her slumbered sounds to his brother's. He reached his hand slowly and placed it on her shoulder. He squeezed slightly when she didn't wake, still nothing. A little shake and her breaths changed and finally her eyes opened to reveal a slit of white around her pupils.

"Mama," he whispered. Her eyes closed, and he shook again. "Mama." This time her eyelids opened farther, and her pupils focused.

"What's the matter, baby?"

"You fell asleep on the couch."

"What you doin' up?"

"I had to use the bathroom."

Her eyes explored the surroundings. A bottle of water on the coffee table. The television. Her son kneeling in front of her. She sat up on the sofa, cracked her neck to alleviate the stiffness and patted the cushion and Carmen climbed to her and rested his head against her bosom. The "chef" seasoned a salmon filet. He removed a whole chicken from the hard-plastic contraption upon a metal rack. His co-host's utter amazement as he sliced into a drumstick.

"Mama?"

"Yes, baby?"

"What was my dad like?"

"Your father," and she paused. "Your father was a good man."

A housewife in a kitchen smiled through the television. Suburban plastic glory with shadowy cleavage as she pressed a button on the oven. A thick cut steak through the clear cover. Spotless black marble countertops and a basket of fresh fruit behind her. A plate, a fork, and a knife were at the ready. And in the interim, Carmen fell asleep against his mother.

6

The students were quick out the double doors as the school bell rang and faded. To idle cars parked in the circle drive. To bicycles with tires steadied between metal bars against the grass that lined the sidewalk. To the road and disappeared to the horizon or down side streets.

Carmen released his bike from the metal and faced the handlebars away from the building. He raised his leg and steadied his crotch above the white frame and waited. With a faded black t-shirt two sizes too large. Faded jeans rolled up at his ankles and tired sneakers. A navy-blue backpack slung over both shoulders. Alice followed close behind and pulled her bike back and threw her leg over. Her hair pulled back in a ponytail. An emerald-green t-shirt with a rainbow ironed on half hidden by a maroon hoodie. Jean shorts and ankle socks and white shoes striped in pink. A white backpack scuffed with haphazard care on pavement. On dirt. On gravel.

They pedaled down Spring Arbor Drive and beyond the school grounds. Into a neighborhood of single-story homes that alternated in their upkeep. Gravel driveways with weeds that encroached through the gray and brown. Down Red Leaf Lane. Oakbrook Street. They turned onto Main Street and rode past shuttered brick buildings. A pawn shop. Fast-food establishments. They crossed intersections where drivers pressed the brakes and waited for the light to turn green. Another pawn shop. Cash checking and the buildings ceased as they approached the bridge that led to the highway entrances. The warning signs, concrete blocks, and metal gate that inhibited southern traffic.

They stopped and laid their bicycles in the overgrown grassy embankment. Among the whiskey bottles and spent shells. Before the notice of severe tire damage. Before the keypad that jutted out from a metal pole and hidden from the cameras focused on the gate. They inspected the fence as they walked along with their legs bent to hide themselves in the grass and sought the break with their hands until Carmen stopped. His hand extended through to the other side. Alice squatted down and brushed the dull-green flora aside, yet all she could spy on the other side was more grass. Carmen joined her in the squatting position, and they silently considered crossing over to the other side.

"You liars!" they heard from the tall grass from where they entered, and they both jumped, and their hearts dropped. Through the thicket emerged the front tire of a bicycle, and beside it Michael pushed on the handlebars.

"Goddammit," Carmen said under his breath. Michael set his bike next to theirs and stood over them.

"Squat down, dummy," Alice said. "You want someone to see us?"

Michael did as asked and let the slight go unrequited. "You goin' to see the 'Frog People'?" he whispered.

"You don't have to whisper," Carmen said. "No one's gonna hear us here."

"You goin' to see the 'Frog People'?" he repeated louder.

"We are just looking," Alice answered, "and there ain't no such thing."

Michael took short, squatted steps and joined Carmen and Alice as they looked through the fence. His white t-shirt was stained with an unknown substance of pale brown and his bony knees projected out from the frays in his jeans. He broke off a piece of tall grass and stuck it in his mouth.

"Nah," Michael started as they stared at a cut fence and grass, "we ain't just looking, we're going in." And he turned, crawled to his bicycle, and dragged it to the opening.

"What are you talking about?" Alice asked. "We can't go in there."

"Why not?"

"They'll arrest us," Carmen said.

"So? They'll just take us home, we're minors," Michael responded.

"We don't know what's in there," Alice added, "and what if someone sees us as they drive by?"

Michael heard the excuses and ignored them as he squeezed and contorted the handlebars on his bicycle through the opening. The seat, and with his hands on the rear tire the bike started to slide down the steep grade that went unnoticed in the grass and from their vantage point. "Shit," he said as he caught the tire between the metal spokes and stopped its descent. Halfway through the opening with his fingers through the tire and prone on his stomach he looked back at Alice and Carmen. Each was hesitant in their own way, Alice with her eyes and Carmen the contour of his mouth.

"No one cares anymore," Carmen said softly. "It really doesn't matter, does it?" Alice understood. Not that no one truly didn't care, their parents cared deeply about them. Her teacher cared. It was the town as a collective, she sensed, that lived their lives on the literal edge. There was an undertone of hopelessness and holding on, of which had seeped into the unconscious. That had been passed down to her generation. The near-death of mind and the physical manifestation through damaged lungs and scars and prosthetics. Through sustenance requested by number. Through the concrete weeds and tall grass. With this insight she pulled her bike to the opening and Carmen followed her, yet without the philosophical recollection of mind. He had simply been outvoted.

They slid down the steep grassy hill, around and sometimes over discarded bottles and rocks half buried in the earth. Michael alit on the curbed border of the highway shoulder first, with Alice and Carmen soon after. They picked their bikes from the ground and balanced the wheels on the new, smooth pavement. To the north, concrete barriers lined the highway under the bridge they had just left and stretched across all lanes. Across the six-lane road was the entrance that led south, blocked by the gate and severe tire damage. To the south, lay the barren highway that seemingly remained only to transport prisoners to The Fields. There were no cars and no semi-trucks. There was nothing except for the dust that had settled and should have been brushed away by rush hour traffic.

Michael hopped onto the bike seat and started pedaling. South. Fast. He was determined to get as far as he could before he had to turn around to be home in time for dinner.

"Wait up!" Alice screamed as she ran next to her bike and then jumped on with Carmen not far behind. He slowed to allow them to catch up and again set a quick pace. The empty highway ran straight, and each child pedaled hard yet took the time to look over their shoulder for the comforting sight of the bridge. Of vehicles and streetlights and human movement as they shrunk with every push.

The words had been covered with black spray paint on the green sign that hung from the first overpass they approached. 'We are not dead... yet' had replaced whatever the sign had once conveyed. Further along, there was an exit with thick concrete barricades. 'We are dead,' scrawled across the entirety of the barrier in thick red.

The safety of their bridge was gone from vision. There was only the unknown and the barren highway. The only comfort that remained was the familiar feeling of the handlebars. The individual responses from the brakes. The connection between the seat and their buttocks. Carmen had taken a commanding lead again, and as the road veered right, he pulled the brake levers and came to a quick stop.

Ahead, at mile marker 171, the flawless road became the untamed of rumors and tales. Of cracked gray and exposed rebar, discolored brown in rusted decay. Sedans and semi-trucks and SUVs sat dormant against the median barrier, the reinforced steel set into the ground that ran the length of heightened sections. Each vehicle dented hard on passenger sides from where the bulldozers pushed them from the lanes, their tires absent air, pressed flat rubber against pavement. The cars that were pushed to the right to grassy shoulders were dinged and punctured on the opposite sides. Vehicle passage was constricted to the center lane for both northern and southern travel. The road sign read 'Aberdeen, Exit 171,' yet the town name was partially hidden by an 'x' painted over.

Carmen and Alice cautiously moved forward atop their bicycles, navigated the center, and studied the high-level. The road ahead. The reflective green signs. White speed limits and weight restrictions. The thick plywood laid over treacherous breaches in the concrete. The quiet.

Michael stayed left and took a more critical view. The types of vehicles: Cadillacs and Jeeps and Toyotas. Fords and Hondas. Above his eyeline, the Mack trucks, Freightliners, and Kenworths. Their state of decay after years of abandonment. Push-button ignitions and those with standard key cylinders. He peered in windows for the personal—purses, backpacks, sunglasses, and loose change. He thought about rummaging through each but knew the treasure he hoped to return with would not fit in his backpack. There was too much, and he held his giddiness in check.

Carmen maneuvered his bicycle to the right, alongside an F150. A Camry rusted at the wheel wells. Peterbilt with its dirty windshield. He pushed the bike with his feet between a Honda Odyssey minivan, its sliding door ajar, and a Jeep Wrangler with its concave soft top that sagged onto the interior headrests. He picked up his bicycle and portaged it over the concrete barrier, then slipped his legs over the spray-painted letters 'sa' of 'don't save' and stood ready to climb Exit 171.

"C'mon guys!" Michael screamed to Alice who was approaching the barrier and to Carmen who dawdled by the vehicles. "We gotta go!"

Alice cut between the Odyssey and a Jetta and lifted her bicycle two feet in the air, which was not enough clearance to pass. Michael set his kickstand, grabbed the handlebars on her bicycle and heaved it over.

"C'mon Carmen!"

"I'm comin'!"

"Do we have time to go up there?" Alice asked.

"Yeah, if big dummy hurries up," loud enough for Michael to hear.

"Screw you, Carmen!" Michael yelled as he directed his bike between two cars, slow enough to look inside the windows. "Help me," he demanded as he lifted the bike up with his skinny arms.

"You ain't a girl," Carmen responded without making a move to assist. Michael let it go and tossed the bike over the concrete and joined the other two.

"Where you wanna go?" Carmen asked as they were all back on the seats. "We got McDonald's, Burger King, Arby's," he read off the sign for amenities halfway up the exit. "We don't need gas..."

"It don't matter," Alice said. "Just gotta be quick."

She was right, Carmen thought, they'd need to head for home soon. He pushed hard on the pedals and they reached the top and the intersection. They turned left onto the access road and stopped at the bridge that ran perpendicular to the highway. "Guess we're not gettin' McDonald's," Carmen said with faux sadness.

"Or Arby's," Michael added as his front tire pushed small blocks of concrete from the edge of the destroyed bridge. They fell to the highway below with dull thuds. Carmen examined the twisted rebar and the rusted golden arches steadied on a hundred-foot pole, bent and resting atop power lines on the other side.

"Let's go," Carmen commanded, and they turned around and the vehicles here had not been bulldozed to the sides of the road. They remained where they had been abandoned. Some with doors open, others with windows broken. Between each, Michael peered inside and Carmen led the way and Alice took to pointing out hazards in the road. Debris and broken glass and cracked concrete created one to two-foot barriers and forced them to walk their bikes over.

The overhang that had before shielded the gas pumps from the elements lay on its side. The three pillars, once in line with the pumps, extended vertically toward the station shop. 'Sinclair' in faded red and barely legible. The dinosaur logo too, but in green. The pavement had opened up and Michael looked into the crevasse at the rusted fuel tanks and spit on one.

The station's structure was skewed, as if a superhero had pushed on one side and simply walked away, which left the shorter walls at forty-five-degree angles. The strain had shattered the windows and glass doors that lined the front. Laminated paper signs were still taped to a shard here and a shard there. The glass crunched under the kids' shoes as they approached the entrance.

Carmen pulled open the door and stepped inside. There was no chime, which meant there was no clerk. Which meant there was no eye contact and calculation based on his skin color with the penultimate contrived smile. He walked further, disappeared into an aisle, and felt off without the sense of being watched.

The shelves lay at the same angle as the building, and all that remained were cardboard containers that had once held specific quantities. For Juicy Fruit and Hershey's Milk Chocolate and Kit Kats and Altoids. Empty red pallets for soda bottles and white wire end caps scattered across the floor.

Michael pulled open a cooler door along the back wall and climbed through into the dark back room. Milk crates, scattered cardboard, and the stench of animal feces reinforced by the small, enclosed space.

Alice slid behind the front counter and pulled out drawers and read the pile of receipts that originated before she was born. For gasoline and hot dogs. For soda and beer.

Potato chips and pork rinds and pre-packaged ham and cheese sandwiches. There was no cash register, which took away her joy of pretending to be a shopkeeper.

Michael slinked back through the cooler door, met Carmen in the aisles, and they looked over at Alice. "Buy something or get out!" she yelled to them with a smile, which elicited smiles in kind.

"We are!" Michael yelled back.

"I'm watching you!" And she waved her finger at the boys derisively, "I got cameras!"

7

"Let's keep in mind that the kind of magnitude we saw was the same as this country saw in the early 19th century." Her words rolled as if rehearsed from the corner of her mouth. "Powerful enough to shake windows hundreds of miles away, so there's absolutely no proof that fracking, or any man-made activities, was the cause."

She sat comfortably at the clear glass news anchor desk, her fifteen minutes of fame had dragged on for years and in that knowledge, she spoke with immunity. No matter what she said, she would be shielded from consequence. She was full-figured and wore a conservative white blouse under a row of pearls. Her top was complimented by a knee-length black skirt and matching pumps. Her eyes were shadowy, almost hidden with smoky mascara and thick eyeliner and matched her hair, curling down to her shoulders.

"Look, I get it," the journalist responded with conviction animated with his hands on the desk, "but why did it take over ten years, *ten years*, for you to take action? How many times have you come on this show and told me that New Madrid Energy is a 'good corporate citizen'?"

The journalist was clean-shaven with toned skin and graced with the symmetry of handsome men. His tailored black suit fit snugly over his commanding frame, a maroon and white striped tie over a white dress shirt that followed the form of his neck. He had thick, black curls that were gelled perfect and covered the entirety of his head.

"As I've stated many times," she answered, "we have been in compliance at all times with the New Madrid Committee..."

"But being in compliance and doing the right thing because you should are two different things."

"We are taking the lead in rebuilding..."

"With prison labor. Why not employ those who have experience in The Fields to restore the area?"

"Again, we have been in compliance with the New Madrid Committee."

"Is it because if you hire, or had kept the employees, that NME would be on the hook for their medical expenses?"

"Like I've said, any specific questions about current or former employees should be directed to the NME legal counsel."

"We've reached out to them, numerous times."

"We are very active within the boundaries set out by the New Madrid Committee and will continue to be in compliance with their, and any, government requirements."

"Do you owe, and I mean this as a 'good corporate citizen' and not legally, do you have a responsibility to those employees who continue to suffer with debilitating injuries? To those families..."

"As I've stated..."

"Let me finish, do you bear a responsibility to those employees, to those families, who we, to this day, don't even have an official count of the dead because NME has steadfastly refused to turn over any data? Do you bear responsibility for their health situations? For their loss? For the millions displaced and so far, it's been taxpayers who bore the brunt of relocation?"

"I've answered you five times already."

"No, you haven't."

"Just because you don't like the answer doesn't mean I haven't addressed it."

The young man had had enough of the television and turned his attention to the nebulizer motor as it whirred from its plastic contraption on the coffee table. Cluttered with magazines and empty soda cans and beer cans and plastic cups. Used tissues white with stains of brown mucus and dried blood. The clear plastic tube bridged from the breathing apparatus. It lay over the potato chip crumbs pressed into the worn moss shaded carpet and ran up the brown recliner cushion to the man's mouth. He pressed his lips against the sky-blue mouthpiece.

He turned his attention to Janice in her green scrubs and the nametag that bounced against her breast. She delicately picked up the stained tissues with latex gloves and placed them in an orange plastic bag with black biohazard print. He watched her expressions for pity, yet she remained dutiful in her charge.

He turned his head to the window. The dust and pollen glinted off the sunlight that filtered through the faux wood blind slats.

His body illuminated by the sun was fair and freckled, though the opposite in shadow appeared livelier, with a peachier color temperature. Stringy, unkempt hair ran down the back of his neck and his stubbled cheeks were formed of neglect in lieu of style. The dreamcatcher tattoo on his left shoulder was faded black and the three feathers pointed to his elbow. His right shoulder was inked with a scaled dragon who wrapped himself around a cross, and as with the former it was faded. The mythical monster contrasted with his meager arms. One pectoral bore another cross and on the other were the initials "M.D.F." in gothic lettering.

"Lemme open a window Tommy, please?" Janice asked in the stiff, uncirculated air and brushed more tissues from the armoire into the bag. She picked up a birthday card atop the pile of unopened mail. "Don't give up on your dream of being famous just because you're 30." She carefully pulled open the card, "You could still commit a weird crime or something. Love, Mom and Dad."

"No thank you, ma'am," he said with the tube still in his mouth, pressed between his lips.

"I promise you, the air is good out there and it'll be good for you."

"Ain't no need for you to clean up," he responded after a pause with a different subject.

"Ain't no problem at all."

As she bent down to retrieve an errant tissue Tommy stole a glance down her shirt and saw her cleavage, her white bra exposed from his vantage point. He involuntarily bit down harder on the mouthpiece and then without warning he coughed hard and deep and the mouthpiece dropped to his lap. He felt the phlegm stuck in his scarred airway and in that pressure, he forced more coughs to alleviate the pain, and each time an uncontrollable fit would follow. His body convulsed as if in seizure, and he ripped a tissue from the box in his lap. He cycled through the fits, spitting thick phlegm into the tissue and catching his breath. Janice sat down on the coffee table and the bag hung loosely between her legs.

Several minutes passed, his breathing slowed, steadied and he looked to the window. Janice gingerly took the tissue from his hand and placed it in the orange bag. She removed her gloves, placed them in the bag and secured the opening. The hopelessness on his face made it impossible for her to remove emotion completely. She turned her thoughts to the next patient on her schedule to try and mitigate the feeling.

The clinical odor of hand sanitizer melded with the stale air as she explored his neck with her fingers. The ridges of his esophagus as he turned toward her. The hard angles of his collarbone. In the proximity she could hear the coarseness of his breaths, she could feel the struggle under his skin through her fingers. He raised his arm from his lap and grasped the television remote from the arm of the chair.

"Today we're looking at a high around 73 with increasing clouds this evening and a chance of thunderstorms overnight." Click. "Later, in 'Jenny's Corner,' we'll see the latest summer trends and how you can beat the heat while turning heads." Click. "Elmo sees Julia is playing with a stuffed rabbit. Fluffster!" Click. "Plus, cleanup is a snap after the meal. The Turbo Oven Pro is not a microwave oven but uses three kinds of cooking power."

8

On the buckled pavement and several miles south of the coiled razor wire where the kids had traversed on bicycles a day earlier, Michael shuffled between the first abandoned cars pushed against the concrete rails. The comfort of artificial light was gone, left back beyond the fence opening near the neon signs on pawn shops and the bullet-proof exteriors of cash-checking stations. In its place, the half-moon illuminated the highway and dirty vehicles with a grayish hue filtered through the passing clouds. It was the silence, rather than the darkness, that pressed on the heart. The absence of distant low rumbled traffic. The absence of squeaky insects and nested birds stirred from slumber.

Among the shadows and armed with a car thief's tools, he seemed more to embody his father's sleaziness, of whom, in drunken slumber, he easily evaded as he slipped out of the house in the late hour. He wore a sweat-stained tank top that left his arms unencumbered. Cargo shorts for extra storage and his backpack hung over his shoulders.

He walked silently along the cars, aimed the small metal flashlight through dusty windows and pulled on the door handles. The first several doors were unlocked, and he slid inside. He checked the seats and under them. He opened center consoles and glove boxes but found nothing of value.

The interior of a luxury SUV lit up as he pointed the flashlight through the window. He tried the doors but found each locked. He took off his backpack and crouched down near the driver's door, then put the flashlight in his mouth and pointed it down towards the bag. He unzipped the smaller front compartment and sifted through a handful of metal pieces. He grasped one and held it in front of the flashlight. The bump key was flat, with one end that resembled a vehicle key but without the grooves. In the middle, a piece of metal extended perpendicular to the 'key.' On the other side there were two thin pieces of metal with knobs set on a wider piece of metal which was marked with lines and numbers from one to eight. Michael flipped the tool over and read "Ford" which was written in permanent marker. He tossed it back in the compartment and chose another, 'Chevy.' The third read 'BMW,' which was correct.

Still with the flashlight in his mouth he pushed the 'key' into the door lock and held the perpendicular piece as a handle as he adjusted the knobs. Slowly and methodically the knobs moved inward toward the lock as thin wires within the mechanism filled in the grooves. Within a minute the 'key' turned, and the door unlocked. He stepped into the cavernous leather-appointed interior and sifted through each compartment. He repeated the process with the next and took what he could carry. Sunglasses, coins, and dollar bills. Then the next. An aged cellular phone and a laptop, each with depleted batteries. Then the next. Another pair of sunglasses, half a bottle of whiskey and he got out of the sedan and unscrewed the cap. He put his nose to the opening and took in the aroma that he had only smelled on his father's breath. With a heavy sigh, he put the bottle to his lips and the caramel brown liquid flowed into his mouth. The gag reflex immediately followed the swallow and he heaved onto the pavement. His eyes watered, drool dripped down his chin, and his ribs pulsed with every deep breath as he struggled for composure. Once attained, he threw the bottle against the concrete barrier, watched with satisfaction as the glass exploded and the liquid splattered, then set his eyes on a minivan.

9

The April heat of summer had settled in the air as Carmen docked his bike near the Walmart entrance. He walked through the automatic doors and found a seat in the small dining area near the registers and customer service desk. He wiped the salty sweat from his forehead with a wad of napkins—eyed an obese mother jealously as she siphoned off soda through the plastic straw deep in 64 ounces. The Icee machine. The chilled soda bottles. The rotund daughter chewed down a hot dog slathered in ketchup, then began the process anew. A teenage employee bent over the counter and started to speak to his female teenage counterpart but instead blathered and stared down her shirt.

Having felt that the sweat had subsided sufficiently enough, Carmen stood and began his exploration of the store. Kitchen, through the carafes and single-use coffee makers. Thin glassware and cheap metal cutlery. Her name tag read 'Miranda,' light-skinned, maybe Hispanic. Average height and nice breasts.

Bath, through towels and shower curtains. Cartoon character toothbrush holders and suction-cup soap vessels. The security guard made his presence known and flexed his muscles by rearranging toilet seats. Acne-scarred cheeks with buzzed dirty-blonde hair and the discerning look of one whose intensity far outweighs their pay scale.

Housewares, through home air filters and light bulbs. Laundry baskets and off-brand tools. 'Jack,' white and old like Robbie. Same gut. Smelled funny.

Baby, through diapers and wipes. Strollers on display and the boxes stacked below. An infant screamed from a child seat, secured with a black strap snug around his chest. He kept reaching for the food stamp card that hung from a plastic bracelet on his mother's wrist as she pushed the wobbly blue cart. The security guard's forehead crested over toddler shoes, and his eyes peered through Velcro.

Groceries, through the coffee tins and cereal boxes. Frozen dinners packed deep in the freezers and artificially flavored pre-made waffles. Aunt Jemima syrup bottles in a brown box sat on a gray cart with wheels between the row of freezers and the last aisle of shelf-stable goods. Hungry Jack and Log Cabin.

Robbie pressed his fingers under the top flap of the Aunt Jemima box and pulled it open, then repeated the process for the other one. He set the bottles on the shelf and rotated the older ones to the rear.

"Mr. Wilson?" Carmen inquired from a safe distance near the pancake mixes. Robbie stopped opening the Hungry Jack box and looked up.

"Oh, hey there Carmen," as he returned to the stock. Ain't you supposed to be in school right now?"

"My ma said I could stay home," as his eyes darted to everything but Robbie and his mind kept stuttering on Career Day, his bare, scarred chest.

"So if I called her that's what she'd say?"

Carmen looked to his shoes for a good answer but only found regret. He had come seeking answers. Without Alice at his side.

Without Michael having followed him. Without his brother's dismissiveness.

"So," Robbie continued, "what can I do for you son?" Carmen remained quiet. "Obviously you need somethin', or it's important since you're skipping school and come right up to me." Still nothing. Robbie set aside the syrup bottles and closed the distance. "What's the matter?"

"I wanna know," he started and then paused. "Know what?"

"See, um, I don't know nothing about... I mean you worked with him. You were friends."

"What?"

"I wanna know about my dad," Carmen demanded with a fast cadence and he looked up and met Robbie's eyes, "that's all."

With a wince Robbie lowered himself into a crouch to meet Carmen's eyeline. "And I suppose, I suppose that your ma don't wanna talk about."

"No, sir."

Robbie exhaled slowly with thought and remained in silence. He considered his place in the matter. Carmen's mother had chosen not to answer him, what right did he have here? The child obviously wanted answers to his questions. Was he old enough to hear the whole truth? Should his words be edited?

While Robbie pondered, a rebel bead of sweat ran down Carmen's cheek and fell from his jaw to the tiled floor. He realized that if Robbie acquiesced and told him, then reality, or at least a fallible retelling of such, would render his daydreams about his father moot. The family outings, playing ball in the backyard, his father's comfort... all these thoughts would be tempered by whatever Mr. Wilson told him. Maybe his mother was right to keep his memory to photographs, and maybe she was right to limit his experience to thirty-second video clips on the computer. Maybe that's why his brother had always hushed him when he broached the subject. Maybe coming here was a big mistake.

"You hungry?" Robbie asked.

"No sir."

Robbie sensed the lie, stood up and removed his wallet from his back pocket. "Go on over to the cafeteria and get something to eat," he directed Carmen as he handed him a few bills. "I'll see if I can get outta here a little early and give you a ride home."

"Are you going to tell my ma that I skipped school?" he asked as he took the money.

"Nah, consider it your one 'get out of jail free' card."

◆◆◆

The sun moved westward across the sky as they sat on the bed of the white pickup truck, Carmen's bike placed further up towards the cab. They were parked on a deteriorated gravel parking lot and hidden from view by the abandoned tire shop. 'Central Tire Co.,' in faded paint along the façade. The windows sharp with glass remnants or boarded up. Robbie reached into a light-brown plastic bag with 'Walmart' printed in blue. He took out a tall can of soda and handed it to Carmen. A tall can of beer for himself and they pulled the tabs and took first sips in unison.

"My old man worked here, right?"

"Yup," Robbie started as he rubbed a few dribbles of beer into his store-issued blue polo shirt.

"I really don't know nothin'," Carmen said as he stared at the dilapidated building. "Mama won't talk about it and my brother ain't got time he says."

"Well," Robbie said as he stared off, "your dad... well me and your dad we went back a ways. Like you said, he worked here, that's where I met him. Funny guy, that's what drew me to him at first, probably what drew your ma, too. Man he was big, picked up truck tires as if they were nothin', rims and all. I remember my first day, I was walking across the garage floor and he starts yelling at me. Says 'maaaan,' he always said 'man' like that, 'maaaan, why you gotta drag your feet?' He told me that the boss drags his feet when he walks through the garage, and that's how they knew he was coming. After that I made sure to pick up my feet. The boss, he'd always say 'chop, chop, guys,' and one time he had a whole pig just sittin' in a tub in one of the bays. One of the sales guys, big goofy white guy, we called him 'Twinkle Toes,' not to his face of course, kinda walked with his ass swinging."

Robbie chuckled to himself at the memory and turned to Carmen, which made him realize he was going off-topic. "Anyways, me and your dad we got to be pretty close. Used to grab a beer after work sometimes and he would use the 'n-word' 'round me, which I think means he trusted me a bit. Well he got married to your ma, and I was already married by then and right off she gets pregnant with your brother. My boy Johnnie was a few months old, and

about that time he got to thinking that bustin'
tires wasn't gonna pay the bills. Which got me
thinking. And you got New Madrid, cause they,
you know what the EPA was?"

"Naw," Carmen responded as he hung on
each word.

"Stood for 'Environmental Protection
Agency,' but they got rid of that and then you
got all these companies that ain't got nothing
stopping them from doing whatever. It was
perfect cause of what your dad was saying
about money. Now you got all these ads on TV
saying you can come down south a bit and work
on a fracking rig and make, well we would make
three, four times what we was making bustin'
tires. Didn't need any experience either, we
could just sign up online and they'd tell you
where to go and you got a sweet job. Called us
'roustabouts.'"

Robbie took a long sip from the can as the
earth shook, which rocked them on the truck
bed and then subsided.

"Your dad was a good man."

"That's all my mom says!" Carmen said
angrily and was caught off-guard by his own
tone.

"Well maybe that's all that matters
sometimes," Robbie said without responding in

the same tone, choosing instead to let the transgression pass. "Maybe all the little things fade away after a while and all you remember is if someone was good. If they made you laugh. If they were nice."

"I know, but I just, I don't know... I guess I can't picture him."

Robbie hopped off the end of the truck and walked to the passenger door. He reached in, unlatched the glovebox, and pulled out a pack of cigarettes and an opaque green lighter. He walked back to the bed and jumped, which made the shocks bounce.

"You won't tell Mrs. Wilson, right?" He asked Carmen as he lit the cigarette.

"Promise."

Robbie took a long drag from the cigarette before he spoke. "I don't know what to tell you. There's nothing, I don't have some heroic story or anything. He didn't save a family from a burning house, didn't save the world or nothing. I guess not everyone's a hero."

"I guess."

"But that doesn't mean... He was always... We looked after each other when we went down south. We were in it together, it was hard work, hard as hell, but I knew that I could make it if he could, and I think he felt the same."

Carmen gulped down his soda and leapt from the truck. He walked to the front door of the tire shop, cupped his hands beside his eyes and peered in through the dusty glass. Cheap, black plastic chairs were strewn across the waiting room. A metal television bracket hung from the wall. The sales counter was empty, save for a few pieces of paper.

"We should get going," Robbie yelled to Carmen who didn't respond.

A rectangular piece of plywood covered the bottom pane of the door where the glass had been broken. Carmen pulled on it with the tips of his fingers and felt play. He pulled harder and the wood came off without much effort.

"C'mon, Carmen, let it be."

Carmen crouched down, looking through the unobstructed entrance.

"Leave it alone, son!"

Carmen ignored him and crawled through.

"Damnit Carmen!" Robbie growled as he slid off the bed and cupped his own hands to see inside. Carmen had disappeared into the interior. "Carmen!" he yelled through the broken door. No answer. "Carmen! Come on back!" He waited a few moments then crawled through the opening.

"Shit!" he yelled as a shard of glass on the tile sliced into his palm. He came through, stood up, and inspected his hand. The cut was long but not deep. He held the palm toward the ceiling and, by memory, made his way to the bathroom. The faucet handle turned, squelched, and went silent. He tried the other. This one too failed to supply water. Even if it had, he thought, the liquid from the spouts were most likely acidic. The paper towel dispenser was empty. He pushed open the stall door, a half roll of toilet paper sat on top of the toilet. He unfurled it and wrapped his hand, soaking up the blood that originated on his palm and ran down the creases and was dripping on the pale gray cement floor.

The bays were as he remembered them. Four lifts with yellow pads. The green and red buttons that hung from thick cables for raising and lowering the cars. Near the back was the alignment rack, where the mechanics could step down into a rectangular hole to access the bottoms of cars without the need to raise them.

Robbie walked along the bays near the balancing machines. The tire mounting apparatuses. Bins that once held lead weights. He looked up at the empty steel racks that held tires and the equally industrial staircase. The environment brought memories. The time Mikey didn't tighten down the lug nuts. The old men who would stand at the tall garage door and watch your every move. Danny's wife enraged, screaming at him when she caught him cheating and she stood under a raised car. They all thought she might get crushed, but they didn't dare say a word. They were all fleeting, slices of life without any philosophical theme.

He stood over the alignment rack and looked down into the darkened space. In shadow Carmen seemed smaller than usual, strangely more exposed as he sat on the cushioned stool with squeaky wheels.

"Why'd you come in here? Make me come chasing after you?"

"I don't know."

"You don't know? Shit, son, I cut my hand up chasing after you."

Carmen looked up at his hand wrapped in toilet paper. "I'm sorry."

Robbie sighed and stepped down into the pit. He took a seat on the other stool and air whooshed out of the cracked black cushion.

"Why won't anyone?" Carmen asked. "I mean I'm not really, I'm not a kid anymore. I just want someone to talk to me like I'm an adult."

Robbie wheeled his stool backwards until it hit the wall and he rested his head against the cold concrete. He drew in a breath, held it, then exhaled fully. "Me and your dad were assigned to 'XL1-Violet,' they named all the well pads by size, this being extra-large, meaning we were drillin' more than 40 wells on the pad. The number meant what state we were in, we was Arkansas, and then they just picked random colors, I think. There was aqua, crimson, olive, just random. Seemed like they started drillin' all at once. Commercials came on the TV saying we could go down. Said they needed workers."

"What was it like, on a..."

"Pad?"

"Yeah?"

"It was hard work, first of all. And you were away from your family, but like I said I had your dad and he had me. There was always a hundred things going on, and you had to keep your wits about you 'cause of all the dangerous stuff around. Then the quakes started. Once a week or two, then more, then they got harder. We'd have to hold tight onto something or get down real low to the ground. You couldn't really feel them if you were in a truck or had some heavy shit you were doing, so it really didn't bother us none. And after a while, they put up sirens that gave us a little bit of warning. It was, we had these temporary trailers that we lived in a little ways off from the pad. That's when it freaked you out, when you were laying on a bunk and the whole thing starts shaking. But when we were working? Nah, didn't matter none."

"What was my dad, I mean, where was he..."

"You want to know about 'The Day,' huh?"

"Well, yeah."

"Before I tell you, you gotta know that I hadn't seen your dad since the morning, and I don't know how, I mean I don't know where he was on the pad. If I'm gonna tell you, you have to accept that, in the end, I still don't know what happened to him."

"I want to know."

10

The siren rang out from the small steel structure that rose up near the entrance to the well pad. It faded in, slowly, then reached a decibel that would cut through the drilling and the mixing and fracking. Movement slowed of the men, screams elongated, filtered through ear protection yet audible. In this time, the men were alive. Truly. Beasts of beasts. Breathing. Unified limbs, supported by hard hats, coveralls, steel toes, gloves. The metal and fibers and bolts of men must, at this time, and within said time, become two and separate their bodies from the man-made structures and save their mortal vessels. It was in these moments that men decided their fates. The tremors had become commonplace, and they treated them with desensitized thoughts. They knew there were seven to ten seconds from alarm to rumble. No more, sometimes less.

Layered with concrete and cut out of the forest, the XL well pad, creatively named XL1-Violet, spanned 15 acres. Upon its expanse the trucks hauled, the pumps pumped, and steel casings drove into the earth. It was set up to hold 50 well pads, 22 of which had been fracked.

The semi-trucks that held equipment were parked compactly and near the center of the XL1-Violet well pad. Fracturing pumps, red and emblazoned with 'Halliburton' in white lettering, belched diesel near the center of the XL1-Violet pad. Then the blenders of identical size and color, built to mix the fracking fluids with polymers. The silver sand cans full of silica and the orange sand kings. Moving east, the liquid storage tanks. At the easternmost point, and beyond the pad, lay the impoundment, a rectangular, man-made lake that held five million gallons of water.

They knew they had seven to ten seconds to find haven. Away from the semi-trucks. Far from the storage tanks. Seven seconds, and then one minute at most to hold on and survive the tremor. They scattered from the trucks.

From the well head and from the burning flare a hundred feet high. And as they ran, held back by their thick coveralls and hard hats they grinned that stupid grin that men get when adrenaline kicks in and they revert to boys, and every boy wants to be a cowboy.

One second. Two. Three. Four and the world set afire. The ground shook with anger, as if all the previous earthquakes were warning the men to stop, but they didn't listen—they never did. Three of the six storage tanks fell to their sides and burst open, which sent a river of poison towards a group of men running for safety past the berm. A river of hydrochloric acid. Terpene hydrocarbons. Cesium-137 sources, hydrotreated light petroleum distillates, isopropanol, ethylene glycol, paraffinic solvents, sodium persulfate, and tributyl tetradecyl phosphonium chloride.

A single spark flicked from a steel casing that rubbed against its brother and slipped through a crack in an upright tank. It exploded in orange anger to smoke choked plumes. The second reacted, then the third, and the liquid river set aflame and chased the men. The flames licked their coverall-covered backs as the river spread unconstrained and they kept running to the berm.

It was the caustic air that slowed each, and its effects showed in the rear first. The deep exertion that was required of the men sped the chemical coating down their throats and into their lungs. It seared windpipes and stuck firm to quicken breaths. One by one the coveralls over their kneecaps made contact with the wet gravel and dissolved as they fell to their knees. Blood spewed from their mouths as their bodies convulsed to fight but they collapsed in the shallow pool of wet chemicals and blue-yellow flames and their oxidized red.

Sparks caught the wind across the pad and the wells in production exploded, then settled in steady flame and billowing, thick black smoke that hid the sun. Skulls cracked under hardhats. Limbs severed and alit in their corrosive world. Steel weaponized and pierced abdomens through and through.

The agony was muted, muffled under ear protection and struggled to overcome the explosive decibels of pressure released and afire. The men near the impoundment were spared the panic of suffocation as the holding pond had breached the berm. The millions of gallons struck them. As they arced through the air, they went unconscious before the steel cracked their bones or the fires consumed their flesh, or their lungs filled.

And so, it went, from XL1-Violet and west through the Fracking Fields. At XL2-Violet. At XL1-Aqua. At XL2-Emerald. The earth consumed them and took its share in fire and constriction and suffocation.

It went northeast into Tennessee. XL3-Crimson. XL3-Olive. Into Illinois. XL4-Coral. North into Missouri. XL5-Goldenrod. It went, and it went, and it went.

And it was the rustling in the leaves that Robbie heard first, that first conscious reminder of life. Before his eyes had opened. From farther beyond the tree line. Then he smelled the impending rain that displaced the acrid chemical stench on the slow breeze. He felt tightness in his chest and a burning clench upon his abdomen and his eyes closed tighter. Released and tightened and then released to a blurry sun on azure sky. He gasped, which compressed his torso and put inward pressure on the wounds. He held the inhale for the duration of realization then released in absolute agony. Into the sky and to the sun as it became focused and in turn focused his mind into understanding.

He tried to sit up, but the pain kept him prone and his breaths were heavy from the effort. A line of puffed white clouds blocked the sun as he heard men's voices. Prayers. Gasps. He turned his head and saw a man he was unable to recognize near the mangled drill rig. His hardhat was several feet away and caked in dirt, the blue flame atop a half-circle of orange emblazoned on its front. His collared gray jacket, thick and also caked. His dark-brown boots halfway up his calves and tucked into blue jeans. Blood pooled under his lifeless body and spread out atop the gravel. A steel pipe jutted out at an angle stuck through his chest.

Robbie forgot the pain as instinct forced his unwilling body to his knees. In his immediacy there were random metal shards and rods that littered the ground. Pools of unknown liquid. Further the black smoke rose. The burnt shells of the red mixers and silver sand cans and orange kings, all now identical blackened steel stripped down to their frames. Further sirens of the towns in the periphery that buzzed in his still recovering ears. An amalgam of police and ambulance and tornado in alternating pitches. Each distinct to him, until they melded into one elongated tone and his mind faltered and he lurched forward, and his body hit the gravel with one last wide-eyed attempt and then shut down everything non-vital and waited in comatose for an intervention by man or God.

11

It was a birth defect that gave Jeremy Sonwu his peculiar look. More accurately, it was the surgeries to correct said birth defect that altered his appearance. The alternative was death, of which he experienced several times sedated and under the knife, the saws, and the tubes.

His left eye was set lower than his right. His left earlobe was fused to the side of his neck, and the right had a piece cut from it. When he spoke, the right side of his face stayed mostly in place while the left moved freely, which made it appear as if he was always smirking.

An ill-fitting suit over his slender frame and frail appendages furthered his peculiarities. The pastel-flowered tie clashed with his dark eyebrows and thin, slick-black hair which fell and rested at the top of his ears.

For all his oddities, both in appearance and in personality, he was hardly an outsider. He was 'Wu,' owner and proprietor of 'Wu's Army Surplus and Pawn Shop.' It was on Main Street in an old brick building next to an auto supply shop and further attached to a store for rent. Shopping within its walls was a rite of passage for the children who heard the rumors first. Who built up the courage to stare hidden behind the racks of bomber jackets. To stare at the odd man reading dog-eared comic books behind the counter with beaded lady's reading glasses set at the tip of his stubby nose. Who went home and snickered in front of their parents at the dinner table. When pressed, revealed the impetus for their braying and felt the full impact of a father's wrath, a mother's slap. 'Wu' was to be respected, and any deviation would be met with swift, physical repercussions, even from the hands of pacifistic parents.

The door chimes rang with soft tones as Michael entered Wu's Army Surplus and Pawn Shop around noon. He was sweaty from the bike ride and heavy backpack which pulled on his shoulders. The front of the store was stocked with the green, beige, and camouflage. Racks of jackets. Cots closed up and cot pads rolled tight. Helmets of various vintage set on soldier mannequin heads stacked on metal shelves. Flak jackets. Hats on displays and empty metal boxes denoted with what ammunition used to be within. Gas masks, goggles, and a wooden box filled with replica grenades. A display case with knives for hunting, fishing, camping, and murdering.

Near the middle of the store the merchandise ceased abruptly, and Michael found himself exposed in the large open area. Counter-size display cases lined the walls, filled with jewelry, power tools, watches, laptop computers and towers, and handguns. The larger items hung from the walls: guitars, banjos, violins, and trumpets. Televisions, long guns, and crossbows.

"Well good morning, Michael," Wu said as he looked up from the comic book and checked his watch, "or should I say, 'good afternoon.'"

"Hello, Mr. Wu," Michael responded politely.

"Ain't seen you around in a while, or your pa."

"My dad went full-time."

"Well that's jus' great, great news. What can I do for ya?"

Michael slipped his backpack off his shoulders, which left sweat stains on his tank top where the straps had been. He hefted it onto the counter and made sure it landed softly. "I got some things I'd like to sell, ain't got no use for them no more."

"Well let's see what you got," Wu said as he unzipped the backpack. One by one he set the items on the counter. Sunglasses, smartphones, several laptops stacked, and a DSLR camera.

"Oh, Mr. Michael," Wu started in a stereotypical Asian accent, "you think Wu stupid?"

"No, sir," Michael responded nervously.

"Then why bring Wu stolen merchandise?"

Michael felt warmth overcome his cheeks and knew that they were flush. He felt the naked exposure amplified by the emptiness of the pawn shop portion of the store. He wanted to hide within the bomber jackets. He wanted to run, to leave his backpack and treasure and jump on his bicycle and ride. Anywhere. In any direction.

Wu, who had built his empire on mind reading and understanding his distinct advantage with each pawn transaction, felt the balance tip further in his favor. Upon this realization, he himself felt exposed. He felt embarrassed that he had the advantage of age and had caught the child in a lie. He casually picked up one of the cell phones, sat back on his stool and reclined to alleviate any imminent threat the boy might feel.

"It's only recently," Wu said in his normal voice, "that I started seeing these. These decade-old things, this phone, these laptops. Do you know why that is, Michael?"

"No, sir."

"It's 'cause they stopped caring. Sure, they make a big fuss with all the cops and the trains comin' in, but they stopped caring. Used to be anyone slipped through the fence they'd be picked up in a minute. I seen 'em. Teenagers, mostly, used to go through the fence and then you got helicopters circling and Humvees and they'd be picked up. Now that don't happen. The sensors they buried stopped working. Pilots ain't there no more, I guess. You can pretty much go wherever. But that begs the question. Do you know what the question is?"

"No," Michael answered after careful deliberation.

"The question, Michael, is why would you want to?"

"Want to what?"

"Well want to go into The Fields?"

It had never occurred to Michael to ask why, as his young mind had gone straight to adventure and rebellion. This, he had learned, was never an acceptable answer to his elders. "For this stuff," as he pointed to the aged electronics, "so I could pawn this an' get some money."

"This stuff," Wu responded as he motioned over the pile with his palm towards the ceiling. "This stuff ain't worth nothin'."

"Nothin'?" Michael answered quickly and with exclamation.

"Well I certainly can't give you cash, can't sell it except maybe the sunglasses. Maybe on trade 'cause I can maybe get something on the parts."

Michael set his hand on his flat stomach and it growled involuntarily as if it knew there were no hamburgers in its future. He looked in the display cases and then stared through the antique lamp which cast yellowish light through the glass below. He had intended to leave with an empty backpack, not replace its contents.

"How 'bout a guitar," Wu said as he pointed up and behind.

"Ain't interested."

"A knife? Boys need a good knife."

"Nah."

"Well tell you what, you look around and then tell me what you think is fair for what you brought."

Michael nodded and started to walk around the u-shaped setup of cases. Fishing gear and hunting accessories. Handguns that Wu would never give him. Power tools for which he had no use. Wu set the old comic book aside and put his effort into a crossword puzzle book, marking each letter carefully with a blue ballpoint pen.

Michael wandered into the army surplus section of the store and picked up a replica grenade. He pulled the pin, pretended to lob it over a trench and made an explosive sound with his mouth. Pulled through the jackets that were way too big for his frame. Pressed his fingers into the foam sized for cots. Put on a helmet and struck himself in the head with his knuckles to test the protection.

Satisfied with his selection, Michael set them on the counter in front of Wu who looked at the items from his peripheral. "Ain't nothin' from the army surplus, gotta be from the pawn side."

"You didn't say that."

"Well I'm sayin' it now."

"That ain't fair."

Wu thought about telling him about life, but let it slide. "Nothing from the army surplus."

"C'mon Wu... Mr. Wu, it ain't much."

Wu set his pen down with a sigh, looked at the items, then at Michael.

"These, sir, and that jumper cable thing and that air thing right there." Michael pointed into a glass case at a dusty portable jumper cable tool and next to it an air compressor.

"You're askin' a lot."

"I got all this stuff myself, wasn't easy."

"And you think this is a fair deal?"

"I do sir."

12

The home dugout on the baseball field was marked by a pile of bricks, only the wall toward right field remained erect. The outfield grass grew in random patches, and the infield was an amalgam of rocks and bottles and fast-food leftovers. The visitors still stood, albeit with a large crack and hole, cut out in right angles from displaced bricks down the middle. Alone, with their backs against the dirty wall, Carmen was acutely aware of this moment. Uncomfortable. Sweaty. Odd. He put his thoughts to the cloud laden sunlight low to the west. Into the pastel depth at the horizon swathed in orange and pink and purple. The cleansing virgin aura of the untouchable. He put his thoughts there and took a swig from the

40-ounce bottle with the paper bag. "I'm going in," he said to the clouds and handed the bottle to Alice who took her sip.

"We did go in," Alice responded with a hard swallow. The beer was cheap, and it was warm, though she didn't know if that had any factor on her distaste.

"Nah, we went just a bit in, that wasn't nothin'."

She took another sip before handing the bottle back to Carmen. "Why? There's nothing in there but busted houses and a bunch of creepy prisoners cleaning it up."

"That ain't it."

"Then what is it?"

Carmen started to speak, then thought it wise to refrain. "I want to see the 'Frog People,'" he continued. "Is that wrong?"

He turned his head, took in her eyes, and watched them sullied with guilt. "Nothing wrong with being curious, I guess, but you know they ain't real."

He averted his eyes, and, in that moment, she slid closer to him. Having felt the near imperceptible vibrations in the wooden bench his heart jumped. He racked his brain for guidance. From his brother, no. From his father, impossible. In the waning light, he was left with the images of fictional romantic encounters. The perfect kiss in closeup at prom, the background dancers reduced to soft focus. The jock football player as he slipped his arm behind her and she pressed against him as the lights shifted against the big screen. The nerd who came to understand himself, and the popular girl who fell for him. Impeccable skin. Flawless, soft brown eyes. Scripted lines that always hit.

The warm beer had settled deep into his empty stomach and pressed a subtle chill through his core. It shook him past the threat of rejection and drove him toward her with deep heartbeats. He leaned in slowly and the worn, rotted bench bounced millimeters as he approached. Her eyes darted across the contours of his face while the sun realized the gravity and paused his descent, which left the aura aloft.

Those sweet, strawberry lips imagined through screens slipped into nothing, and the first feeling of another's lips flashed into Carmen's memory. The bitter warm taste of cheap beer. The salty aroma from dried sweat at the remains of the day. It was everything to him, and he pushed his lips harder against hers and she reciprocated. And as he released to read her eyes, the sun winked and clicked his metal gears into motion heading west.

Her eyes again studied and, in the end, gave their approval, which in turn fixed a smile she had forgotten. He, in turn, smiled in relief and, draped with confidence, leaned in with clutched eyelids.

"Carmen!" he heard with eyes closed from beyond the ball field dugout. He hoped in the darkness the voice was imagined. "Alice!" she heard and took the same strategy to make it go away as Carmen. "Guys!"

"Mother fucker," Carmen said for Alice's ears.

Bicycle tires over gravel. Brown, brittle grass. Glass shards. The tires as they skidded to a stop. Handlebars that hit the ground and finally the heavy breaths. "Guys," Michael panted as he appeared just inside the brick walls, "guys, I went back."

"What?" Carmen asked.

"I went back," Michael shot back, then paused to catch his breath. "I went back and I went further and we can, I think I can get us a car workin' and we can go. I mean we can actually see The Fields."

He grinned through the breaths, proud that he got it all out and slowly his body relaxed with steady intake.

"No one likes you," Alice responded curtly, which broke Michael's anticipation, yet not in the way he had considered. She glared at his greasy black hair and salty skin. The black dirt collected under his jagged fingernails. His dirty tank top frayed at his waist that was pulled down over his left shoulder where the black duffel bag hung. The openings that ran the length of his sneakers between the canvas and the rubber soles. "No one likes you, Michael. You're gross and dumb, and you need to stop following us."

He looked at Carmen for something, anything, but simply stared under the kiss' spell. He looked back at her and regretted immediately. "I said no one likes you!" she screamed, and dust puffed as she rose from the wooden bench. "Get out of here!" She grabbed his arms and pushed on his thin frame while he had no reaction readied. "You stupid weirdo! You creep!" She released her grip and shoved him. Once, twice, and then beyond the dugout. "Get goin'!" And she pointed to his bicycle next to theirs.

Michael lifted the bike by a handlebar and swung a leg over. In a moment, he found the balance with the duffle over his shoulder and pushed forward. In a moment, he navigated through welling eyes and tears that washed the dirt from his cheeks.

Alice returned to the dugout, took the 40 from the bench, and drank with large gulps. Carmen watched her and knew that his silence would keep him from sleep for the eternal. The deep guilt that cut a wound through which nothing would ever heal. Alice belched with carbonation and conquest, and he replayed what really mattered, 'we can actually see The Fields.'

Michael pushed down on the pedals and into the neighborhood. Past the shirtless, obese man who mowed his lawn even when the stalks were too short for the blades. Past the rusted caravan in the empty lot with flat tires where the prostitutes took the scarred, the limbless, and the awkward. Past the Jesus house.

He squeezed the brake handles at the edge of the porch, a small patch of concrete slanted to one corner. A rain-stained mattress among the leaves angled against the peeling wooden frame. Rotted firewood. A red Radio Flyer wagon rusted at the base and curved edges. He ran along the pathway that pushed along the side of the house and led to the backyard. A rusted lawn mower. A white car door. Black plastic bags filled with aluminum cans and half-empty bottles. Through the chain link fence, he sprinted over the dead grass to the back of the yard.

The white paint was weathered but held on the metal shed, with only the corners rough and caramel with rust. 'Stay Out!' was scrawled in marker across the doors. Michael turned the simple latch and pulled the door open in the dying light. He shut the door tight and his world came into darkness until he pressed the button on a small LED lantern. The darkness evaporated and cast shadowy light throughout the cramped quarters.

The interior was impeccably clean and neatly organized. A faded charcoal recliner and small couch. A nicked coffee table with exposed particleboard over a shaggy emerald rug. An antique boombox on the floor. A U.S. Army issued footlocker locked with a silver combination lock. Three wooden shelves lined the back wall vertically, each stained a dark coffee, each glinting from the artificial light that bounced off the hard angles. The top shelf was lined with books. Plato and Aristotle. Lao

Tsu and Sun Tsu. Dog-eared army field manuals, mostly United States, but a couple Russian and one Japanese. Electronics manuals and schematics. Comic books stacked on the left side of the middle shelf, and notebooks rose up the right side. The third shelf was empty except for a single candle surrounded by its thick glass casing etched with the image of Jesus Christ. Yet there were two pictures taped to the corrugated metal above the shelf. There was a young man in both, with short, cropped black hair and chiseled features about his face. In the first, he was seated on a recliner and held a newborn baby in his arms, the small figure enveloped in the muscled embrace. The man held his eyes steady on the sleeping child. In the latter, he was shirtless, and a toddler's feet dangled over his tattooed shoulders. The toddler grinned that gleeful toddler grin as the man reached up and held his sides.

Michael threw the black duffel bag on top of the footlocker and climbed into the recliner. He turned sideways and pulled his dirt-stained knees up to his chest. He stayed in that position for some time, with his breaths pushing against his knees. With his mind fending off thoughts, any thoughts. Just his breath and the serenity of the clean solitude that was afforded him. In a shed behind his decrepit house in Nowhere, America.

It's the voices without hope that have only quiet resignation and amplified madness. To that end, the screams from the house started at a reasonable decibel, then steadily rose. Anger that was precipitated by some action or situation that had been repeated ad nauseam. It was this anger that cut through Michael, and he broke and he wept into the gray fabric worn smooth from years of use. He had, at such an age, felt the hopelessness of circumstance and chance. And so, he wept. He wept to the soundtrack of middle-aged hatred and profanity, though he could not discern the object of their rage through the shed walls.

The tears flowed steadily, his nose ran, and then the cacophony ceased. There was a quiet that settled into the air and allowed him to regain his composure. He turned and straightened his limbs until he was sitting normally in the chair. He stared into the nothing until an echoing knock rattled him into consciousness. His heart jumped at the intrusion, and he decided to ignore the trespass. Another knock, this time quieter, less jarring.

"I ain't hungry," Michael said through the closed door.

"It's Carmen."

"What do you want?"

"I just," he started, "I just wanted to say I'm sorry."

"You didn't do nothin'."

"I know, I mean I didn't say anything, but I didn't stick up for you," Carmen said, then waited for a response that didn't come. "Can I come in?"

"If you want," Michael responded after an extended delay.

Carmen undid the latch open and swung the door open. The light from the lantern lit his face as the dusk was transitioning to night.

"Man, I'm sorry, I really am," he said as he stepped inside and closed the door behind himself. He noted the reflective streaks on Michael's cheeks and the sniffles.

"It's alright."

"Holy shit," Carmen said as he looked around.

"What?"

"Nothing, I mean, I was expecting a shithole."

Michael ignored the comment as Carmen studied the tight environ. The footlocker and the books and the notebooks and the photos. The stark contrast of what he spied through the partially open door when Michael's mother answered.

"It's not alright," Carmen said as he pushed aside the duffel and sat down on the footlocker. "She was being mean."

"I'm used to it."

Carmen looked at him and hoped for some clue as to how to respond yet found none. "I mean, I mean maybe," he started with a comforting tone. "Maybe if you, you know, showered more and had clean clothes, maybe you wouldn't get picked on as much."

Michael stood from the recliner and turned his back to Carmen. "We ain't got no water," as he studied the book spines.

"What?"

"At least not out of the taps."

"How do you not have water?"

"My dad don't work at the dog food factory, he got fired a while ago. Can't afford the filter fees, all we got is the dirty water. Tried showering with it but it hurt real bad and I got all red." He pulled the *Tao de Chang* from the shelf and flipped through the pages. "Once a week he goes out and steals as much water as he can so we can get clean and wash some clothes."

Carmen hadn't considered that his appearance was due to circumstances beyond his control, which made his initial guilt return tenfold. Having already apologized he looked to the nuances within the structure. The folds of the metal. Its color. The brand name printed on the lantern.

"You said we can go? We can get to The Fields?"

Michael replaced the book, turned around and sought sincerity in Carmen's eyes. "Yeah," he said once satisfied, "I can get us there," then turned back to the shelves.

Carmen stood up, walked a few steps, and stood next to Michael. "Who's that in the pictures?"

"That's me and my brother."

"I didn't know you had a brother."

"He's a lot older, he was a lot older than me."

"Oh."

"I was 'the mistake'."

"The mistake?"

"That's what my parents call me when they think I can't hear them."

"What happened to him, I mean, if you don't mind me askin'?"

"The Fields," Michael said in monotone.

"How are we gonna get there?"

Michael stood for a moment, then handed the black duffel bag to Carmen who unzipped it on the coffee table.

"Holy shit, Michael."

"We must be prepared, mustn't we?"

Carmen sifted through the duffel and explored the contents. "Two bump keys," Michael said to the shelves from memory. "One Sputnik. One Slim Jim. One transmitter simulator. Three knives, one for me, one for you, and one for Alice. Three flashlights. Three gas masks, for the 'Frog People.' One set of portable jumper cables. One air compressor. A Geiger counter. Bottles of water. A cell phone. Candy bars. A GPS that kinda works."

"You know we couldn't go tonight, right?" Carmen asked as he closed the bag.

"I know that."

"Then why'd you bring the bag with you?"

"Just wanted you to know I'm not... that I was serious."

Carmen stood up and the voices resumed in the house, unintelligible but the intent was known to the boys. "You want to eat over at my house?"

"Tonight?"

"Yeah."

"I don't wanna be a bother."

"You ain't no bother."

"C'mon," Carmen said as he opened the metal door to the darkness and the screaming, "grab a bag of clothes too, you can use our washer."

Michael felt the embarrassment and stood still in thought. The dirt was his, as was his worked skin. He had compensated with knowledge and ingenuity. He was the guy who could get things. Alcohol and cigarettes. Hiding places. The resources for The Fields. He stared at the open door. A friend, a real friend even with lingering doubt. He listened to the words as they echoed from the house. The last chirp in the branches. Yet it was only when he saw the dewy sincerity in Carmen's eyes that he moved to the door. And he snuck into the house and filled a black plastic bag with his clothes and joined his friend who was waiting in the front yard. And Carmen held Michael's bike steady by the handlebar, so he wouldn't have to bend over with the bag. The two boys rode off into the darkness, navigating from memory with the only conversation a warning for potholes. Suspect houses and armed drunkards.

Unleashed dogs and abandoned vehicles encircled in glass shards.

Part 2

13

The clouds at the horizon were either darkened apprehension or simply the morning warmth in the distance. Nature's deception to the early risers. In either case, the kids were not concerned as they stopped their bicycles at the edge of their last exploration. Far beyond the gate and fence within the interior of the restricted zone. Too far to hear the blue-collar workers in their rusted sedans and workhorse pickup trucks. Here was the cracked and buckled cement. The faded white lines and vehicles stuck with bulldozer holes from where they were pushed to the medians in haste.

Alice stared past the dirt embankment and up at the faded green dinosaur roaring over the abandoned gas station. She thought about running after Carmen through the aisles. Michael exploring the empty refrigerators. Michael, even after Carmen explained his story, she did not like Michael. There was something about him that struck her core. She heard his voice behind her interspersed with Carmen's and the clank of tools against sheet metal. Each grating and playing off each other, pressing her mind into regret as she stood in the reflective quiet.

Carmen ran his fingers above the rusted punctures in the luxurious black SUV. They covered both the driver's side and the rear passenger door. He imagined the man who drove the spikes into the metal with his bulldozer. His head dripped with sweat under a hard hat. Safety first with an orange vest and steel-toed boots. Did he worry that the tremors would take him too? Did he work in The Fields or was he someone else? What did he think when he pushed the first car against the embankment? The second? The hundredth?

"Alright," Michael told Carmen with his head buried under the hood, "let's see if this works." He left the jumper cable box attached, walked around the black duffel bag on the cement and hopped up to the driver's seat. He pulled a small plastic contraption out of his pocket which was similar to a keyless start remote, yet only had two buttons, 'run,' and 'stop.' Michael pressed 'run' and numbers began sequencing on the rectangular LCD screen below the buttons. Ten-digit combinations that changed over in milliseconds. He set the device in a cup holder and sat back on the sun-faded black leather. Ran his hands around the steering wheel and then his fingers over the buttons, the imprinted horn icon. He rummaged through the center console. Receipts and travel-sized tissues. He pulled the glove box open. An owner's manual, proof of registration to 'Mark Inhoes,' and an unopened pack of Marlboros.

As he closed the glove box the SUV came to life with a jolt, which caused Michael to fall back into the seat. "Holy shit!" Carmen exclaimed as he appeared in the driver's side door swung open.

"Why's it sound like that?" Carmen asked Michael while listening to the knocking engine.

"Old gas I think."

"That gonna be a problem?"

"Don't think so, but it don't matter."

"Why's that?"

"This one breaks down, we just get another."

Carmen looked past Michael and through the windshield at Alice. She had her back to the boys, as she had since setting down her bicycle. Carmen walked over to the edge of the pavement and stood next to her as Michael inflated the tires. He made sure she felt his presence, and she made sure not to acknowledge it.

"You know we don't have to go if you don't wanna," he said to her with locked eyes on the faded green dinosaur. "I mean it's dangerous, but I mean if you don't wanna go."

"It's not that."

"It's not what?"

"It's not that I don't want to go. I've always wanted to go."

"Then what?"

"It's him."

"I told you he's just had a bad, you know, go of things or whatever."

"I do not trust that boy, Carmen. He's a squirmy little shit, and it always feels like he's trying to get something."

"No he's not."

"You only say that cause he's got you believin' his shit. He's scamming you."

"Scamming me how?"

"That's the thing with pieces of shit, you don't know what their angle is until they got you already."

Michael disconnected the jumper cables and slammed the hood shut. He picked up the black duffel and threw it in the backseat. "You guys ready?" he yelled as he settled into the driver's seat.

"I wanted it to be just me and you," Alice continued without responding to Michael.

"It can't be just me and you, unless you want to go on our bikes?"

"I know."

"C'mon! We're burning daylight or some shit!"

Carmen and Alice turned and looked at Michael in the driver's seat as the hard engine bounced him. He was indeed tall for his age yet still seemed childlike at the wheel.

"You do get the feeling when you're with him," Carmen said. "You know, that you're gonna die."

Alice laughed, and Carmen smiled at succeeding in breaking her anger. They walked to the idling car. Michael pressed the "CD" button and "Once in a Lifetime" by the Talking Heads came blasting through the speakers.

"But it'll be an epic death," Carmen yelled over the music and Alice let a smile crest the edge of her lips. Carmen took the front seat, Alice got in the back.

Michael shifted into drive, pressed down the gas pedal and the SUV lurched forward. He had only driven a few times, but the empty road gradually gave him confidence. Straight south as the sun came up over the haze. Deftly he maneuvered around dusted buckled pavement between the sedans and the pickups and the semis adorned with rusted horizontal puncture holes. His passengers looked out the windows as the abandoned towns appeared and faded. Amenities promoted on billboards in various states of sunburnt and gravitational decay before exits. The reminders at ramps with arrows that aided the navigation of hungry travelers and those with full bladders. Indestructible fast-food logos aloft on metal poles that pushed into the sky as if the Tower of Babel. The names of hotel brands bolted to hotels above windows of dirt and dust above the broken glass of the lower stories. The green reflective sign hung from the bridge that informed of Corning, Exit 77. The tattered bed sheet next to it exclaiming 'Corning is Dead'; with a frowny face in black spray paint.

'Death was here' at mile 81. 'Zombie apocalypse is real' at 87. 'I miss mom' at 95.

Michael slowed the SUV, maneuvered around a massive buckle in the pavement, and stopped. The highway forked at a junction and the signs had long ago fallen or been taken as trophies. The car jittered with the bad gas as they looked for spray-painted clues.

"I say left," Carmen said.

"Go right," Alice retorted.

"Well that ain't helpful," Michael thought while straining to see further down the roads.

"Left looks better," Carmen added.

"Why an' how?" asked Michael. "They look the same to me."

"Just a feeling."

"That don't reassure me."

"Go right, Michael," Alice commanded from the back seat.

"Why right?"

"Cause right is always right."

Michael took a moment to consider this nonsense and where she might have learned it.

"Go left."

Michael turned his head and looked at Alice who scowled. At Carmen who implored with his eyes. At the gas gauge with 87 miles estimated then slowly pulled his foot from the brake and steered left on the fork as Alice seethed.

The concrete buckles that were before a nuisance had now become fluid and crested like waves with several foot drops. Some rose as ramps and the others impenetrable walls. The SUV's high clearance overcame some, yet they felt the concrete scrape the steel underbelly. The worst lifted the back tires and Michael had to press hard on the gas to clear them.

Michael leaned forward in the leather seat and squinted to see further down the road. He registered a collapsed overpass, yet he lacked confidence in this assessment.

"Oh, shit," Carmen said, beating Michael to the confirmation. The bridge had broken and collapsed on both sides. This left only twisted steel rebar and the odd edges of concrete jutting out from the dirt embankment and into the air to nowhere. A semi-truck was left with its cab dangling over the western edge, the trailer still with 'shop, smile, save' in bold green letters.

The large pieces below had been moved by the bulldozers. Pressed against the barriers along the shoulders, against the vehicles with the rusted puncture wounds. Michael drove over the crunching remains that had been left on the flat of the road and upon the buckles and over the faded white lines and the embedded ridged reflectors.

Alice stared out the window smug at mile 101. 'Where is FEMA?' at 103 and Michael stepped on the brakes at 107.   Absent   the road   noise   the   clattering   engine   echoed throughout the cabin. The boys took stock of the road ahead while Alice leaned to the center to see through the windshield.

Michael was the first to open his door and step to the pavement. Carmen next and then Alice. They left the SUV with open doors, walked slowly and left footsteps on the dirt-swept road.

This time it was their bridge that had gone. Their cracked concrete and rebar impasse. A hundred feet below them ran a lazy river, lined with trees that bowed over the banks with lush greenery, and the water baked brown from sediment. Small rapids ran in whitewater directly below the former bridge where pieces of the structure had sunk into the riverbed and stood inches above the waterline as if miniature icebergs.

"We shoulda gone right," Alice stated.

"No shit," Michael said before spitting over the edge.

"What do we do now?" Carmen asked.

"Gotta go back."

"Way to state the obvious," Alice said with venom.

"C'mon," Carmen started, "let's just go back to the car and go back."

"Back home?" Michael asked.

"No, just to the fork in the road."

"What a dumbass," Alice muttered under her breath.

The kids got back into the SUV and shut the doors. Michael veered right then turned the wheel left and headed back over their tire tracks. Even with traffic absent it felt uncomfortable to drive the wrong way. The road signs were opposite the concrete barrier that divided the traffic flows. Bisping, exit 105 covered with a black 'x'. Pawnee, exit 103 under skull and crossbones. A sarcastic smiley face at 101. An apt frowny face at 99.

"This time," Alice said when they reached the fork, "go right."

"I know what to do here, Alice."

"Good, then do it."

Michael turned tight on the wheel and set them on the right fork. Colter crossed out with black at mile three. The remnants of an American flag draped over the chain link of a pedestrian overpass. 'Hell is Real' a faded imprint on a billboard. 'Jesus is THE WAY' a mile further. 'Shampoo saves lives' at mile seven.

And at mile ten the impasse they found bore no structural failures. There was not a collapsed bridge. The pavement ran smooth. Yet what lay ahead blocked any hope of passage. The engine idled, yet they did not exit. There was no need. The road ahead was a twisting interchange that soared over the overgrowth below, a bridge that had inexplicably survived. And at its apex stood a copy of the same metal gate that was visible from Main Street. A warning for all but authorized vehicles. Severe tire damage. Red lights on each side of the structure. The metal keypad from within a concrete pylon. All was identical to home, except the razor wire extended across the top of the gate and down the sides, whereas the other continued to the horizon with chain link and barbs.

"This is hopeless," Carmen said despondently.

There was a quiet acknowledgement from the driver and backseat passenger. Innately curious are the youth, yet, without opportunity and reward, that curiosity wanes quickly. Each pondered the blockades set in their path and the rewards that would be reaped. At the least, a story to tell. At most, some semblance of closure, whatever it meant.

More practically, Carmen and Alice had a hard deadline of sundown. They kept the time on their minds as the day progressed. The hours traveled south and the commitment they'd have to make north.

"We're outta gas," Michael said after the quiet came over the cabin.

"Hopeless," Alice added.

Michael pushed open his door and stepped softly to the ground. Alice exited, Carmen followed, and they watched Michael's figure shrink as he walked further from the SUV and up the incline of the bridge. Further and his figure halved in size and at the gate halved again.

He studied the keypad and ran his fingers across the black metal bars. Through them he saw the rusted tire spikes, and above him the aged razor wire. The pavement beyond was free of debris and the abandoned vehicles were noticeably absent. He surveyed the land, the unsettling quiet of neighborhoods in a town without movement. The expansive roofs of big box stores collapsed inward. Nature's reclamation, which encroached on the reassuring straight lines of human planning. He walked to the edge of the bridge, set his hands on the concrete barricade, and looked over the edge. The lazy, brown river several hundred feet below. The shade trees with their emerald canopy plumes.

Michael's figure doubled, then doubled again as he neared the SUV.

"What's the plan?" Carmen asked him.

"Huh?"

"What's the plan? Use that thing to open the gate?"

"What? Oh, nah that gate is old school. I ain't got the tools."

"Then that's it?"

"I guess."

"So we just go home? Screw that."

"I don't know. If you want to get home by supper, we should get a new car and get going."

"You don't have to be home for supper."

"You wanna keep going?"

"We got a cell phone, we just call our parents."

"And say what?"

"I don't know."

Alice watched the young men parse the situation and then set her eyes south. The sun streaks through the dirty air. The adventure promised in peril, and when she opened the rear door and took out the black duffel the boys did not notice. When she flung it over her shoulder and started up the bridge, they remained focused on themselves. She started up the grade, methodically and with purpose, the duffel substantial against her small frame.

It wasn't until she was halfway to the gate, her figure halved, that they realized her absence. "Alice!" Carmen yelled, "C'mon, let's go!"

She kept going. Methodically. Purposefully.

"Alice!"

She stopped and slowly turned around. "Let's go you pussies!" and again turned her back to them.

"I guess we're going," Carmen said with a hint of trepidation to Michael.

"Yeah."

They started for the concrete apex. For the first time, the boys felt the unease press into their skin. Alice's reluctance was their out, the one way they could turn back with bravery intact. Beyond the gate, this was real. Unknown. And when they arrived at the border, Alice had her hands grasped tightly on the bars with her cheeks pressed against the indifferent metal.

Carmen took a bottle of water from the duffel, cracked it open and took a long sip, then handed it to Alice who ignored him. He set the bottle to his side and pressed his cheeks through the gate to match her stance.

Michael went to the edge where the barrier divided the bridge from the drop. He looked over to reaffirm the exposure below, then reached up to the black bar at the gate's terminus and pulled himself up on the barrier. There was a gap where the gate extended, and another where there was no concrete on which to step upon on the other side. A careful grip and he stuck his left leg out, swung around and lowered himself the several feet to the bridge deck.

"Hey," Michael said to Carmen through the bars, "pass me the duffel."

Carmen took a moment, then a step back from the gate. He stole a glance at Alice who gave no signal, then picked up the bag and walked to the end of the gate.

"Pass it over," Michael instructed.

Carmen clutched the bag by the strap and extended his arm over and around to Michael's waiting hand. As soon as he felt the slightest touch he released and shuffled fast away from the edge.

"Shit!" Michael yelled as the slack let out and the duffel dropped in the empty air above the precipice. The weight yanked on his arm and as it pulled down, he grabbed for the metal bars. His shoulders extended, and his body contorted over the edge until he gained control and heaved himself and the bag to safety.

"Tell me," Michael said with shortened breaths. "Tell me if you're gonna let go."

"I'm sorry."

"Do you know how fucked we'd be if we lose this?" He held it aloft.

"Calm down, Michael," Alice responded for Carmen and stepped up on the concrete ledge with her hands around the metal, then deftly jumped down to the other side. "You comin'?" she asked Carmen, who hadn't moved an inch closer to the opening since retreating.

He thought about moving and even commanded his legs into movement. He looked at Alice, then Michael, then the ledge, and swiftly back to them.

"Guys," he said, "I've never been up this high before."

"Me either," Michael responded. "So what?"

"So," as the air thinned for only him. "So my legs ain't working."

"What do you mean your legs 'ain't workin'?"

"I mean I want to be where you are but it's like I'm standing in concrete."

"You are on concrete."

"In concrete, you dumbass."

"Carmen," Alice said softly as she approached the gate. "Take a deep breath, Carmen." She waited for him to comply, "Now, forget where you are."

"I can't."

"Yes, you can. Close your eyes."

"I can't go forward," he said with eyes closed, "and I can't go backwards."

"Think about me and you. Think about the dugout. Remember drinking beer in the dugout? Just me and you?"

"Michael showed up."

"Yeah, don't think about that part, just the first part."

"My heart's going real fast."

"Breathe, Carmen. Breathe."

He took a deep breath.

"Now hold it for a second, then breathe out."

"My legs feel tingly, like bugs crawling up me."

"Don't talk, Carmen. Just breathe."

"I think I need some water."

"You gotta come to the gate to get some water," Michael said.

Alice shot him a glance and he returned to silence.

"My heart's going real fast."

"Breathe, Carmen," she implored motherly from opposite the gate as Michael looked on nervously, "breathe."

He closed his eyes and he took deep, controlled breaths while he coaxed his mind to not think about the breaths. The pressure from his chest pulsated. He drew a breath, held it, then released. Comfort in front of the television. Settled under blankets.

"You alright, Carmen?" Michael asked.

The heart slowed, another breath, and he opened his eyes.

"You alright?" she asked.

"Yeah," after a few moments, "I'm good. I think." He took one last deep breath, but this one was for courage, and he took his first step toward the precipitous entry to The Fields. And his second faltered.

"Tremor!" Michael shrieked and in a second, he fell hard to the deck where he could hear the hidden metal structure flexing as the bridge swayed and bucked. Then Carmen lost his balance, hit the concrete, and sprawled out face down to ride the motion with silent prayer. Alice kept her hands wrapped around the black metal bars and her grip firmed.

Far below them the earth rumbled, and the trees shook, their green canopies convulsed. The river adjusted and rode the trespass. The town in the distance had no more to cede, the structures remained in their current disrepair.

Time slowed, trapping them in an elongated faux eternity, with fingertips dug into the harsh, man-made material and whose engineers they were now reliant upon. Ten seconds passed, or a minute or fifteen and as quickly as it came it ceased. Though at its egress, Carmen and Michael's fingers stayed pressed, Alice's knuckles white. Each took turns seeking clues in the other's eyes. Michael stood first and dusted off his knees. Alice relaxed, and Carmen remained prone.

Michael walked to the gate and stood next to Alice, and they were both impatient for Carmen's first move. He waited, as if building suspense, then shot up quick and walked with fixed gaze to the gap and grasped the gate and swung to the other side. Alice met him near the edge with a tight embrace as he held in the emotional release that had swelled from the panic and the earthquake. Michael watched them until the situation lingered and unzipped the duffel for a bottle of water.

As they separated their eyes stayed fixed until Carmen turned and started down the bridge. "We doing this shit?" he asked the two still idling near the gate with confidence, then turned and continued. Alice smiled, and Michael slung the duffel over his head and onto his shoulder. He handed her the bottle and she took several gulps before handing it back.

He smiled with the simple interaction she had granted him. A near-death experience it seems, he thought, makes people not care so much about stupid things.

Michael and Alice doubled their pace to catch Carmen, and the three walked abreast down the slope of the bridge towards the town. Steady in their gait with purpose. Steady through the aftershock. Steady south.

14

The bedroom window faced east, the navy-blue drapes were open, and the panel of the beige race car wallpaper opposite had faded from the sunrises. American classics—Mustangs, GTOs, Corvettes, and Chargers from the golden age of muscle. The bedframe was plastic, molded in the shape of a non-descript stock car. A blue comforter with a matte finish of dust set over a twin mattress. The wood toy chest stained a caramel brown and "Brandon" in stylized letters along the front. The dresser was similar, yet noticeably a different tint. Model cars among pro wrestlers next to a worn leather glove with an eggshell-white baseball tucked into the webbing.

Carmen crouched down and picked up a half-built robot of Legos near an assortment of pieces on the maroon carpet. Reds, blues, and greens. Long yellows and stubby purples. He stood with the toy in hand and stepped over the uneven floor where the tremors had cracked the foundation. A ridge, a foot high, had raised the carpet and pulled it from where the floor met the walls. He picked up the fallen photographs on the dresser and set them right in their frames in slow reverence.

A wood pier jutting out towards a small lake. A boy holds an olive-green bass by the fishing line next to a smiling father. The boy posing in his baseball uniform, white with an olde English "D" in dark blue.

The bottom dresser drawers ajar and overhung, the top ones having come free and on the floor. T-shirts in Arkansas Razorbacks maroon with white lettering and the lighter Cardinal adorned with baseball bats. Superhero underwear. Worn white socks with stripes at the calves.

The eggshell-white refrigerator lay face down, the handles pressed into the tiled floor and the mechanics in view. Drawers open, drawers felled with silverware scattered and layered in dust. The table glass had shattered which left shards under and within the legs. Alice tread softly over the glass and centered it in the dining area. She picked up the chairs and arranged them around the table.

Michael sunk into the plush plaid couch and held the television remote toward the overturned flat screen that hung by its cord. A painting remained on the wall, having survived the initial horror and subsequent reminders. A whaler out at sea, askew as it crested the whitecaps under blackened clouds.

He thought about the men. Their fear cocooned in adrenaline. Arms tightly wrapped knowing overboard was death amid the screams and saltwater breaches over the deck. The deceased artist.

Façades in vinyl siding, in brick, in wood—each spray-painted with x-codes near front porches. Numbers for the search unit. Numbers for the date. The time. Those found alive, and those found otherwise.

Each door they entered was concealed by wild grass, and every arrival was met with the same quiet. The same solemn aura. Scattering cockroaches. Nests of twigs and leaves near broken windows. Nature trespassed at every opening.

Bottles, their liquids long ago evaporated, escaped through the hidden pores in polyethylene. Pots and pans and dinnerware debris. Video game controllers on couches, on floors, and on beds. Report cards, trophies, and posters felled from their adhesives. Of rock stars and sports figures and princesses. Hushed cribs within pastel interiors and plush animals strewn across the uneven floors.

Support beams cracked, door frames splintered, the sharp edges exposed in hallways. Dirty clothes in hampers, clean in dryers—some upright and others crashed over. Novels piled on den floors, storybooks in the children' rooms, and pornography under mattresses where teenage boys had slept. Old school magazines and flash drives.

Each home was a replication with one more discovery that pulled each kid deeper into reflection. Carmen clung to his mother's love, of which he realized his ignorance. Alice tried to put her hatred of Michael in perspective, yet it still clung, for societal compartmentalization gripped her pubescent mind tight. For Michael, he found similarities between these abandoned homes and his own, which tempered any revelation, and these situations normally put him in a philosophical framework, he found his thoughts shallow.

"What do you think?" Carmen asked the others while standing around a kitchen island.

"About what?" Michael asked.

"About this. Should we keep going?"

"What time is it?" Alice inquired.

"Don't know," Carmen said. "Maybe two, three."

"Do we have enough time to keep going?" asked Alice.

"We gotta get a new car," Carmen responded. "Any of these cars out here work?"

"I don't know," Michael started. "Gotta try 'em."

"Bunch of cars on the road," Carmen said.

"Best if they're in a garage."

"All the garages we saw were caved in."

"Well let's find one that ain't."

"Wait," Alice interjected, "where are we going?"

"What do you mean?" Carmen asked, for the boys hadn't considered a purpose.

"I mean where are we going?"

"South," Michael answered.

"To the next town," Carmen added, "to see if the prisoners are there."

"And if they're not?"

"Then we head home so we can be back by dark."

"I don't wanna get in trouble."

"You're not gonna get in trouble."

"How do you know?"

"Cause we'll be home by dark, I promise. My mom'll beat my ass if I'm not."

Alice found sincerity in Carmen's eyes and ceased her objections while hesitation remained in hers.

"I drive fast," Michael reassured. "One more town and we'll speed home. Be there for dinner."

Her eyes examined Michael's and then Carmen's. Their expressions and their posture. She lifted her elbows off the island and stiffened her joints to seem taller, which gave her a superficial burst of courage. "All right, one more town."

"Let's get the hell outta this shithole," Michael added for good measure as they followed Carmen out of the house and into the wild of the neighborhood.

15

The red Toyota hatchback sped down the country road, and its 4-cylinder engine whined under the request from Michael's foot pressed hard to the carpeted floor below the dash. Raised from hibernation, it fought him with knocks and pings and skipped pings within the pistons. Whereas the SUV was refined with an air of audacity, the Toyota was a hyper child, and the kids felt its essence and matched it in kind.

Michael kept steady as the speed pushed the car left and right into the overgrowth that had turned the two-lane road into a narrow passage. Carmen ducked his head back inside the window whenever the high grass brushed against the frame and stuck his head back out when the car straightened out.

"I want shotgun next time!" Alice yelled from the backseat, over the whir of the engine and the wind, then returned to singing along with the CD left in the stereo slot. She stuck her arm out the window, let the grass punch her palms and watched the blue horizon over the blurry tips of green.

Breaks began to appear in the overgrown expanse. Rusted mailboxes that marked blacktop and gravel driveway entrances. The faltering siding and roofs turned in on quaint single-family homes X-codes in black spray-paint. A herd of deer fed on grass near an RV. An ice cream truck tilted along the hidden ditch. Water towers tilted against the horizon; their largess realized by the proximity. Welcoming script painted on dirty white cylinders. The lively movement of an elm as an extended family of birds lifted off into the air as the car went by.

As Michael drove the sparse acreage of lawns and trees, both erect and felled, became more cluttered. The speed blurred the x-codes next to front doors on the homes that still stood and made the rubble impossible to process.

Michael slowed as they approached a stop sign and an intersection. None of them questioned the action. Weeds had overtaken the shoulder and grew tall with invasive vigor. The shattered glass below large window frames at a gas station. 'Fresh Corn' painted on a wood sign that hung from a dilapidated wood-framed stand. They looked left, then right, and finally back to center.

The turn signal chimed and Michael turned right. An auto mechanic shop. More homes with cars idled in driveways. Collapsed roofs. X-codes. Fallen trees with thick trunks from lives lived next to saplings young and ambitious.

And somehow the vinyl banner, although tattered, had remained hung aloft above the street as the brick buildings along Main Street appeared. 'Harvest Days' in bold black font which partially hid hand-painted corn stalks and bushels of apples. 'September 19–21.'

The Toyota creeped along. Over broken bricks. Around a decomposed mattress with metal springs exposed. A soda fountain machine laid on its side. Plastics of human consumption. Automobiles, charred steel skeletons breaking down in the air—and with every rainfall, another layer of rust shed and slipped into the soil.

Broken windows in shops and restaurants, and the glass shards reflected from the sidewalks. Flag poles sans flags, save for a few ragged American flags that hung by threads and slumped in the night still. Cracks ran down the front of brick buildings that remained upright, symbols and numbers spray painted on doors. The wooden buildings tilted at odd angles or collapsed in a heap of splintered timber, rusted pipes and furniture.

There was a difference here, a seriousness that the kids felt and respected. This was more than an abandonment, something happened here. And as they attentively closed the car doors and felt the crunch of the ground, they knew that something was happening here. The faint waft of burning, resembling a campfire, settled on their nostrils. They sensed the turning of the day and realized the urgency. Each surveyed with intent, yet none moved. Each establishment only identified by furniture and fixtures, or, in some cases, the surviving signs. Restaurants and coffee shops. Insurance providers and dentists. Second-floor businesses and clothiers. Still, it was the marquee extending out from the cinema that consumed their attention. None could remember the last time they sat in a movie theater, and Michael was convinced he never had.

The black, block letters scattered among glass shards under and around their feet. The broad picture window through which they saw the darkened lobby. It was decided with a look between them, and Michael crunched his way to the Toyota. He unzipped the duffel, took out the flashlights, and handed one to Carmen, one to Alice with eyes averted.

Carmen led the trio though the window, and the spotlights darted across the lobby, compartmentally illuminating the setting. The empty candy counter. Flat screen televisions detached from the wall behind the counter and hanging from electrical cords. Crushed popcorn tubs. Soda fountains. Fallen metal stanchions with snaking red, velvet ropes.

Michael split off down the hallway and aimed the flashlight over the double doors for 'Theater 1.' The door squeaked as he pulled it open and entered the quiet rows of seats. Drink cups left in cup holders. Decaying popcorn browned and shriveled at the bottom of white paper bags. Hardened Dots and Sno-Caps and

Raisinets. Slits cut into the screen, shredded with knives.

The door squeaked as Carmen pulled the door for Theater 2 open. The silent rows of seats, empty of any refuse and still awaiting the next audience. The screen was intact, and as he panned the flashlight from left to right, he stopped at center. Someone had painted a 'smiley face,' and below it, 'Hello, Stranger.' He kept the face illuminated while trying to parse any meaning.

Theater 4's door did not squeak nor make any sound. As with 2, the seats were clean and the cup holders empty. It was the screen that gave Alice pause as the door closed behind her. Similar to Carmen's theater there was spray-paint on the white backdrop, yet hers had a different message.

'Those who stay here, die here. We will find you.'

She stepped cautiously down the darkened, elongated steps and kept the light on the screen. As she drew closer, she noticed the paint tinged maroon, and the thin boundaries that faded into the white were noticeably reddish in color. She reached the landing and turned the flashlight to her right and down.

Michael shone the flashlight on the digital projector opening above and behind the seats. He thought about finding the entrance but thought better of the effort and the reward. Back up the stairs and into the lobby.

Carmen slipped down to the landing in Theater 2, slowly pulled the screen forward and shone the light behind. He jumped, shrieked, and drew deep breaths as a pair of rats scurried from the intrusion. Embarrassed, he looked around and listened for any witnesses. Satisfied that his involuntary cowardice was his alone, he headed for the lobby.

Each boy stood with their backs to their respective theater doors. Carmen looked over at Michael, then to the other doors for Alice.

"Alice?!" Carmen yelled. No answer.

"Alice?!" Michael echoed.

"Three or four?" Carmen asked Michael.

"I don't know," he answered hesitantly.

"Alice?!" Michael tried again.

Stuck in indecision Carmen took to Theater 4, only because it was closest to him. He pushed slowly, for he knew that inside was the unknown. Michael held the door as he followed behind, his flashlight wild as the door hit his shoulder and then composed. They treaded lightly down the steps and the lights fixed on

Alice. She stood in trance, fixated with her head tilted down with the flashlight aimed and the seats obstructed her focus from the boys.

Carmen again found himself forcing his legs forward. They slid across the thin gray carpet of the extended steps with Michael behind him, satisfied with the pace. Alice illuminated; they saw the steady shakes in her shoulders. The frozen trepidation that rendered her immobile, less the primal that overcame her being. And Carmen's eyeline crept over the first row, and Carmen's heart stuttered. And Michael self-separated from his body and in an instant was back in the shed amongst the safety of books and trinkets. Eyelids tight then wide, and his self was back. In an abandoned cinema surrounded by the quiet across the border, and in The Fields.

She had seen a dead body once. Her grandfather, but arranged in sleep, his cheeks blushed artificial and dressed in Sunday best. She remembered the khaki dress she wore and the black sandals that pinched her toes as her legs dangled in her father's arms. Held above the white casket, she stared at the body in half understanding surrounded by elderly relatives with their handkerchiefs, bent backs, and thick lipsticks.

Here they were contorted, left in death in the shadow of a cinema screen. They remained in the tortured hold of last breaths. A family together with matching thin black rubbery skin hung from the skeleton which made their clothing seem three sizes too big. The mother on the floor posed in fetal, her mouth agape from the witness. The father reclined in a seat, slits in his t-shirt where the knives had punctured. The baby splayed out, having fallen in mid-crawl towards mother and the opening in her pink onesie ran the length of her back.

The cartoon monkey stitched into the lavender blanket. The baby bottles and diapers. Decayed food amongst fast-food wrappers.

Michael stepped with reverence over the bodies and bent to pick up a flower-print comforter folded yet disturbed. He unfurled, pulled it with backward steps and as he covered them, tears streamed down Alice's cheeks. Carmen took in her profile and with his own swollen eyes wrapped his arms around her. She sobbed into his shoulder as Michael set the end of the comforter to the floor.

While he stood stoic, Michael fought back tears as well, though he was more adept at catching them before they manifested. He stared at the bodies covered with stitched flowers of which his mind removed. The rubbery skin etched into memory. "It's time to go," he said in monotone.

For a moment Carmen and Alice kept the embrace, then slowly disconnected with sniffles and sleeves wiped along cheeks. Michael led the way up the stairs, through the lobby, and out the windows to the street.

Without words they pulled open the doors to the Toyota. Carmen did not protest, even jokingly, as Alice took the front passenger seat. Michael slid the sputnik key shaft into the key slot. A tool of thieves, akin to his bump keys, the sputnik had one end that mimicked a normal key. There was a metal cylinder in the center. Five metal prongs ended with rubber balls and stuck out of the back similar to the antennae of a satellite. Within each cylinder were small wires that could be adjusted to fill in the gaps to mimic the true key.

With the key set from before, Michael turned the device away from him. Click. Back and then forward. Click.

"Shit," he said.

Again. Click. Again. Click.

"Is the battery dead?" Carmen asked from the backseat.

"Don't know."

Alice scanned the street, the debris and burnt-out automobiles, and the sun low in the west.

"Well use your charger thing," Carmen instructed.

"I know what to do," Michael snapped back.

"Mother fucker," he mumbled as he found the hood release. "Well?" as he turned to Carmen.

"Well, what?"

"You got the duffel back there, hand me the jumper cables."

Carmen started to retort, realized he had no standing and passed the device forward. Michael took it, pushed open the door and closed it with purpose. He propped the hood and set the cables on the battery terminals. He watched the machine for a minute after turning it on, then returned to the driver's seat.

They sat in silence. Reflective and all wished for the sound of spark plugs to push the pistons. Michael stared at the steering wheel. Carmen, the cinema marquee and Alice, her hands. Michael turned the ignition. Click.

"Guys!" he yelled with a whisper. "Guys!"

Carmen and Alice each straightened in their seats and looked around. "Behind us," Michael said with his eyes pointed at the rearview mirror. They turned around and looked out the back window and saw the lights of a vehicle slowly approaching. It swerved around the obstacles as the Toyota had.

"Get down," Carmen commanded.

"They're gonna see the hood open," Alice said. "Close the hood!"

"It don't matter," Michael responded. "We're the only car that ain't burned up."

"Who is it?" Alice asked.

"Don't know," Michael said, "looks big though."

"Let's run for it," Carmen suggested.

"They'll see us, they're too close."

"Not if we go now."

"Go where?" Alice inquired.

"Back in the theater," Carmen said.

"Fuck no," she said before the thought had formed in her mind.

"Shit," Michael exclaimed, "looks like one of them charter buses."

"What charter buses?" Alice asked.

"From the train station. The ones that take the prisoners."

"That means we're near a camp," Carmen said, half excited and half fearful.

"Maybe," Michael tempered, "might be a long ways off still."

"We have to get out of here," Carmen said. "Try the car again."

Click.

The charter bus drew nearer. Its largess spread across the road and amplified by the debris that started on the sidewalks and pushed into the street. The color disguised by the darkening eastern sky. The kids sunk low into the seats in an attempt to hide their forms. Not quite dusk though the headlights made a noticeable difference within the Toyota interior. Still the hulking engine was yet to mask their breaths.

Michael pushed himself up in the seat, his eyes set at the bottom of the rearview mirror and looked intently through the reflecting back window. He watched the bus navigate between the mattresses and tables and ashen cars.

"I don't like this shit," Carmen whispered as the headlights lit up the interior and the engine rumbled nearby. Alice balled herself up pressed against the back of the passenger seat with her head tucked between her knees.

"I don't like it either, man," Michael affirmed, and Alice just breathed.

The men didn't feel it, they thought it was just the rough road that rocked the charter bus from side to side. The driver, he was more attuned to the engine. Its normal grunts and its quirks, and he could feel minute differences through the prosthetic against the pedals and up to the nerves at his kneecap. Nate was more attune to the earth. The slow rolls that meant nothing and the gentle rolls that foretold a more perilous spell.

55 seats available and 50 taken. Mostly young, yet some had the quickened wrinkles and long stares that accompanied imprisonment. The blacks self-segregated, as did the whites, as did the Hispanics, though brought together with loose-fitting white cotton shirts printed with 'D.O.C.' and 'CAMP A' and pants that matched. Brought together with red bracelets on their left wrists with a green LED that blinked once per second. Joined by uncertainty coupled with the opportunity to live outside the prison walls. The reality set in waves as it coalesced with second and third-hand stories.

A jaded Nate pulled back his off-white shoe from the gas pedal and placed it firmly on the brake, which guided him with pressure through his thigh. A shift into park, the engine turned off, and the bloated white bus with the blue flame atop a half-circle of orange logo stayed to absorb the tremors. 'New Madrid Energy' in bold that matched the flame. The debris along the road and sidewalk popped and slid. The buildings shuddered, and the hard materials crunched and threw pieces of bricks to the sidewalk below. The poles that held the "Harvest Festival" banner bent and swayed.

Some of the men sat stoic as the bus rocked, others were wary. The ones who had yet to accept the inevitable of their lives held tight to the armrests with sweaty, white-knuckled hands wrapped tight around the plastic molding. The newbies pushed their bodies up from the seats and strained to find some comfort in Nate's eyes in the oversized rearview mirror. The wrinkled lines below his oily-red hair specked with gray. Any movement from his goatee-covered chin. Settled or darting sunken eyes.

Yet as the wheels lifted violently from the left, then from the right a newbie sat and stared out the window without worry, without the white knuckles and sweat. He had the same pale skin and awkward, gangly features as Nate, yet his eyes pulsed constantly in search of opportunity. Clean-shaven, with short, black hair receded back from the crown of his head. His thin lips were pursed tight, and the veins on the left side of his neck bulged as his head had been turned right for some time. Meticulous as he had scrutinized the first gate on their journey. The vehicles pressed against the concrete barriers with the rusted puncture wounds. The highway numbers, the bridge and the second gate. The first town and the homes set back and the animal herds. The houses that led to this town and their states of disrepair, and here the burnt shells of family sedans, pickup trucks, and minivans. The remnants of law offices and coffee shops and insurance agents and bars. The cinema without a matinee scheduled and below the marquee, directly out his window, was something that didn't belong. Something that had the glistening sheen of recent life, or at least the lack of death.

With the slightest movement his head turned down and only his eyes moved vertically to compensate for the unsettled earth. A Toyota, he could tell. Dirty red and a mid-level trim at least he knew for the base would not have a sunroof. From his vantage point he could see the top of two heads, and he assumed another in the driver's seat, tucked down and hiding with the others. He knew they were alive, as he was acutely aware of the subtle movements the body makes in fear, with the knowledge that they should be hidden but are not.

His pupils expanded and contracted as he watched and waited. It was this patience that had garnered success, though it was the lack of detail that had caused his current predicament. And while the quake had started with a slow roll and struck violently, it ceased in a moment and the shocks bounced slower and then settled. There was uncertainty aboard the bus and within the car in the new silence.

A fast shudder, a finale from the earth and Nate felt the event had ceased enough to restart the engine. Alice became conscious of her breathing, slowly raised her head, and looked up through the sunroof. Her watery eyes met the man's sharp eyes peering down from the bus window. He did not blink, or at least she did not acknowledge any movement until his reflective tongue slid out from his lips and then returned, as if an involuntary reaction. She took in his sunken features as the bus lurched forward.

The man craned his neck back to keep his eyes on her for as long as possible. Forward, she disappeared from his view and he turned his neck forward and down. For the first time since the first phase of this journey at the train station in some forgotten town he studied himself. The white D.O.C. shirt he wished was a plaid button-down tucked into khakis. The red bracelet locked to his wrist he wished was a digital Timex. He thought about the timers and the stopwatches as he read 'Milton Dwyer' on the display. And then 'Tulsa, Oklahoma.' And then '#158224.' And then '1011 – Kidnap Minor – Nonparental. 1103 – Rape – Strongarm. 1110 – Sex Asslt – Sodomy-Girl-Gun. - 1122 – Rape – Drug Induced. 1114 - Sex Asslt – Sodomy-Girl-Stgarm.' And then 'Milton Dwyer' again as he thought about Alice's eyes and soft features. He imagined her body when it's not compressed between two car seats being rocked by a tremor. He imagined as he considered the buildings and the condition of homes down side streets. They made their way through the downtown, and under white bed sheets tied together and hung from poles above the street, they left the quaint American strip. 'Welcome to Camp Andersonville,' in spray-paint against the sheets, 'You've left the normal.'

16

"I'm so screwed," Carmen lamented as he stood behind Michael and directed the flashlight towards the engine.

Michael unclipped the jumper cables from the Toyota's battery then set them back on the terminals and knew the futility.

"This thing don't work," Alice said while switching between observation and lifting the cell phone into the air for a signal.

"There ain't no towers out here," Carmen explained.

"Nah, I saw them on the way."

"Yeah but they ain't on."

"Oh."

"Cell towers need power," Michael said as he sat back down in the car and tried the ignition. "They ain't had a need for years."

"Well that's stupid," Alice said to Michael.

"That they need power?"

"No, that you brought a cell phone and you knew that it wouldn't work."

"I didn't know that."

"Well you knew that the towers need power."

"Yeah?"

"What's the point of bringing a cell phone if it don't work?"

Michael started to respond but let it go. He turned the sputnik in the ignition and still only clicks. "Fuck!" he screamed as he slammed his hands on the steering wheel.

"Let me guess," Alice said snidely, "it won't work."

Michael felt the seething anger transition from the automobile to Alice. It built through clenched teeth and exhales. He shot out of the driver's seat and into her personal space which repositioned Carmen.

"Why you gotta be such a bitch?!"

"A bitch?" she said incredulously with her flashlight shining in his eyes. "We're stuck here because of you!"

"Because of me? You wouldn't even got this far without me!"

"I didn't even wanna come."

"Yeah right, you can't stop talking about the 'Frog People, let's go see the Frog People.'"

Carmen put himself between his two friends.

"Fine, I did wanna come but I didn't wanna come with you!"

"You wouldn't have got nowhere without me."

"I wouldn't have had to smell you if you weren't here, why don't you take a shower, you're gross."

"Just stop it," Carmen interjected. "Just stop it."

"Your girlfriend's a bitch," Michael said as he spun away to get some space and prepare for the punch that didn't come.

"She's not my girlfriend!" he shot back.

"See, Carmen, he's a dick. A poor, stinky, white trash piece of shit."

"C'mon Alice," Carmen started and swung his flashlight towards her.

"Me? You're gonna defend him? Over me?!"

"I'm not taking sides, we're all," Carmen paused, half of him was a peacemaker and half wanted to run and hide. "Let's just figure out how to get home."

"We ain't goin' home," Michael said from a distance, "It's dark, this car don't work and all the others are burnt."

"We have to get home," Carmen almost begged. "I'm dead if I don't get home soon."

"How, Carmen? We don't have a car."

"Cause of you," Alice added.

Carmen walked to the sidewalk and stood under the marquee with his flashlight pointed despondently at the fallen black letters. He pushed them gently with the tips of his sneakers.

"This is all your fault," Alice told Michael and walked to Carmen and stood by him. She put her arm around him and rested her head against his shoulder, hoping the flowery scent of her shampoo would remind him whose side he was on. Michael felt the distance and the hatred he didn't understand. He wished for a distraction, but the abandoned town threw back silence.

Carmen stayed with denial of their fortunes for several more minutes before he dragged his feet to the Toyota, opened the back door and retrieved the duffel bag. He walked it over to Michael and pushed it into his chest.

"I guess we need a place to sleep tonight," he told Michael with resignation.

"We can sleep in the car."

Carmen looked over his shoulder to Alice who registered her disapproval which he relayed to Michael.

"You gotta find us a place to sleep," Carmen said in a whisper, "a good place so she won't be mad."

Michael took a moment to reflect on Carmen's eyes with his hand on the bag and the bottom on the ground. The trepidation formed around the creases to the left and right of Alice's lips, which mirrored his own reflected emotion yet kept hidden. The true darkness that enveloped without the reassurance of artificial light. The infinite stars that danced with Cassiopeia and Orion. And on that deep inhale and deliberate exhale, he picked up the duffel, slung it over his shoulder, and turned to the blue fluorescents in the distance.

17

The fluorescent lights flickered on, spread throughout the camp, and threw blue translucent light in pockets and left shadows in their absence. Rows of white and beige trailers numbered one to thirty under windows nearest the brick rubble of the former high school building. Thin, opaque drapes that swayed in the screenless window openings, for the men chose mosquitos over the suffocating, and wet heat that stagnated through the days and permeated the nights.

Rats and voles, squirrels and opossums found haven under the trailers, each elevated by two car tires stacked at each corner. An economical, if not foolproof, solution to the tremors. Down some rows, a trailer had fallen from its rubber foundation and tipped to one corner. Left there by the men who found housing down another lane. Left there by the superstitious who insisted that, once resurrected to level, the demons of the place would enter. It was meant to fall.

Down the beaten paths between, walked men in their white shirts. No rush with whispered words. Some ate bologna sandwiches in tandem, and others ate alone with cheese-powdered fingers from a white bag, nondescript with "cheese chips" stamped in black on one side.

Outnumbered, and with a preference for the shadows, the corrections officers made their rounds and imagined the ways they could die. It seemed, they thought, that order, structure, and the safety of steel cells were forgotten behind the gate. It seemed, as they caressed their batons and adjusted buttons on olive-green and collared shirts, this was more of a dumping ground for the unwanted. They were wardens of trash, trash that could, in an instant, become the murderer forgotten in this forgettable place. If they doubted, their thoughts turned to the lack of any fence that surrounded the camp. There was nowhere to go, it was reasoned, along with the expense.

They compared, as they felt the sweat dampen their hat brims, the excitement upon learning of their selection. Of triple pay and 3-months on and 1-month off. Of how their small children back in the normal would benefit from a bump in societal class, or, at the very least, a reprieve from frozen dinners and canned meat. It was these thoughts that pressed on them in the night. With the hundred steps required between the illumination of fluorescents that ran from power cords down the lanes to the bank of large generators that lined the outfield fence in an arc.

Segregated and inhabiting the plots west of the football field were the construction workers, the demolition men, and the engineers, drillers, and roustabouts who chose to remain in the fetid, abandoned land where they drew the gas from the rock. Either too young to measure the danger, too ignorant to believe in something better, or those too old to do anything else.

Pristine trailers and double the accommodation. Common areas and full kitchens. Showers and refrigerators and two bunk beds in each bedroom. Televisions with video game consoles and a row of lockers set near the entrance. Telephones and computers with internet connections within the confines of conditioned air. Palaces, to the prisoners, who were afforded none of these amenities.

The prisoners lived in second-hand trailers of various disrepair. Their lunch trays of lower-grade beef and mysterious sides where even taste could not be discerned at most meals. A canteen stocked with white-label staples, processed and packaged equally plain. They could accept this, yet it was the disdain from the Plaids and the scarcity of the officers that gave pause, that pierced the serenity of the most docile.

The air of superiority among the Plaids, the coverall-clad workers, was not subtle. They did not interact with the men in white. Not in the mess hall, where they were served first and left before the prisoners arrived. Not in passing, nor in sport on Sundays. Even on the job, the Plaids would designate a foreman from the prison ranks, and only that man was spoken to. Any inquiries from others were ignored, and, if they persisted, were met with ferocious anger.

Yet amongst the few Plaids and their prisoner foreman counterparts, there had developed a basic understanding that stalled only a few levels below friendship. They would secret the name-brand candy or liquor or real fruit to the prisoner foremen, who would then steal away to the tree line behind the baseball diamonds. Or, if with smoke that would give them away, he would follow the trickling creek up the hill by the moonlight and sit down in the grass that overlooked the camp. From there he smoked his Swisher Sweet or his Marlboro and contemplated the moment when he'd have to return. The idea of running. The unknown time remaining on his sentence, or what would qualify him for an expedited release. The information relayed was half-baked and left questions for the men moved and the families displaced. No one had thought to set a deadline, and once society had adjusted, they simply acclimated to the new normal.

Yellow bulldozers and backhoes and the rusted steel of dump trucks that once worked were idle and silent in the faculty parking lot. Cushman three-wheelers for less intensive tasks. Pickup trucks and fresh diesel and unleaded secured in proper tanks, with strong coiled springs and a base that slid and adjusted for any movements in the earth.

Felled LED lamp posts fifty-feet high and piled against the crumbled brick of the gym, replaced by the twenty-foot portable fluorescents. Compressed cars piled on tractor-trailers with semis turned out towards the camp's entrance. A line uncompressed, some burnt, and others only rusted and waiting for their turn in the crusher.

The men stared from the charter bus windows as Nate deftly maneuvered around a tight corner. He directed the bus between the flatbeds and backhoes and bulldozers on one side and the prisoners' quarters on the other. He held true and slow until he pressed the squelching brakes into service and the bus stopped. A hydraulic hiss, and the doors clunked open as the interior lights came alive. Outside the door, direct, an opening in a chain-link fence where at one time volunteer parents in red rain slickers took tickets on brisk Friday evenings under the 'Welcome to Bison Country' sign.

"Gentlemen!" Nate exclaimed as he stood and faced the rear, his thin frame under soft light. "This is the end of our time together, and although I may look sad, please understand that I am not. Once I step off this bus you are to get off two at a time startin' on my left."

An officer stepped up with proper authority that emanated first from his rubber-soled black boots laced high and gleamed over neatly pressed olive-green trousers tucked. His chest was thick, and his shirt contoured, which made his badge angle and glint in the prisoners' eyes. Hair high and tight and a fondness for militaristic accessories. If they doubted the sincerity in his eyes, they dared not doubt the shotgun barrel directed at them. Nor his equally sober counterparts outside—one in front, one to the left, and one to the right. Each breathing steady and with full confidence of men who've pulled a trigger prior.

"Gentlemen! It is my duty to inform you that if you do not follow my instructions you ain't gonna see the next sunrise. Again, two at a time, starting with you two," as he pointed to the men seated in the front row stage-left.

Set upon the short porch of a trailer, a man's large frame spilled out and dug into the metal handrails. His skin was a deep, brown hue, with plump, clean-shaven cheeks below a two-inch afro of ebony hair. The build of a lineman out of season. His audience sat in a semi-circle, legs crossed upon the patchwork of grass and dirt below. The standard-issue cigar puffed its way around from red bracelet wrist to red bracelet wrist as the man held court. The whiskey bottle—white-labeled with "whiskey" stamped in black, followed two men behind.

"Is he leading this thing?" a man whispered to his neighbor on the ground after passing the whiskey. He looked young, with olive-skin that straddled Sephardim and Ashkenazi. Those who didn't know him assumed Italian. His eyes, dark brown bordering on dusky. Hair thin but strong; short, charcoal, with tight, natural curls. A short stature, with toned muscles hidden behind the loose, standard-issued sleeve.

"Yeah, that's Jeremiah," the neighbor responded before taking a swig of whiskey, and after "you're gonna see some shit."

Juan had a thick frame, more solid than muscular. Black tattoos ran down his arms and up his neck. Both features combined for menace, yet he sat with a calm that came in time. His memories of Humboldt Park and Logan Square in Chicago had faded out as his days in the camps grew. The scars from heated metal and honed blades that once swelled at the precipice of sleep now murmured sweet nothings and went quickly to the quiet. He was at peace in the humidity, surrounded by the blacks and the Mexicans, the Puerto Ricans, and the whites, and now, he assumed, the Jews. Or was he Italian? He wasn't sure.

"I seen some shit," the Jew or Italian said stoically, to which Juan gauged his eyes.

"Yeah?" Juan asked incredulously.

"Here?"

"Nah, at Camp Chase."

"Shit," Juan said before passing the bottle on, "you ain't seen nothin' at that pussy camp."

"How do you know?"

"Cause they only rectify here or at Douglas. Let me tell you something, you see a motherfucker with an outfit like you got on but purple, shit, you run the other way. You run and you run fast, they's fucked up."

The Jew or Italian thought to request clarification yet held his tongue as the whiskey settled into his empty stomach. He looked at his LED bracelet and waited until his name scrolled across the screen. 'Sam,' that was him, and he was here.

"This is Andersonville, cabrón," Juan started and was interrupted by a deep horn blast beyond the trailers. "And you've been blessed by Jeremiah or else you ain't here with us."

The murmurs among the semicircle ceased and each stood, steadiness according to tolerance. Jeremiah remained perched and his breaths shortened, though only perceptible to the skittering mouse, the mosquitos, and the cicadas gone silent that watched from the eaves and metal posts.

Another horn, and Jeremiah pressed hard on the metal armrests to pry himself from the seat. He stepped down from the porch, took a makeshift flowerpot of hand-molded cardboard and inhaled deeply the purple wildflower. Held reverently in the light, then back down to the ledge as he stepped to the earth. Behind him, the men fell in line and followed him down the narrow dirt path between trailers. Under the buzzing lights spread throughout and past the prison officers shelved in the shadows. Down a block, then two, then a left and in the distance, faded yet legible, the sign read 'Welcome to Bison Country.'

18

Three abreast in that pure mortal darkness and Main Street was illuminated only ten feet forward by flashlights. The owl's call over the howl odd as they walked the buckled pavement. Around automobile carcasses and on the glass shards that scratched between the road and the soles of their shoes. Strewn refuse fused, and children's clothing clumped, partially disintegrated and partially within a sewer grate built into the curb.

The stoplights had each fallen inward, ripped from their bolts, creating a symbolic end to the town. Carmen set his light so that both structures of the red, yellow, and green lamps were within the beam, if only at the edges.

And at the precipice between the epicenter of a small town and the country expanse, a rumble came. Slow in the soles and up through the nerve endings structured in every toe. It deepened, and realization came to the kids that the cause was not buried deep in the plates or between shattered aquifers. A far squeal. Then another. The ground shook. Michael turned back to the town. Then Carmen and Alice refused. Nothing yet but squeals and shifting pitches between mothers and fathers and children. Anticipation slowed the seconds and louder. Shrieking. Harder still the ground unsettled. Through rusted metal squeezed the first line, and with the distance closed, there reflected the glint of life in moist eyes against the thrown light which shook.

The rumble came, but not from fractures precipitated by the wells. No, the rumble came first from South Texas pens where they bred them for sport and for game meat gnawed around bonfires and spits near sparse ranch homes. Bred for their speed and size and primeval tusks that pressed adrenaline. Trends, as they do, trend, and once passed the pens fell into disuse. Upon freedom, the warthogs meandered north and east. At boredom they bred, and when The Fields cleared, the only threat left and the foliage consumed brick and wood structures they bred.

"Run!" Carmen screamed. Elongated. Echoed and in a sprint, he cut between the stoplights.

"Wait!" Michael yelled.

"Carmen!" Alice added, "wait!"

Carmen did not stop, nor turn his neck back. The flashlight useless as his arms extended forward and then back. Steady breaths on autopilot over debris and shoes alit on apexes of cracked concrete. Rusted axles. Shopping carts nearing dust with bent wheels.

Michael kept his light trained in decision. He watched the snouts instinctively explore as their animal minds revealed no other choice. Fifty, one hundred deep, 200-pound bodies pressed together through the narrows constructed by vehicles and then dispersed wide in the open road. Onward, onward until a meadow of tall grass and a watering hole and the lone stately elm. And here a boy stood, not with animal instincts but the conscious deliberations of how it will end. What stories could be told in August before the school bells? How he led them to The Fields and was, sadly, trampled by wild boars. His mother would return for the funeral after these years, and she would hear how Carmen and Alice carried his limp body north. Her uncontrollable sobs draped over the casket.

Perhaps it was the daydream that focused him not forward as the beasts neared but behind. How he could, over the carnal din, hear Alice's stuttered sobs. "Ah, shit," he bellowed aloud, turned fast, and ran awkwardly to her with the duffel bag bouncing against his back.

"Alice!" he yelled. "Let's go!" He slowed only to prod her along. To grab her hand and pull forward. Quiet sobs with twitching shoulders and feet embedded. "We have to run!" he shouted over the rumble and pulled.

The squeals transitioned with the proximity. That high-pitch tenor coupled with the bass of abject terror in mortal flight. The shrieks that rattle eardrums. To Alice, who had made the decision not to see the beasts, imagined them as ten-feet tall. Glistening fangs from rabid drool that held sticky to their lower lips and hung until they separated and hit the pavement with a splat. Gnarling demons that had finally caught up to her with razor claws and clouded minds. For the conniving and the disrespect and the ruthlessness of a pre-teen girl. Of which, she assumed her share had been greater than other girls in similar positions, and for which, God had seen enough and written her name in the devil's book.

Michael pulled her arm forward, and she resisted. He looked over her shoulder and it wasn't long now.

"Alice!" he had to scream even though they were feet apart. Her glazed eyes gazed past him to Carmen's shrinking form from distance and darkness. Her vision unable to focus while Michael tugged again, this time causing her to step forward before steadying herself again.

"Alice!" he shouted but no words were heard—the beasts were almost upon them. He dug his grip into her wrist and this time pulled down. As she fell forward, Michael wrapped his free hand around her back and followed her to the ground. Her shoulder hit first, and then her cheek. It was the broken glass which sliced across her cheek that broke the trance, but now she was trapped. Under Michael who covered her as best he could with his thin frame and he himself was covered partially by the duffel over his back.

The quiet sobs dissipated with the pressure. Through the openings in Michael's embrace she felt the bristled hairs of the beasts as they rushed by with the now guttural grunts as if inside their heads. Michael accepted all of this and breathed steadily, if he was to be killed, he preferred nature doing the killing.

Yet the beasts did not trample. Those same instincts that pressed them into panic drove them around the children. The males that massed around 300 pounds were, if you will, the most considerate, and gave wide berth as they felt life below their legs. They were careful with their tusks, as if, had they not been, the females would have words upon sanctuary. The piglets, with youthful indifference, did jump and climb over Michael and the duffel bag, but their small frames made no impact.

It was maybe a minute and the sounder had moved on in search of meadow, and time reset to normal for the children face down on the ground. Breaths calmed, hearts returned to pace, and Alice felt a dull sensation through her cheek and the blood lazily dripping down.

"You can get off a me now," Alice said, only this time there was no bite in her tone. Michael paused for a moment, moved his hands from around her arm and pushed down on the ground to rise. As he stood the bag caused him to stumble, but he regained his balance quickly.

She rose to the distant squeals further along and seemingly off the main road. Her held breaths had transitioned to quick, succeeding gulps of air with eyes to the pavement until her head slowly rose to his. A thought of hatred, and it passed. Of understanding, fleeting. Finally of acceptance, but only enough to move the needle the right of disdain, and as she readied herself, verbalize what would be a small comfort as the pain replaced the adrenaline. She slowly raised her hand to her cheek and pressed, the sting shot through her nerves around and within the gash. She wished for a mirror and was relieved that none were nearby.

Michael, by default, was her mirror, and he stared with flashlight trained at the two-inch gash that ran just beside her eye and down towards her chin. His unflinching stare with the corners of his mouth turned down told her all she needed to know. She set her hand in front of her face and looked at her fingers smudged with blood and pebbles and dirt. For a moment she convinced herself it wasn't real, and in the next, panic.

He ran and grabbed her just as her legs gave out and her blood covered his t-shirt as her cheek landed against him.

"C'mon, Alice," he said as she sobbed. "It ain't that bad."

He held her tight in his scrawny arms until she relaxed and pulled away from him. This was the first time he saw her exposed. Not weak, or in a sympathetic sense, only that her edge had dulled, if only for now. He went down to his knees and bucked his shoulder to get the duffel to the ground. With care, he pulled the zipper until the bag was open, and in the flashlight illumination pulled out a neatly folded green tank-top and extended it towards her.

She stood idle several feet from him, and in the time elapsed two drops of blood fell from her cheek. Slow steps and she was within range of the soft cotton.

"You're gonna have to hold it against your cheek," he said softly as she reached and grasped. "Sorry I ain't got nothing better."

She winced as she pressed it against her skin. "You got everything in that bag but a first-aid kit?" she asked.

Michael waited on bended knee for a scolding, but instead a slight smile escaped her lips.

"Guess I ain't that good of a Boy Scout," he responded as he zipped up the bag. Relaxed, then stood and slung it back over his shoulder.

"C'mon," she said as she turned towards the white light of the camp, "let's go see this shit."

Michael jogged to catch her stride.

"Carmen!" she yelled into the dark air. "Where are you, you wuss!"

19

"We are all survivors," Jeremiah started, "all of us." He paced across the fifty-yard line, or where the fifty was once marked with white chalk and the colored outline of a bison. Behind him stood the men over whom he had held court from the porch of his trailer. Sam, for whom this was new, had the same frightened expression as those before them. With the same hard beats from his chest, he stood several inches further back from the others who lined the football field behind Jeremiah and insulated himself slightly behind Juan.

The light post, near where the charter bus had parked, provided the only flooded illumination. The buzz audible to the three men kneeling, their wrists zip-tied behind their backs, and to Sam in the muted breaths between Jeremiah's words. Slow green flashes from each man's red bracelet. A flashlight trained by one man near Sam. Another by a man further along the line.

The first man kneeling, to Jeremiah's left, was pale, accentuated by the white D.O.C. outfit. His frame intimidating and unstructured, amorphous and built for smothering. A protruding belly that disallowed his t-shirt from resting against his hips and it swayed with the rare breeze. Wild, sandy hair where each strand found its own direction. Oily skin and the unnerving combination of eyes wide, unfocused and tired.

Centered, and seemingly smaller in relation to his large neighbor, knelt an Asian man. Monastic, and the wind flowed through him, yet his heart belied the calm perceived. With eyes closed. Short, cropped, jet-black hair. Taut skin with warm undertones.

The last, the gaunt one who had felt his erection press against the thin, white, government-issued boxers as he spied Alice through the window of the bus. His lips quivered, having not the control over the physical manifestations that originated in his mind. Emotions, for him, were always on display, if not his intentions.

"Survivors of circumstance," Jeremiah continued, "of location, of skin color…"

"That's right, brother," an African American man standing behind him stated, the olive-green backpack slung over one shoulder.

"Of poor decisions," he continued without hesitation, "be they from urges or those circumstances. It don't matter much now, does it? These things of how we got here? But we got here, and that's a blessing."

"Amen."

"It's a blessing because we, you," and he took the time to gesture to each, "you, and you are free of that physical bondage. Are we not? Did you not feel freedom when you left it behind? The bars? The clank of that metal that told you this was real? The real, real? Niggas on one side, Aryans on the other? Me hermanos over there? Look behind me."

He trod slowly to the Asian man centered, who still stared at the trampled sod. "Look at me, nigga!"

The man's chin raised in measured tremble.

"Ain't got a Chinaman over there but you get the idea. And you know what?" as he squatted.

"We ain't gonna have a Chinaman over there. No, no, not today."

Jeremiah stood and stepped between the Asian man and the slow-witted one until he was behind them. He knelt and wrenched his bound wrists upward with one hand while driving his knee into his back to keep him in position. The man winced with a quick, uncontrolled yelp. With his free hand he pressed into the sides of the red bracelet with softness that countered the pressed force otherwise utilized. The gray LED alit in a muted yellow, and across it ran the numbers and letters that connected man's understanding with sin.

"You are aware," he whispered close and into the man's trembling ear, "that we cannot abide a child-killer amongst us."

He released, and the pressure abated from the man's shoulder. His back throbbed, mimicked by instinctual gasps. "You understand, right?" he yelled into the emptiness of the field. "You understand that it was not luck that brought you here? But it's men like you that are so fixated on the present that they cannot see the future. That cannot see other men's intentions cause you're pulled along by your own urges!"

He yanked the thin man's arm as he had done the previous, and the stimulus aroused only a slight smile. "By your urge," as he illuminated the bracelet, "to..." and he paused, "shit, this just keeps going." The man's smile widened, as if he was reading along with Jeremiah.

"He smilin', Taco," the African American chimed, and Jeremiah took both hands and lifted the man's wrists backwards and over his head until both shoulders cracked out of their sockets. He held them there as the man flopped while screaming as the pain shuffled between the shock. His legs flailed to find footing for his feet and that relief did not arrive. Jeremiah gauged the looks of his cohorts and only when they broke, winced, did he release the man to the ground to flounder in the dead grass over the sod.

Jeremiah regained his composure and paused over the Asian man who had returned his gaze inward. He walked around the obese dimwit and as he lifted his wrists, he felt an unnatural compliance, as if this man was not afraid. Barely the knee pressed into the largess of the man's back and his posture broke. His breaths had maintained throughout the ordeal. He did not cower, and he did not defy as

Jeremiah read the LED readout and then released his arms.

"What's your name?" Jeremiah asked, squatted in front of him as he found it difficult to meet his eyes. "It's alright," he continued. "Look at me."

The man's eyes still darted.

"It's alright," he repeated, this time in a slightly higher register. "What's your name?"

The broken man's sobs fell into the background as finally the two considerable men found a connection.

"Leonard," he said meekly. "My name is Leonard."

"Alright, Leonard, what'd you do?"

Leonard stared.

"What'd you do, Leonard, to get here?"

"I took a bus," he responded with the same simplicity and quiet, "the white one."

"Nah, man. Why'd you go to prison?"

Leonard deliberated, "Because I took a bus."

"Do you," Jeremiah asked, "do you like girls?"

No answer.

"Leonard," he pressed, "do you like little girls?" as he looked for his eyes to avert. A swallow. The twitch of an eyebrow. The raised corner where the lips meet. Nothing.

"Like, girls who are shorter than me? They are all shorter than me."

Jeremiah smiled, "They all shorter than me, too," then stood up and sighed a sigh that heaved his frame. A turn and a moment for the men who stood behind him. The Mexican who twitched with each syllable that put him further from what was to come. The aged man who responded, who answered as if before a sermon, for these opportunities were close to that memory. The new man who, like all new men who knew not a social order, took to minimizing his involvement until he understood the structure. The other few who were either numb or accepting.

Satisfied in his reflection, he turned back to the men on the ground. The thin man had lost consciousness. The Asian man had made peace. "Take these two to the trees," a deep inhale, and on release, "untie Mr. Leonard here, he's one of us."

It's an odd place, straddling childhood and responsibility, however limited. Monitored. Structured by elders who have seen what men are capable of. Cuing only on the reactions to events by parents. By teachers and by strangers. Dangers, for those children under shelter, once presented are processed as an opportunity to explore. To absorb that which is foreign, to always push to borders farthest from the breast.

Under these auspices of curiosity, the three kids stood rapt. Under the Bison sign. Unaware that the blue aura from the single light above exposed them to sight, regardless of their silence. Michael, with the duffel secure across his body, his right thumb dug under the strap and knuckles fast over the top. Ritual, to him, was foreign. He had hardly experienced it, and was therefore more adept at parsing the act, rather than the comfort derived. The intention, or desired outcome, was secondary, and often moot.

Alice held the t-shirt against her cheek, yet the blood had hardened and could have stayed pressed without the pressure. Still uncomfortable, still vulnerable, her posture slipped slightly, and her shoulders hung just a little lower. To her, the strange scene before them did not recall adventure, it reminded her, in tandem with the dull sting across her face, just how far she was from home.

It didn't matter how many times Carmen replayed it, or how many times he had told the others that he thought they were right behind him. Set eyes on Michael. Implored Alice. How he had told them he had not heard them scream to wait. Or had he heard them? Had he turned and saw? Did he run out of subconscious fear or that which was in him fully aware? There was no recollection that alleviated. Only the rueful, embarrassing heartache that pushed him forward from the precarious comfort of the light and onto the football field.

As he walked, he watched as the men in white t-shirts and pants and sneakers lifted a man from his knees and guided him towards what remained of the visitors' bleachers. How he went with his head slumped and with shuffling feet yet without protest.

He watched as two men knelt behind the biggest man. One was idle and the other cut away the zip-tie and helped the man to his feet. He saw the bracelets he saw on the men when they would get off the train and transfer to the white bus.

He watched as they dragged another by his feet across the turf and after twenty feet the man awoke. The shrieks and kicks brought the men who had untied the large man to aid in subduing him.

"Help us!" one man said to the now freed giant, and without hesitation he climbed on top of the spastic prisoner. Through the weight he still screamed, and the large man put his gigantic hands around his neck and shook him until his body went limp.

"Good job," a man said to him, "you did real good," and then helped him up while the original two men tasked with pulling continued.

"Guess we ain't gotta hang him now."

The men busied with their tasks did not notice, but Jeremiah did, as was his charge. It was the conviction in the young man's gait that held him steady in observation. The oddity of what he was witnessing. A child in this place. Comfortable in the distressed night. He took heed and thought to halt the activities witnessed, but it was too late. What he had seen, what the two a hundred steps behind him saw, could not be unseen. It was time, he determined, to endeavor to this new situation.

20

Alice winced in the sterile white under fluorescents as the man carefully removed the shirt from her cheek that had bound fast. He was patient, leaned forward on a padded, wheeled stool, with both meticulous and nimble fingers behind latex gloves. His crimson hair, even having been awoken at the late hour, was full and combed back and the tips flowed down towards the back of his neck. A full beard of equal hue with a spackling of a color that straddled the red and a new gray, as if youthful features were combating the inevitable.

He wore a plaid shirt of saturated blue and black, with sleeves rolled up neatly above his elbows that exposed his defined forearms. Blue denim and beige steel-toed boots loosely tied as if they were always worn, even in relaxation. Technically, he was not a doctor, trained only through experience and internet videos. Yet, in the absence of society known, that detail was moot.

They were in a double-wide trailer, all of them. The main room, of which was the most spacious, resembled an examining room at a doctor's office, if the waiting room were included. White cabinets with metal locks that hugged the wall over a sink and counter space. The vinyl examination table was covered with white paper that rustled whenever Alice made the slightest of movements. The stool with wheels. The glass jar filled with tongue depressors, the other cotton swabs. Blood pressure cuff. Stethoscope. A privacy curtain.

Yet there were additions, those which were more suited for a hospital room. IV poles. Various monitors on carts with ample locations for tubes. Two padlocked refrigerators.

Unlike Carmen, who had seemingly disappeared into the chair, Michael was rapt, and wished he had not been relegated to the row of chairs that served as the waiting room just inside the front door. Jeremiah had positioned himself near the chairs, with Michael's black duffel slung over his shoulder.

Michael pressed to the very edge of the chair to see clearly, to watch the doctor's every movement. The direction he pulled. The strength that he applied. The two trays on the counter of which he could not see the contents. The final tug that removed the cloth, how he cleaned the wound and calmed her with a firm palm on her shoulder.

"I have a daughter," the doctor started with a comforting voice while continuing, "about your age." He tilted her neck, which exposed the wound to the light and then took a needle and suture from one of the trays. "Got a son too, younger." She grimaced as the needle slid through her skin, but quickly relaxed as the traumatized skin had numbed itself. "When he was born," he continued as he sutured the wound, "the doctors and the nurses did their thing but every time one came into the hospital room, they found something wrong with him. Nothing crazy, but something." She watched his eyes to avoid any peripheral sight of the needle or string. "See here, one said, his big toes are too big, you should get that checked out. His eyes, maybe they're a little too far apart. See this line on his palm? Look at yours, you got two. Hmmm, his ears might be a little low."

Carmen unwrapped himself slightly, the man's story had removed him from the current environment. "But what's weird is," he continued, "I wasn't worried, and I've thought about that 'cause it's something I think about now and again. Of course I was concerned. But why? Why wasn't I worried? Why wasn't I petrified? Was it because I already had a kid? Was it because we just went through all kinds of crazy and I couldn't take on any more at the time? I mean, what was wrong with me? What kind of parent...?"

In an instant the lights turned from the fluorescent cool to flooded red, held for two seconds, then returned to their normal state. Michael and Carmen looked to the ceiling, here, there, seeking the source of a chime that rang through an unseen speaker. The doctor paused and held the needle as the room began to sway. Gently, as if a ship upon calm seas.

Michael turned and pressed his head between the opening he made with his fingers in the slats of the vinyl blinds. Carmen followed, and they watched the trucks with their shocks struggle in the violence. The lampposts as the earth gave her all to extricate the metal poles and support wires. The bleachers, pushed and the entire edifice angled several feet to the right, rested, resisted, and was then pushed back beyond normal to the left, the bolts and soldiers strained.

"And then I thought," the doctor continued with both his words and charge, "what if it had been my daughter who they kept coming to tell me about? What if they said, 'your daughter has strange toes, your daughter has these abnormalities?' And that's when the worry came, that's when I felt that pit of something I could not control that would, that, I can't really explain it."

The intimacy of the encounter had made her acutely aware of his voice. The faint aroma of hours-old toothpaste. The machinery embedded in his flannel, impervious to the washing machine. The two-second switch of lights to red and chimes that, to her, extended and yawed in the consequence.

"What if, instead of you," he said as only a few loops remained, "it was my daughter sitting here, and I was stitching her up? I think I'd be having a much harder time of this."

He snipped the remaining suture and the needle clanked inside the metal tray once dropped. "Not because she's my daughter and you're not. Nah, it's not that." He removed the latex gloves and held them. "It's because I was in The Fields, and do you know what kind of women are on a pad?"

A tighter grip on the examining table was the only response she could muster. Carmen and Michael with ears trained and even Jeremiah set aside subsequent thoughts.

"Badasses," he almost whispered, "only badasses. And you, young lady, are a badass, and I don't need to worry about badass women, do I?"

With a smile half-hidden behind the beard he put his hand on her shoulder. The fluorescents faded again, but this time bathed them in lime green. Chimes, yet this time reassuring with a rising intonation and then back to the bluish-white.

"Do you get to see them?" Alice asked. "Your kids, I mean. Cause you're here."

"Yeah, I do," as he sat back. "Once every six months I get to go home for a few days. Sometimes Christmas."

A knock roused the doctor from thought, and he cleared his throat and stood. Discarded the gloves and set upon cleaning up the examination area. Carmen watched Alice slide off the table and position herself in the center of the room as Michael turned his attention to the door. Jeremiah stepped forward to allow entrance as the door swung open and Carmen took his eyes off Alice.

From the darkness the figure appeared and was immediately judged. Alice went to Nate's oily, stringy hair and saw in him Michael plus twenty years. Carmen saw a white man who had yet to earn his trust. Michael felt something familiar in him and inspected his features which brought no connection until he saw the prosthetic jutting out from his blue jeans and recognized the limp. The train station. The white charter bus that delivered the prisoners from rail to road.

Nate, too, paused to assess. To judge. To inspect. The wound on the girl's cheek. The black boy. The white boy. The inconvenience of their presence and how he found it hard to believe when told that three children were in the camp.

"She came here with that wound, boss." Jeremiah announced to the ethereal, "We just fixed her up."

Nate lingered on Jeremiah, as if to give him space to elaborate on the situation, yet he remained pursed. Sheepish. Passive as the doctor scrubbed his hands under slow-moving water. He took soft steps and in front of Alice, he squatted with a bent neck to the stitches.

"What's your name, miss?" he whispered.

Her eyes glinted on his, yet Alice did not answer.

"It's alright, you ain't in any trouble. What's your name?"

A pulse of time, then another. "Alice."

"Alice, that's nice."

On a qualified breath he returned erect, the prosthetic which made his stance subtly uneven and reflected for only a moment. "Mr. Palmer," he said to the doctor.

"Yeah?"

"Take Alice and her friends to 12 East."

"No problem. C'mon, kids," and the doctor directed the three out of the door, into the faint light that separated sparsely the darkness over the rolling earth of the camp

"They just came up on us," Jeremiah started, having dropped the subordination in his voice as he handed the black duffel to Nate.

"What'd they see?"

"Enough."

"Enough to say something?"

"Enough to have nightmares."

"That doesn't answer my question, Mr. Caste," Nate pressed.

"You know they're not supposed to be here, and they know they're not supposed to be here. I think whatever is seen stays between them."

"Is that something you are prepared to guarantee?"

"Why is this something you'd need a guarantee for?"

Nate searched for an answer.

"They seen what they seen," Jeremiah exclaimed definitively.

"Yeah, we've all 'seen what we've seen.' Can't go back on that, can we?"

The two men stood reflective in the shadowy linger of the last syllable until Nate had the strength to take a seat along the windows. Jeremiah felt compelled to follow him, and each faced the same faux wooden cabinets pressed against the far wall.

"They sent us another retarded gentleman," Jeremiah said to the cabinets.

Nate answered by pulling a silver flask from his jeans pocket, unscrewing the lid and taking a swig.

"Knew right away."

"That's why you're the best," and he handed Jeremiah the flask.

"Yeah," and he sipped, letting the whiskey pool under his tongue before swallowing, "but sooner or later they're gonna slip one by me."

"Maybe, or maybe this place will be burned to the ground before that happens."

"We can only pray, right?"

21

The last of the steam rolled out from the bathroom in 12 East, clung to the ceiling of the trailer before it became nothing. Before it reached the room alight by a single LED lantern on a wood coffee table. Before the fading freshness of generic green shampoo and harsh white soap would have been noticed by those not yet acclimated.

The quarters were designed with utility top of mind, and in the main room there was a kitchen area which consumed a third of the space. Beige cabinets that matched the beige drawers. A metal sink. A white refrigerator, absent the sound from its motor. Not an item set upon its counterspace.

The remaining two-thirds had the feeling of a hotel, in that the furniture had, in fact, been in a hotel room at one time. It had the vain attempt at an identity while attempting to placate every guest. Designed with an absence of thought, for there was no need for one. A brown couch along the back wall. An olive recliner angled and separated by an end table.

The coffee table that almost matched the hue of the couch. The television stand without a television under the windows and next to the front door. The dining table and chairs where three children sat with oversized, white t-shirts with the New Madrid energy logo printed on the breasts and the white D.O.C. pants hemmed short with safety pins. They ate greedily, Bologna on white bread with yellow mustard and plain potato chips on paper plates. Each bite, each crunch, was audible in the silent room. Every gulp from a plastic water bottle as if a microphone was held within an inch of their throats. The lantern's falloff barely made it to their dining area, yet none thought to move it closer. Light was a secondary concern, if one at all.

Six chairs around the table, two at the heads and two on each side. Alice sat at the head further from the windows. The two boys sat nearest her along the length, their faces hidden under the bills of white, adjustable baseball caps with the blue flame atop orange stitched. Carmen reached for another sandwich from the pile centered and as he pulled it back to his plate he paused, a mechanical *thunk* preceded the fluorescents that flicked on in the trailer and overtook the lantern.

"No," Alice said to Michael as he reached for a third sandwich and grabbed his wrist.

"Why not?"

"We have to save them."

"Carmen got another."

"Yeah, another, not a third."

He thought about pushing his arm forward.

"Leave it," she added as she released, and he pulled his arm back to pick at the potato chip remnants on his plate.

His face was hidden as the trailer door swung open. Behind a stack of alternating plaid blankets and three stiff pillows each their own plaid color combination. Yet the white prisoner's pants and tawny hands adorned with black tattoos meant he was someone new, and for this they all settled in attention. The man took several steps into the room and stood, and Nate entered several seconds later with the black duffel over his shoulder and a satellite phone in his hand.

"Feelin' clean does a world of difference," Nate started, between the door and the table. "You kids feel better?"

"It's like a reset, ya know?" he continued, having not received any response besides stares. "Whatever happened in the day... it's all washed away. Washed away to do it all over agin' tomorrow."

He stepped softly, and the faux wood under his foot was quiet but clicked with the prosthetic. He sat down on the chair opposite Alice and set the bag on the table directly in front of his chest, the phone next to it.

"What's your name?"

She pondered the ramifications of responding truthfully and found none. "Alice."

"And you?"

"Carmen, sir."

Nate grinned at the formality. "And you?"

"Michael."

"Alice," Nate said aloud as he pointed to each kid, "Carmen, and Michael. This," a beat, "this duffel here, now it's got some interesting items in it. Whose is it?"

No answer returned.

"That's alright," Nate uttered with a wry smile. "I know whose it is. It's yours, isn't it, Michael? You're the trickster here, ain't you? The wiry little son of a bitch who makes your parents go crazy, right?"

Nate realized the futility of the united front. Explored first under the principal's height, then the policeman's badge, and then honed, finds itself before any perceived authority. "Juan," he said, "why don't you take these two, Alice, and Carmen, take them and have them help you set up those beds. They gotta be tired from the day they've had."

"C'mon," Juan implored, muffled behind the linens.

"Alice, Carmen," Nate said sternly with that hint of compassion when they did not rise, "please go with Mr. Juan, now."

Slowly the two did as instructed, stood, and followed Juan, who craned to his left to see through a gap between a pillow and a blanket. Past the kitchen area and the bathroom and they disappeared through an open door.

Through the entryway there were two bunk beds, each pressed against a wall to leave a two-foot walkway between. On each were small triangular plastic tables, like those on an airplane, stuck out, attached to the fabricated metal frames and nestled near the heads of the beds. Juan set the stack on a lower bunk, Carmen saw the black tattoos running down his neck over a Hispanic tone, and he shuffled back an inch. And Alice saw his sullen eyes and the creases that explored age beyond accurate numbers, the scars that stung her cheek in preparation, and she crept forward two inches.

"You got the quakes where you live?" Juan asked as the lights went crimson, the chimes rang, and he handed a blanket to each child.

"Call your mother," Nate instructed as he slid the satellite phone across the table, "she's gotta be worried about you."

The phone slowed, then stopped several inches from Michael's fingers. He glanced at the bulky black plastic for a moment, then returned his silent gaze to Nate.

"Go on, call your mama."

"I ain't got a mama," with eyes averted.

"Alright," Nate said with a heavy exhale and a relaxation in the chair, "then your father, you got one of those?"

"Yeah," Michael snipped, "I got one of those."

"Call him, he's got to be worried about you, right?"

Michael didn't reach for the phone.

"Call him, son."

"We ain't got a phone, asshole, and don't call me 'son'!"

Nate settled, and after considering the trajectory of the conversation, slid the duffel to the edge of the table. He unzipped it, reached in, and pulled out each item one by one. The tools of a car thief: the Sputnik and the transmitter and the bump keys and the Slim Jim.

"So, Michael, what does your pa do for a livin'?"

He looked at Nate, then at the tools, and finally, away.

"You know these expire, right?" Nate asked as he set down each gas mask, each an antique and slightly different from the one before. "May I ask why you have these?"

The reason fluttered, then stuck, and the impersonal truth made Michael's lips part. "To see," he paused, as he realized the stupidity of what was yet to be said, "to see the 'Frog People.'"

"The 'Frog People'? Who, pray tell, are the 'Frog People'?"

Michael felt the involuntary heat upon his cheeks, having realized he'd never explained them to an adult. Nor had Alice, he believed, and he knew not Carmen. "You know, the people, the people down there. The ones that have, like the things on their necks, on their throats."

Nate scrunched his brow and his eyes hid behind the narrow slits.

"The things," Michael tried to clarify, and put his hand in front of his throat like he was holding a cup, "like from the radiation, like from the fallout."

"Wait, are you talking about a tumor?"

"Yes, a tumor," excited that the word had been found. "They all got tumors on their necks. I mean on their throats."

Nate pulled the flask from his pocket as the child waited for either confirmation or denial. He unscrewed the cap quickly, yet the swallow came only after the eternal and was followed by a giggle. A deeper, guttural and then finished with that laugh deep from the stomach. Hard, with tears and a long recovery.

"Oh, young man, it's good to know that reality still gets bent out of shape in this day of age, and in this place of all places. 'The Frog People,' you know, I miss that."

"Miss what?"

"A child's imagination. The-the dark and scary house at the dead end. The quiet janitor who's got a house full of snakes and a freezer full of heads."

"It's really only Alice that believes it, that's why we're here. It's Alice."

"Don't go throwin' your friend under the bus now, that ain't right. And you believe it too, else you wouldn't be here."

Nate took another small sip from the flask and slid it back in his pocket. "So, tell me the story."

"The story?"

"Yes, tell me the story of the 'Frog People.'"

22

Camp Douglas resembled, for the most part, Camp Andersonville. Set upon vacant fields instead of a high school, the rural expanse remained the same. The single-story structures that surrounded. The few modern trailers for The Plaids with their anti-shock technology. Opposite, the rows of derelict trailers set on horizontal truck tires to absorb the earth's movements and in such a way to form makeshift roads between. Faded green and yellow panels. Door hinges that clung, worn down by the years and springs that could barely spring.

Backhoes and dump trucks and bulldozers neatly set along a tree line. The trampled land far afield. Nondescript, where no activity should occur yet one's hair would raise walking near the firepits flush with ash and charcoaled logs. The white prison guards' office. The white-paneled mess hall.

The full moon filtered through the cracked window shade and into the trailer, muted from dust and the dirt that clung to the window and slightly obscured by a thin wood dream catcher that hung down from the ceiling. A line of linty moonlight cast down between the bunks and the ground grumbled, which made the shirtless man take notice of the dreamcatcher's shadow drawn on the tiled floor.

He breathed slowly, and the light crossed the indentation above his pursed lips from his seated position at the long side of the twin mattress. He noted his sleeping bunkmate across the aisle, then the one above. He heard elongated breaths overhead, a slight wheeze.

Between genetics and his proximity to barbells, his chin had remained sharp under subtle scars into middle age. Blue veins protruded from his biceps down through the crooks in his elbows. His hair was cropped, full, a sandy brown and gray mixture. Eagles rose over his collarbone, sun-faded and black. A dragon in profile between them, and its tail ran down under his solar plexus shaded in grayscale. 'Maggie' in olde English lettering across his stomach, the ink deeper. Newer.

Shaded clouds in darkness that led to lightning to a pine filled forest down his right arm. The unimpeded sun that rose behind mountains and valleys and the tree line down his left.

With his eyes acclimated to the limited light, he stood and walked silently to the dresser along the short wall near the door. He pulled the middle drawer—labeled E. Mason with Sharpie on masking tape curled at the ends—and dressed. Loose purple pants. The loose purple D.O.C. shirt that proclaimed, 'Camp D.' White socks with three forest green stripes at the calves.

When Mason had finished urinating, he did not flush the toilet. A slow turn of the faucet and he cupped his hands under the reluctant running water until it pooled, then splashed it across his cheeks. Rubbed his eyes with the wetness. Cupped his hands again, slurped. Swallowed and shook the excess into the sink.

At the front door, he slipped a dirt-stained sneaker onto one foot, then the other. Spied through the panes in the door out into the dimly lit road created by repetitive steps and little else. Held his breath and strained his ears for footfalls. Cautious as he turned the knob. Wary as he exited and then quick to close the door in his solitude.

His back rubbed against the vinyl siding as he sidled along the trailer exterior. At the corner of the structure he went to his knees, then to his back and pulled himself under the trailer. There were several feet of clearance made by the rubber tires set at the corners to absorb the unsettled earth. He reached up and ran his hand over a wood beam that helped support the build.

The prison guard made his pass down the road that separated the prisoners' mismatched trailers. An olive-green uniform like his Andersonville counterpart, yet he held his semi-automatic rifle tight because here, here they were honest with their fear. An AR-15, sleek black, a full clip.

Mason stalked him in the shadows. Behind the wall of a trailer. Along its length when the distance was right. Closer still and the guard passed under the hum of a floodlight. Mason sprinted through the exposure and hid himself behind the stairs to the front door of a trailer. He waited several seconds then raised up, the guard was still unaware, still daydreaming in complacency.

He felt the moment and quickstepped at an angle from the trailer positions to the road. Ten feet. Nine. Seven. The serrated kitchen knife handle secure in his fist, the blade flush against his forearm and the point almost to his elbow. Five feet. Three and his unencumbered arm readied. One and it reached out, over the guard's shoulder, tight against his mouth to muffle any response and he pulled his body in tight to his own. He exposed the knife and drove the tip into the guard's neck as his veins pulsed. Deeper until he felt satisfied and twisted the blade. He felt the guard's gurgling struggle and when he turned his head saw the confusion in the young man's wide eyes. And when the acute encounter ceased Mason was careful to set the guard's body down gently onto the ground. As he removed the gun strap, he was keenly aware of the few surviving blades of grass along the path that rubbed against his arm. He took the extra clip and tucked it several inches inside his pants. He crouched over the body, stared, then closed the guard's eyes and posed his arms over his chest. A solemn moment, then a retreat to the shadows.

Down the next road and another lifeless body. Two clips added, one from the stock and one from the guard's belt. He slid against the white-walled guard's office and spied the idling guard set upon the top step of the porch. Cupped his chin around the back of his neck, pulled him tight against the metalwork handrail and slid the knife through the lattice. Pulled smooth on the return and held his shoulder to recline his body in repose upon the stairs and let the blood drain properly to the earth without man's creation interfering.

He sidled to the base of the stairs and increased his ammo before taking the guard's keycard from his pocket and entered the building. He took a small vinyl bag from the back of a chair—half full with a variety of energy bars—and added to it the key fobs for the pickup trucks. All of them. Number one through number ten. A case of bottled water.

Mason was now encumbered, most vulnerable, and he knew it. Hands full. The metal clips that rubbed uncomfortably against his hip bones. The AR across his back. He was in it and any guard he had miscalculated would not hesitate to end this, and end it fast. He could play it safe against siding and betwixt the shadows, which would give him cover, yet perhaps give them more time to stumble into it. He could run straight, follow the roads with a quarter of his speed reduced, in which he would arrive quicker, yet perhaps provide an opportunity to be spotted. He had removed all known barriers, yet he did not know what he did not know. The guard that just needed some air. A first night of insomnia or his opportunity to drag a contraband cigarette, his legacy habit which followed him from the real world. An inopportune medical emergency.

Time, he concluded, was the more threatening enemy, and he pressed with a quick trot. Awkward and stiff with the gear. Down the rows and through the prisoner's trailers. Into the open field that separated the living quarters from the construction equipment. The moonlight gave visibility to the line of white trucks, the glint off the reflectors and the hard corners of the high arches of the backhoes and the buckets and the pails.

His eyes pushed the edge of the peripheral. Ten feet. Nine. Seven. Stood in front of the trucks he set down the water, pulled a fob from the bag and pressed a button. The ambers flashed twice on Truck Number Four.

Water in the bed. He hefted the two red gas canisters and concluded their weights were sufficient. Candy wrappers and crushed coffee cups strewn about the passenger floor. AR-15 on the seat proud poppa to the clips and the key fobs. Flask clamped between the roof and sun visor and clipped a metal box with two rectangular red buttons. An NME Energy baseball cap with a mesh backing and an adjustable plastic strap. Three-quarters on the dashboard. Satisfied.

Serene.

Accomplished.

Mason pushed the 'Start Engine' button and the truck turned over. He held for several seconds in the dash illumination, then released the brake, a slight nudge on the gas and then steady. Through the open field. Onto the patchwork road that divided the prisoners' trailers and the ten-foot fence topped with razor wire. To where it intersected the wider road that ran the length of the camp and segregated the prisoners from the Plaids and the guards.

He stopped in the intersection, gave reverence to the metal gate to his left before driving past its center. Reversed and turned the wheel until the truck was facing the gate. Had he the desire, this was the time to imbibe from the flask. Instead, he pulled the AR closer and ran his thumb along the two rectangular buttons over his head. Waited. Visualized what would come next and then found the fortitude to press one of the buttons.

Nothing. He considered that maybe his choice was guided by a divine hand, then dismissed the notion and pressed the other button. Crimson glows lit each side of the gate, faded out, returned, then repeated the pattern. A buzzer rained down decibels on the camp. Mason switched his focus between the slow gate as it moved from right to left and the rearview mirror. In the intolerable seconds he sat stoic.

Focused. Gate. Mirror. Gate. In the mirror there were figures, trivial still in the distance but closing fast. He figured ten seconds for egress. The lamps that run along the main road behind him grew in brilliance to a level he had not seen. The guards' gates were stuttered, as if they were sure they needed to take aim but did not know when that transition should occur.

Five seconds, and several guards converted from sprinters to shooters, but their compatriots had continued, blocking the line of fire. Mason heard them barking orders in frustration and would have found the idiocy amusing had his circumstances been different.

Shots rang out at two seconds, one of which hit the tailgate. Mason slammed his foot against the accelerator. The truck dug into the dirt, found traction, and slipped through the gate as it was still reluctantly opening. Another bullet hit the taillight; the rest errant.

He released an almost imperceptible sigh of relief when the lights of the camp were no longer aiding his course and he flipped on the headlamps. He pressed the navigation on the screen and was prompted for a password, a viable fingerprint. He had no solution, so he turned his attention to the flask and the dryness of his mouth. No worries lit his face or contorted his mind—he knew where he was going, and he knew how to get there.

23

"Hey."

Michael didn't flinch.

"Hey," Alice repeated a little louder and shook him a little harder.

"I don't want bubbles in the bathtub," he mumbled.

"Hey, weirdo. Wake up."

He stirred and his eyelids parted, and he didn't understand until his mind caught the environment and the company. He was on the lower bunk bed, with Carmen directly above him, still slumbering. It was still dark through the opaque blue drapes, though he sensed the nearing dawn. The exterior ambience gave just enough to outline Alice's figure standing in the narrow walkway between the bunks.

"What?"

"Let's go."

"Go where?"

"What do you mean 'where'?"

Michael turned away from her and closed his eyes. "Go to bed."

"We have to go now."

"No, we're gonna sleep and get up in the mornin' and go back home."

"Don't you want to see them?" she prodded sympathetically.

"They don't exist," as he rolled back over, figuring that this conversation was to go on for a while, "and even if they do, who cares?"

"Who cares? If you don't care, why are we here?"

"Boredom."

She relaxed, satisfied by the logic. "You're the one who wanted to see it, Michael. You're the one who got us this far, when they tell us there ain't nothing wrong down here you can stand up and say 'no, I've been there, this is how it is.'"

"Tell who?"

"I don't know, anybody."

"It won't change nothin'."

"I want to keep going, and Carmen..."

"Carmen's only here cause he likes you."

"That's not it."

"Yeah, it is. He's only here so you'll like him too."

She thought about the intimacy of her next words before uttering them.

"I already like him, and he knows that."

"Then he's only here because of you."

"Well it doesn't matter, he's here, you're here, I'm here. Question is, are we going to finish this or give up?"

"Give up," he responded without hesitation.

"So, you are a pussy."

"Don't give me that crap, I ain't gonna fall for it. Besides, how? How are we gonna keep going? He took my bag. He took our clothes."

"Yeah, and we look like we're supposed to be here with these shirts."

"And with these?" as he pointed to the prison initials on the pants. "Plus, I feel really weird without underwear, I'm looking forward to getting them back in the morning. Clean, with my other clothes and a free ride home. So, good night."

Michael rolled again, the blanket followed his body and he squeezed the pillow under his head. She hesitated, then retreated to her bed next to his and explored the metal slats above her bed.

"I want to keep going."

Alice heard it. Michael heard it, and neither answered.

"We have to see it," Carmen continued. He imagined heading home tomorrow, sitting next to her as the coward who ran, who was responsible for the gash on her cheek. Who accompanied yet had no part, no influence on any outcome.

"Did you hear me talkin' to Alice?" Michael asked Carmen.

"Some of it."

"Then you know they took my bag; how do you figure we keep going then?"

"I don't know."

"That's what I thought."

"There's something down there." Alice added, "You know it, and I know it."

Michael pressed his head deeper into the pillow as Carmen slid down from the top bunk and joined Alice on hers.

"Halfway there," Carmen said with true authority, or the sleep deprivation had made him delirious and he was unaware that he was coming across as such.

"Halfway? How do you know it's halfway? Halfway from what? To where? We don't know where we're going, hell, we don't even know how we ended up here. Just luck, that's all this is and that's all it's been."

"It ain't luck that we're here, the shit we saw, her face. I wouldn't call that 'luck'."

"Happenstance. Coincidence. Fate. The word don't matter, it's just, it's just, tell me how we do this, Carmen. Huh?"

Carmen had no answer.

"We only have a general idea of where to go, no vehicle, no way to borrow a vehicle. We're surrounded by criminals and guards and at any moment the earth could start shaking. Yeah," he finished sarcastically, "let's keep going."

"Rock, paper, scissors," said Carmen.

"What?"

"Let's play rock, paper, scissors."

"That's stupid."

"You said it's luck that we're here, so luck will either take us further or take us home."

"That isn't luck, and it's a stupid game, and there is a bit of strategy involved."

"Best two out of three."

Michael sat up, looked across the gap in the beds at Carmen, ready with his fist rested in his open palm. At Alice as a spectator and realized he had already lost two out of three. The lone detractor.

"If we go," Michael started, "you need to promise me something."

"What?" Carmen asked.

"You have to promise not to blame me for everything. Everything ain't my fault."

Alice saw the depth beyond, while Carmen took it literally.

"We promise, Michael," Alice said motherly.

"Aw, fuck," Michael muttered, "let's go. Probably won't make it far anyways, but at least y'all can't be mad at me."

"Hey Michael?" Carmen asked.

"What?"

"I love you, man," in a voice meant to make him squirm.

"You prick."

Carmen smirked, Alice giggled, and Michael stood and stretched.

24

Out the front door with a rusty squeak, under the purple sky to the sounds of ravenous animals close enough to be heard yet far enough to disinvite threat. They slunk against the white-paneled trailers with unlit windows, then ran at every break between, and crept again. They were alight as the faint light reflected off their white, borrowed linens. With nothing but the lantern from the trailer that swung in Alice's hand.

The line of trailers ended at the road that ran parallel to the football field where they first encountered the prisoners. They ran along the fence that separated the dirt path from the wooden bleachers and caught their breath in the ticket booth.

Rusted nails protruded and the planks were soft from water-logged histories, yet the etchings within remained. Teenage, bullshit romance. Erica hearts Mike. Steve plus Jennifer. Jake and Jackie 4ever. Teenage, bullshit angst. Rob is a fag. Kill everyone. Teenage, bullshit hate.

"Wait," Carmen instructed as he caught his breath, "there's no one out there."

Michael lifted himself over the half-door and stretched. "You're right, there's no one."

"No prisoners," Carmen said, "no guards. No one."

Alice extended her neck out of the opening, "I thought this was a prison."

"This place is fucking weird," Carmen added.

"Okay," Michael said, "the trucks are back where we came in. The keys aren't gonna be in them because this is a prison. At least we think it is, kind of. There were storage bays, and the weird guy with the missing leg said they have gas masks here so they've got to have other shit."

"Why'd he tell you they have gas masks?" Alice asked.

"Cause the ones I brought don't work."

"Well that's good to know," Carmen said sarcastically.

"Yeah, well, what I don't know is where they keep the water or the food."

"What the hell, Michael," Alice exclaimed.

"It's been like ten minutes, and you already broke your promise."

Carmen furled his eyes at Alice.

"My bad, seriously."

"We can't go without at least water," Carmen said.

"What do we do?" Alice asked neither and both.

Michael stepped out from the booth through the splintered half boards that remained and from the middle of the road looked left, where they were headed. He knew that was the way, beyond the shabby trailers to the trucks and the equipment. He looked right, to the east, from where they had come. The dark purple sky had become fuchsia, and in front of that backdrop he saw two larger buildings. Or maybe he didn't, as the morning light is a trickster child.

"We didn't see anything coming up here like a cafeteria or nothin'," Michael said as he climbed back into the booth, "it must be that way."

"How do you know?" Carmen asked.

"I don't, but if I reckoned a guess."

"That doesn't make me feel too confident."

"I'm sorry."

"I'm just messin' around, Michael."

"So, who goes?" Michael asked.

Each waited for the other to volunteer, with Michael abstaining as the only one capable of driving.

"I'll go," Alice said. "If I get caught, they'll go easy on a girl."

Michael looked at Carmen and waited for an objection, then climbed out of the ticket booth. Alice followed spryly with Carmen despondent, last, and shuffling his feet to the arbitrary meeting point in the middle of the dirt road.

"Okay," Michael said, "here's the plan. Me and Carmen are gonna get to the storage bays, get our gear, steal the truck, and meet you in the front of the building."

"Which one?" Alice asked.

"I don't know. I'll just stop in between them and you come on out. Quick, we got maybe a half-hour, forty-five minutes before sunup."

"This is insane," Carmen exclaimed, "a half-hour to break into a building which we don't even know where it is, steal food, break into another building, steal a bunch of random shit, find keys to a truck that we don't even know exists and then what? Drive off to where? To what? For what?"

"Don't puss out on me now," Alice said.

"I'm not 'pussing' out, I just don't think it will work."

"What, you just want to go home?"

"Yeah, I do."

"Then go home, go back to the trailer, and go to sleep, and wait for that creep to come wake you up and take you back to your momma."

Alice stared him down with pursed lips, and he looked away. Found the dirt and the pebbles and pools of yellowed light spread along the road.

"But what if," she continued, now with an empathetic tenor, "what if you could do something that no one's done? What if you could be an outsider to see them? To meet them? To see how they live, and to go back home and know you did that? Your brother, my brother, ain't none of them got the balls to do what we're doing. We've made it this far, if we turn back now, we'll never get another chance."

Michael wanted to stop her halfway through the soliloquy, to correct her. To tell her, and Carmen by proximity, that there are no people 'down there.' That they didn't let anyone stay on the contaminated land, that all they're going to find is wasted earth abandoned and the clicks of a Geiger counter. All they were going to do was drive south, further from home.

Carmen looked up at her, then Michael, and they all felt a chill as the wind finally breathed through their loose shirts. He thought about how he had frozen on the bridge, how he had run from the boars. How he was running now. How easy it is to run. To hide. To give up. How he had said he wanted to go and how easy it is to say things.

"Let me get the water," he said, unable to hide the tremble in his voice. "You two get the supplies and the truck." And before they could respond he turned and sprinted towards the two buildings.

His urgency triggered theirs, and they ran west hard and fast. Down the dirt road and through the pools of soft light from the portable streetlamps that hummed the only sound besides their footfalls. To their right the aging trailers designated for the prisoners, a stark contrast to the construction reserved for The Plaids, the skilled workers, and the guards fast asleep.

The road curved right, and to their left appeared the yellow bulldozers. The backhoes and the dump trucks where teachers once parked their modest sedans. The pickup trucks, white and dirt-splattered and adorned with the New Madrid Energy logo on each door. Next to two storage sheds of white siding and doors rusted at the corners and pressed shut with padlocks and metal latches. Breathless, the two stopped in front of the first shed. Michael pulled down on the lock, and it stayed true. Several more forceful tugs and it did not budge.

"Goddammit," he screamed as he pulled, and the lock held firm to the metal. He released with force and walked swiftly around the structure. He hoped for a window or an entry for his scrawny, weaselly body, but ending up next to Alice who pulled at the side of the door above the lock. She had pried it an inch, then two, then it slipped from her fingers and snapped back into place. She pulled again, with the lock clenched in her fist to make the gap and this time Michael slid his hands in to assist. Four hands each with four fingers inside the grated door and they pulled. Released. Pulled. Each time the gap grew another centimeter.

"Pull hard, then release a little bit," Michael instructed, "then as hard as you can, the latch is coming loose."

They released in unison, then yanked hard and repeated. Once. Twice. A third, and the silver metal separated from the rusted corrugation and reverberated that thunderclap true to its nature. Michael steadied the vibration while Alice stepped inside and lit the lantern borrowed from the trailer.

It was small, maybe ten feet by ten feet, but orderly with wire shelves that ran along the side walls. The back was lined with hooks that held shovels and rakes and pickaxes. Red gas cans and oil drums and cases of various oils and lubricants on the floor pressed against the wall. A black gun case secured with both a keypad and fingerprint scanner. A large red toolbox with a workbench top set in the back-right corner.

Michael yanked a black trash bag from a box and concerned himself with the shelves. He rifled quickly through each box, each storage bin. Nails. Nuts with their bolts. Straight pipe, L and J in PVC and copper variations. Couplings. Females made for the males, or the other way around. Manuals for the backhoes and dump trucks and the one-cylinder carts. He could find uses for it all yet kept restrained for the journey ahead. And tucked away, half-hidden from where the toolbox jutted out, he found a cardboard box taped tightly. He pulled it forward and, with a screwdriver from the convenient toolbox drawer, sliced through the top along the center of the tape where the two sides merged. He pried the two flaps apart and found what he was looking for. Unused, unwrapped, and an expiration date further than the present.

"Keys," he shouted. "You find keys yet?"

Her pounding heart had blinded her to the task and she immediately circled, scanning the walls. For hooks. For a small shelf. The shelves for a metal box. A misappropriated cereal bowl. A clear container.

"There's no keys," she whispered.

"What?"

"There's no keys," she whispered a decibel above, which was enough.

Carmen ran. He ran like running home against the setting sun. Against the rusted sedan and the speed limit to be home before her. He ran as if the white kids who called him "nigger" were behind him.

Quick past the worker's quarters and quick to the first building. Prefabricated, with the same failed attempt at individuality as the trailers before it. White siding. Machine-perfect windows, each two-paned, horizontal, and placed center on each long wall.

He tried the first gray metal door he came upon, along the short side of the building. He turned the surplus knob and looked at the flat, black plastic rectangle for identification cards against the frame as his efforts failed.

His shoulder pressed hard against the building as he turned the corner, peered inside the window, and tried to decipher the shadowy shapes within. His palms pressed against the lower panes and he pushed upwards. Nothing slid except his palms, which became uncomfortably covered in a thin layer of dirt which he brushed off quickly against his white pants.

The door opposite the first, again, locked. He crept around the corner to the last of the walls, here half-hidden under wild growth that filled the pathway between the building and a chain-link fence. The foliage rose to his knees and he pressed with his palms, which did not nothing but dirty them further.

"Shit," he muttered, and kept walking and as he followed the fence line his foot caught on something under the brush. He stopped, kicked lightly, lifted a wooden handle from the foliage and up came the rusted shovel. Grasping the tool with two hands in the echoes of songbirds in preparation, he walked back to the window with his eyes on the pointed termination. He held it aloft, aimed it at the lower pane and with breath held he thrust it through the glass. Shattered, his breath held for the last crash against the floor. His eyes creased in wait for the alarm, yet none rang.

Recomposed with full vision, he ran the edge of the blade across the wooden pane to clear the remaining shards. He tossed the tool aside and hoisted himself through the opening with his body shrunk as best he could. He pulled himself through and felt along the desk pressed up against the wall and under the window. Tried his best to avoid the shards that littered the surface amongst the papers and the pens and the lamp and the coffee mug.

Once his legs cleared, he turned himself around and slid down until his feet found the floor. He surveyed fast. Desks. Chairs. Large rolls of papers and those unfurled with blueprints. Plans. And in the growing light he found no food stocks. No pallets of bottled water and no time to search the other building.

Yet on a desk just inside the first door he attempted, there was something familiar. Something that brought him back home, to the journey's beginning, and with a sprint he had the black duffel in his possession. He unzipped it, tossed the useless gas masks aside and with it over his shoulder, searched the building. Half-filled water bottles from desktops and full bottles from a mini fridge set along the wall. Soda pop cans and a sandwich. Several candy bars stashed in the drawers.

All that he found and felt of worth he shoved in the bag and zipped the top. Weighed down, he walked towards the first door he had tried, closest to the way he had come, and as his hand reached the knob he paused. There, to his left and a foot above his head hung a pegboard stuck with brass hooks. Sectioned by permanent marker. By equipment—those that dug and pushed and drilled. Those that transported liquids and building materials. Hung on each hook a silver key and its identification tag attached with a metal link on the coiled ring. Each except the lowest rung labeled "Pickup Trucks" numbered one to five with dark gray keyless fobs and their corresponding pegboard numbers etched below the buttons.

Carmen tried to slide fob number one into his pocket and then realized, or remembered, that the white D.O.C. pants had no pockets. The keyring secured through his finger and the fob grasped in his left palm he opened the door to the grayish dawn of the songbirds at full attention. Of muffled voices partially awake and in need of either connection or sustenance. He closed the door quickly and pressed his back against the metal with eyes alive. To the other door. The broken window along the back. The ceiling with its height. He shuffled to the front window exposed to the open area and watched as a guard sauntered leisurely in his duty. Two prisoners walked by towards the other large building, then three more.

Carmen's eyes strained at the distance to determine if the man who appeared in his purview did, in fact, have a limp. While the sun had overcome the horizon, there was still the doubt, and he concentrated wholly before making any decision of understanding. Closer still, and there was maybe a discrepancy between the man's feet. Closer, and he was almost certain it was the man from the night previous. Closer, and it was him, and he was headed for the building.

"What do we do?" Alice asked Michael. Her nose pressed against the corrugated door two inches ajar with her eyes set on the movement along the road.

"You tell me," Michael responded, his butt on the floor with his legs extended, "this is as far as I usually get."

"What?"

"With a plan, or idea. I usually get this far, and then something stops me."

"Stop being so dramatic," she said without looking to him, "and let's think of a plan."

He stood up, slung the garbage bag over his shoulder and peered out the opening with her. The prisoners walked down the road and from their vantage point they couldn't see faces, only the black D.O.C. printed on white and the colors of their skin. A guard stood at attention near the bend in the road.

"I don't think there's anything we can do. We're kinda stuck here."

"Michael?"

"Yeah?"

"If it does end here, I'm glad we did this. I mean together. I mean you, me, and Carmen."

He waited a moment to respond. "I'm glad I came too."

◆◆◆

Carmen acknowledged the slippery sweat as he gripped the knob and considered being cornered in the building by the one-legged man. Being tackled on the street by prisoners. By guards. By the doctor who stitched Alice's cheek. Stung by the guards, or shot by the guards, or taken to the trees like the men who were on their knees hours before.

He acknowledged it all and shoved it all down as he found the traction to turn the knob and swing the door wide open. As he ran, he could hardly see but what was in front of him, his peripheral shut down except when needed. He sprinted, darted, as if the duffel's weight was somehow elevated. Veering left to evade three prisoners, right to evade two. Each confused by both the early fog about their minds and the oddity of a child running through the camp, and when their minds had decided to react it was too late.

"Guys!" Carmen yelled. "Michael! Alice!"

From within the storage shed Michael and Alice heard something, felt the tenor of the camp constrict and watched the guard at the bend turn fast to his right.

"Let's go!" he yelled again.

"Shit," Alice said to Michael, surprised, "that's Carmen. What do we do? Do we stay here? Does he come here? Do we go get him?"

The adrenaline faltered and Carmen felt the duffel push down on his shoulder, yet he ran on. A prisoner reached out reflexively as he ran by and grasped his shoulder but couldn't keep the grip. Carmen tripped momentarily but regained his footing. "Alice! Michael! Get to the trucks!"

"What'd he say?" Michael asked Alice, still with their faces barely out the door.

"Get to the trucks!"

"The trucks!" Alice said excitedly.

"I got the key!"

"Hell yeah," Michael said, "we got ourselves a truck."

"Stop!" said the guard as he ran to the middle of the road, put out his arms and lowered his body.

Michael shoved the metal door open and ran out into the open with Alice close behind. They ran towards the trucks parked to the right of the road, nearest the bend where the guard had positioned himself. Carmen came into their view, made his move to avoid the guard who lunged at him and grabbed onto the duffel bag strap and pulled him down to the ground.

"Carmen!" Alice screamed.

He put out his arm to soften the fall, and his face hit the graveled dirt. Stunned, the guard wrapped him up in olive-green covered arms. "Stay down, boy!" the guard ordered as Carmen found his wits and started to resist.

Michael dropped the garbage bag without breaking stride, launched himself at the guard and ended up on his back with his arm around the man's neck. Alice grabbed the guard's wrist and started pulling.

"Let go of him!" she screamed at the guard. "Let him go!"

Several prisoners had stopped to watch from the shadows, not willing to be a corroborated witness. Not willing to get involved based on code, or risk of punishment, or the inability to unequivocally deny involvement later.

The guard freed his arm from Alice. He took Michael's hand and shook him off his back and recommitted to Carmen, who, while the guard was preoccupied, had scooted out from under him.

"Michael!" Carmen yelled.

Michael turned his head to him from where he had been flung and saw his arm outstretched, the key fob dangling from his finger. The guard retrained his eyes on Carmen, lunged and found himself on Carmen's back, the duffel disconnected from his shoulder.

Alice jumped on the guard as Carmen tried to crawl out from under him as he felt the badge and the belt, and the baton dig into his skin.

"Throw it!" Michael commanded.

The guard's weight abated as Alice pulled on him, and Carmen slid the key fob from his finger and flung it in Michael's direction. Alice lost her grip and groaned as she fell to the dirt while Michael bear-crawled to retrieve the key.

"Truck one," Carmen said, muffled under the guard, "go!"

Alice scampered to her feet, grabbed the duffel bag, and ran towards the trucks. Michael followed, yet detoured to retrieve the plastic garbage bag. Neither looked back, for they both knew they were going back.

Five pickup trucks in a row. White, regular cab standards with the New Madrid logo on each door and below in reassuring font 'Powering Lives, Safely.' Alice and Michael scanned each number either on the quarter-panel or the tailgates. 112-SS. 152-MW. 103-DC. 189-MF. 125-CS. No single digits, no truck number one.

"What do we do?" Alice yelled. "There's no 'one'."

Michael looked at the buttons on the fob and pressed 'Start.' 189-MF turned over and hummed. Alice felt a tinge of embarrassment, and Michael could sense it. She tossed the duffel in the cargo bed as he placed the garbage bag. He pressed a different button to unlock the cab and climbed in.

Clunk, he lowered the steering wheel. Click, whoosh, he pulled the bench seat closer to the dash. Quick into reverse the wheels spun the dirt and then Michael pounded the shifter into drive which let loose a cloud of dust over the excavators and backhoes and bulldozers. Down fifty feet, the Cushman's, the dump trucks, the diesel, and their unleaded counterparts. Hard left out of the faculty lot, and the tail went. He adjusted quickly on the wheel and it came back.

Carmen scrambled to his feet. The guard recomposed. Stood and slid the baton from his belt. Held the wooden shaft to his side. Both in view through the windshield. A steady clip, and the truck drew nearer. A hundred feet. Seventy-five. Michael's foot pressed down hard, and the tires caught the dirt and dug in.

Carmen's neck adjusted and watched his friend with intense eyes turn the steering wheel slightly to the right. Watched his crush's eyes follow without hesitation nor any audible instruction to the contrary.

The guard turned his attention from Carmen and saw the front bumper as it angled towards him. Vicious in its speed. Volatile in its direction. True in its intent. His boots stuck in the dirt for a moment before his mind could properly instruct his body and then leapt as the truck was seconds from finding its mark. The headlight struck his knee, spun him midair and his forehead crashed against the New Madrid logo on the door.

He fell lifeless to the ground. Michael slammed on the brakes, Carmen took hold of the edge of the cargo bed and jumped inside.

"Go!" Alice commanded as she looked back and saw Carmen within the bed, hands secure on the long edge and the tailgate. Michael pressed on the gas pedal, turned the truck hard left, and sped away from the football field. Down the rows of prisoner's trailers and out the entrance from which they came hours before. Through the town where the glass cut. Where they hid from the charter bus and where they covered the family with blankets.

25

Nate had awoken earlier than usual. Crafted his thoughts in bed while staring at the tiled ceiling. Ignored the prosthetic next to the bed and denied the empty space past his knee where the blanket sank to the mattress. Felt the difference in the day after the many echoes.

Leisurely, he walked to the front door of the building designated as the camp office. With the desks and the chairs with wheels and the plans. He walked across the open space where the dirt road expanded into an accidental parking lot, devoid of vehicles, save the charter bus. The lot opened to the office and the cafeteria, its larger counterpart. He spent his vision on the ground, purposeful in his avoidance of any prisoner in their haze or any Plaid in his blue-collar determination.

He reached into his pocket, pulled out a gray keycard, and set it against the black card reader next to the doorjamb. The door chirped, clicked, and as he pushed it open, he heard what he thought was the other door shutting. He stopped, the door angled thirty-five degrees, and listened. His ears brought forth nothing new, yet through his nostrils came the normal staleness of the air less stale. Through his skin came the stillness that was less still.

He cued on the subtleties and pushed the door with suspicious care. Stepped lightly with the near imperceptible limp, took an LED lantern from a shelf near the entrance and pushed the button. Eyed the rummaged desk to his right. The one to his left and the one further still. Crunched over the glass shards and examined the windowpane on the back wall. The open fridge and over leisurely to the pegboard as he listened to the commotion rise along the road and move further away.

The commotion outside rose several decibels in seconds as Nate opened the side door. His ears strained and he thought, maybe, he heard a vehicle turn over. The struggle was beyond his line of sight. He smiled and closed the door, lifted his hand and touched each key fob with a finger until he reached the empty peg for truck number one. He reversed and pulled the fob for truck three and held it in his hand.

"Sir!" a guard yelled as he appeared in the open doorway. "Sir, we have a problem."

He was pale, with a thin, lanky frame which made his uniform resemble a Halloween costume rather than form-fitted for an authority figure. Blonde hair buzzed tight that made one think twice if he was bald.

"Do tell," Nate responded with his attention still on the board and slyly slipped the fob into his pocket.

"There's a, there's a kid running through the camp."

"Hmmm."

"Well, there ain't supposed to be a kid."

"I know about the kid."

The guard stood quiet, unable to reconcile his next words with Nate's demeanor.

"What should I do?"

"I'll take care of it," Nate assured him as he walked to him.

"There shouldn't be a kid in here."

"There shouldn't be a lot of things, should there?"

"Sir?"

"What's for breakfast this mornin'?"

"Excuse me?"

"What's for breakfast?"

"For us or the prisoners?"

"For us."

"Um, I don't know."

"I hope it's pancakes, it feels like a pancake day," Nate continued as he turned to face him, "can you do me a favor?"

The guard waited for instruction without offering an affirmation.

"If it is, in fact, pancakes, a tall glass of milk would be nice. If it's eggs, orange juice. Also a tall glass."

The guard stood still; he heard a child yell out in the distance through the open front door. "And if it ain't pancakes or eggs?"

"Surprise me," faux anger, then a smile, and this was all the guard needed to feel satisfied and leave with a plan of his own design.

Nate continued in his leisure. Closed the front door. Pulled a chair askew to a metal desk and cleared the space of notepads, plans, and pencils. Ran his hand along the surface to remove any unseen dust or speck or crumb. Came to attention, as this time he was sure that a truck was loose along the camp roads then returned.

Returned to youth, those memories that, in retrospect, were pure. The only ones that made life an acceptable pursuit. Shuddered when the embarrassment crept. Solace as those thoughts transferred to the kids and especially Michael. Was interrupted by fast footfalls he knew were guards. Was interrupted by thoughts of responsibilities and pushed them down to return himself to the memories. He stared at the door. The pegboard. His rights as an employee. Worker's compensation in large letters and the legalese in illegible font from a distance. The blur as he stared without staring.

"It's French toast," the guard announced as he pushed the door open with his back.

"French toast," Nate said without turning his head to face him, "so what have you decided goes with that?"

"Huh?"

"What did you bring to drink?"

"I got milk, cause it's kinda like pancakes, so I figured."

"You figured?" with a raised voice.

"Yes, sir," the guard responded meekly and set the plate and glass down.

"Well, that was a good call," and he smiled.

The guard chuckled uneasily.

"You shoulda brought two plates, we could've ate together."

"But you told me to bring you breakfast."

"I'm just messing with ya, pull up a chair."

"But the trespassers."

"Don't worry about the kids," Nate said sternly, "and don't call 'em 'trespassers', they ain't that."

"I'm sorry, sir."

"And don't call me sir," Nate smiled, which relaxed the young man.

As the guard took a chair from a nearby desk, he noticed the broken window and felt the lack of intuition contradict his profession. He pulled to the opposite side of the desk and sat down across from Nate.

He watched as Nate pulled the end of the butter packet and spread it on the toast. Repeated the process and spread the soft yellow across before applying the syrup.

"Where you from?" Nate asked the guard as he cut in with the knife, stabbed with the fork, and put the browned sweetness to his lips.

"Delaware."

"Delaware? Ain't no one from Delaware."

The guard didn't know how to respond, hence he didn't.

"So, Delaware," Nate continued between bites, "why are you here?"

"Excuse me?"

"You're new, it's still fresh. What made you leave Delaware? Why us? Why here?"

"I saw an ad online."

Nate waited for a continuation of the thought but could see Delaware was waiting for his retort. "That's it?"

"Yeah, I guess."

"So, you saw a job, far as hell from Delaware, and you applied."

"Yeah."

"And that's it? That's all that went into that?"

"Well, I guess the adventure."

"Adventure?"

"Yeah, to see it."

"Is it everything you thought it would be?"

"Honestly?"

"Yeah, honestly. Off the record, as they say."

"There's no adventure here. It's kinda depressing. No, it's really depressing."

"And you thought it would be otherwise?"

"I don't know, the resilience of America. Rebuild the country. Be a part of something great."

"That's what they told you, huh?"

Delaware looked away, not wanting to admit gullibility.

"And how is it really?" Nate prodded.

"Well, it's not that."

"Is it ever how you think it is in your head? Is it ever how they tell you?"

Nate took several gulps of milk as he waited, "ain't no one gonna offer you adventure. Ain't no one going to give you more than they can get themselves." He took a bite of bacon, chewed. Swallowed. "If you want adventure, if you want to have something in your mind that you can hold onto, you gotta make it yourself. Just gotta take it."

"Maybe I just wanted a job."

"Bullshit, you wanted something more."

"It's easy to say, 'go make some adventure.' It's a little harder to actually do it."

"How old are you?"

"Twenty-two."

"Gets harder as you get older."

Delaware cleared his throat to give his mind that moment to broach the subject of the kids again, this time properly.

"Where did they come from? The kids?"

"Don't know," Nate answered, and seemed comfortable on a full stomach to entertain the topic. "Showed up last night."

"How'd they get here?"

"Determination, I assume."

"Why didn't they get picked up by the sensors? How'd they get past the barriers? The cameras?"

Nate burst with a deep, hard laugh. Delaware kept his eyes on him until the extenuation became uncomfortable and he averted his gaze. Two tries and Nate composed himself.

"This place is forgotten; it was designed to be forgotten. Expendable, just like the batteries in those sensors, in those cameras. Gates still work just for show. This place, this is just a dumping ground for the unwanted. The undesirables."

"What about The Plaids?"

"Simple men," Nate said as he leaned in, "who find meaning through physical labor. Simple men who find themselves on the lower rung of society anywhere but here. Men who know no matter what they say, what they do, as long as it don't break the law, they know they got a safety net below them who wear red bracelets."

"I met a bunch of them, and they seem really nice."

"Oh, real nice, every last one of them."

"So where are they going?"

"Who?"

"Those kids."

"Well I assume they're going on an adventure."

"And you're not worried about any of this? None of this makes you jump up and go after them?"

"Of course I'm, well it ain't worry, let's say I'm concerned. And yes, I'm gonna go after them, and yes, I'm gonna take them home. Nothing wrong with giving them a little head start."

Nate reclined in his chair, smug in his assumed altruism.

"Why?"

Nate let the chair come forward. "See now, that's the difference between someone your age and someone like me. The further you get from your youth, the more you know that youth was it. That those memories, those are yours. Don't have to share them with anyone 'cept those you were with. No thinking, no responsibilities 'cept to each other. In that time there ain't no success and there ain't no failure. And I ain't about to take that from those kids."

"I'm sorry, sir?" Delaware responded, "I mean you; I mean Nate?"

He waited for Nate to approve the informality, which he didn't, yet he did not disapprove either.

"Do you get what I'm saying?"

"I do," Delaware answered with the tone of a liar wishing to change the subject.

"Sir!" another guard yelled as he crashed open the front door. "Sir," as his eyes found Nate, "we need you in the medical trailer." More astute than Delaware, he processed the broken window and the oddity of this boss privately meeting with a new guard before Nate had responded. His muscles pushed against the uniform, from his chest across to biceps and down to his quads. Hair high and tight and the scarred intensity across his face of one who had seen things.

Nate sat in the nonchalant aura he had created before realizing the oddity to those uninformed and rose quickly. He met the concentrated guard at the doorway and at the bottom of the stairs, he looked back to see nothing but the open door.

"Delaware!" he yelled from the exterior. "Get your ass in gear!"

He heard the chair slide fast, careen off a desk, and then watched as Delaware bounded down the stairs.

26

"Tell them what you told me," the doctor instructed the guard who had attempted to stop Carmen. Prone on the examination table. His head thrashed along the right temple. Peppered with specks of gravel, embedded in raw, exposed skin. His right pant leg cut above the knee, which exposed the cap set at an improper angle.

"I saw a kid running," the guard told Nate, with Delaware a few steps back. Between winces and bottled water through a straw, strained on his elbows and then back down. "He come from the direction of the worker's trailers. So, I told him to stop, but he kept running so I tackled him. Then, out of nowhere, there were two other kids and they jumped on me. Next thing I knew," he continued as the doctor tended to his head, "I see the truck come out of nowhere and I'm flying through the air."

The doctor placed a gauze pad over his wound and secured it with white tape. He stood from the stool and motioned Nate and Delaware away from earshot.

"We got a bit of a problem," he started.

"Yeah," Nate responded. "What's that?"

"Well, as you know, I'm not really, you know, qualified for this. Self-taught, really. Cuts, bruises, stitches, I can handle that. But resetting a kneecap? That's above my pay scale."

The three stole a glance at the disfigured knee.

"Shit," Nate uttered, "guess I'll run him up north. Delaware, you wanna go for a ride?"

"Sure."

"Alright, get him cleaned up, and I'll go get a truck."

"Weird thing was," the guard continued from his bed as if there was no interruption in his thoughts, "he was wearing an NME shirt. They all were."

Nate's head turned slowly.

"Where'd they get those?" the guard continued. "Why were they wearing them?"

There were more words, addendums that ran from the through-line, but Nate heard none. Disappeared, the medical trailer, the doctor. Disappeared, Delaware and the mangled orator. Out went the light and out went the dark. He succumbed to the echoing heartbeat and the stomach drop. How could he have forgotten? How could he overlook, as he spoke philosophically with Delaware, that there was the possibility that they could take a truck? That they had driven this far, and that there was tangible guile amongst them. A truck, full of gas, could at least get them there, to The Enclaves, the nomenclature amongst the camp—and there was danger. Unknown, fluttering through the rumors. He stood in the distant closeness of the words uttered, in ethereal reckoning of his fallibility, and in it he pressed with purpose out the door.

First with a clip that matched the situation. Quicker and into a jog, then a limped sprint as Delaware chased after.

"Sir! Damnit," he muttered, "Nate!"

Delaware followed. Through the busted storage shed door. Watched from the entrance as Nate rummaged through the boxes set on shelves against the back wall. Ran his hands through an open box then through it aside.

Tore open the box behind it, stood and shoved two gas masks into Delaware's chest.

"Wait," Delaware asked, caught off guard but caught them. "What are you doing?"

Two smaller boxes within a larger one, the first empty and the second thrown at Delaware. "Come with me," Nate instructed and led him out of the shed. He lifted a tarp rested against the back of the structure angled out. Two red plastic gas cans. Full as they pulled down on Nate's arms and handed them to Delaware, who struggled to rearrange the load he already had to accommodate.

"Truck three, extended cab, go," he instructed Delaware, then went back into the shed. Dust had collected on the gun case and as he pressed on the keypad those that remained untouched kept their matte finish. Six, four, five, six, two, seven, nine, and then it glowed yellow. He wiped the dust from the fingerprint scanner before placing his forefinger, it glowed green and he pulled down on the latch and pulled the leaden door open.

The lot was half-empty. Diggers and backhoes and dump trucks gone had headed out for the day's work. Cement mixers and haulers. Driven by Plaids with their beards, hardened forearms, and disfigured grips from nails placed by 10,000 hammer strokes. The prisoners bunched thick on flatbeds had left, with metal rails that doubled as a safety feature but built for holding implements. Shovels. Sledgehammers. Stepladders and wheelbarrows. The guards who, on any other day, would have fit comfortably within the pickup truck cabs. Yet two keys were missing, and several men in olive-green were forced to climb into the cargo beds of the unlocked trucks and ride to the worksite in the open air.

"Wait," Delaware asked again, but this time put his hand on Nate's shoulder. There was offense at the intrusion, at the delay. Nate waited for the continuation, yet none came.

"Open the back door," he instructed Delaware.

Without urgency he obliged, and Nate slid two rifles, two 9mm pistols in cases, and several boxes of ammunition along the seats. He shut the door, checked the cargo bed, and was satisfied.

"Where are we going?" Delaware asked as he keenly watched the weapons being loaded.

"We, my friend," Nate said as he pulled open the truck door, "are going on an adventure." He closed the door, pressed the ignition, and rolled down the window. "Get in."

His feet shuffled. Long way around the bed. Spied the gas masks and slowed around the tailgate.

"Get your ass in here!"

Delaware stood motionless. "Where?"

"Godamnit, boy. I told you an adventure."

"That doesn't mean anything."

"You know where we're going," Nate said as he nodded to the cargo behind him.

"I'm not going there."

"And why not?"

"Because no one comes back."

"I've been there and come back," Nate stated while keeping his voice on even keel as best he could to deliver the lie.

"No," Delaware said as he looked away, "no one's come back. Those company men. The National Guard. Hell, the Marines. None of them came back."

"An' how would you know that? They tell you those stories up in Delaware? They know what goes on down here up in Delaware?"

"I know there's a least some truth to what they say. Even a rumor has to come from somewhere, from some truth."

Nate slammed his palms on the steering wheel. "Ya know, if anything, God forbid, happens to those kids I'm gonna, you know when they come for us, I'm gonna be forced to tell them that I asked you for help. That you were right there and maybe, they'd still be alive if it weren't for you. You want that on your conscience?"

"No sir," his voice cracked, "but I'm not prepared to die yet, sir." He regained the eye contact through the open truck window. "Are you?"

Nate pulled the shifter in and then down into drive. The tires kicked up dirt as he had intended, to make Delaware disappear from view before the distance had allowed. Left down the prisoner's road with the ramshackle trailers. Down the road to the chain link, the razor wire, and the stacked truck tires, their usefulness in constant dispute as the main gate never closed, was never locked.

He pushed the truck at a steady clip through and under the Camp Andersonville sign. Out onto the main road of buckled concrete. A sign askew at forty-five degrees, 'Downtown, 2 Miles.' A sign askew, bullet-ridden and once clearly informed the speed limit. At a half mile there was a herd of deer a hundred deep. Half-hidden under wild grass among trees cracked at their lowest breaking point and new teenage saplings stronger in their development. At three-quarters, he slid between rusted automobile carcasses pushed to the ditches. At a mile, there was a sign, dirt white cracked with green lettering and read 'Green Gables, A Friendly Neighborhood.'

He slowed and turned into the subdivision. Took in the soft reverence of decay that never receded. Homes split in half and some only splintered. Brick chimneys that faltered into the abstract on roofs and flower beds below. The FEMA X next to a door frame. Then the next. The next. The natural landscape that only occurred without the mower. Haphazard patterns in stalks and stems derived from chance that crafted beauty. Up through the pavement and surrounded the sedans. The pickup trucks and the SUVs.

Nate followed the road as it curved, enveloping him deeper into the houses. The homes. Wild dogs mangled fighting for alpha through a picture window. Deteriorating mattresses on roofs. The basketball hoop nailed to a garage and how he rooted for the last strip of netting still clinging to the rust. Plastic miniblinds askew through bedroom windows. Plastic everything that survives.

The natural soundtrack dissolved and, in its place, raised slowly diesel engines in decibels.

Metal against brick against wood against metal. Backhoes that bit into structurally deficient walls and inner drywall. Men in plaid deftly destroying. Bulldozers that pushed two-by-fours and shingles and white bathroom fixtures. Ceramic plates. Baseball trophies over family photographs over teen idol posters.

The prisoners in their whites directed the men in plaid. Dig here. Push here. Over there. Ensured their hydration as the sun pressed and the air thickened. They dug with shovels where the machines could not reach. Pushed the dirt where an accurate spread was required. Pulled and wrenched at refrigerators, washers, and dryers.

Through each exertion, they noticed Nate while The Plaids continued unaware with the machines. Through each exertion, they examined the details while careful to placate the guards situated throughout the lot who re-examined their life choices with every bead of sweat.

They examined. Who, Nate who drives the big bus and never comes to a job site. Why, don't know, but this is a diversion from the norm. Where, close enough to see us but far enough to think he's inconspicuous. When, when those kids showed up at the camp. Keep digging. Keep Pushing. Keep pulling. This does not concern you until it does.

At first, Nate tried to will Jeremiah to the truck with his mind. He stared with internal commands. None reached, so he put the truck in drive and inched forward twenty feet, then twenty more. A Hispanic prisoner paused and turned to him, then resumed with the rake. Nate willed again as Jeremiah waited for the final shovel of splintered wood and the cracked porcelain remnants of a toilet to top off his wheelbarrow. Without a grunt he lifted the load, walked it across the uneven land, and guided it up the wooden ramp angled against the tail of a truck. He tipped it towards the front wheel and the contents crashed against the metal floor.

Nate pulled forward again, guiding the truck within a few feet of the ramp and stopped as Jeremiah lithely turned the wheelbarrow and walked it back down the ramp. Nate stared through the windshield, sure that Jeremiah would sense the cue. The closeness and the oddity of his presence.

"Goddamn invisible," Nate muttered as Jeremiah rolled the wheelbarrow down the ramp and turned towards the worksite. He reached back, extended his arm, and grabbed a pistol case. Slowly opened it, slid a clip in the weapon and slid back to press a bullet into the chamber. He pushed the door open, shoved the pistol into his jeans, and followed Jeremiah into the worksite.

The three closest guards keyed on the intrusion, and their right hands went to their batons in unison. Eyes upon, if not for peril, but for the break in routine. Their minds had softened over the many days, the many subdivisions and the understanding that there were no builders here, only destroyers.

"Mr. Caste," Nate said with enough volume to overcome the machines yet soft enough to be inquisitive as opposed to something else. Jeremiah stopped and set the wheelbarrow down yet did not turn. Instead, he waited for Nate to approach, pass, and set the distance between them.

"Yes, sir," Jeremiah responded amiably.

"I need you to come with me."

Jeremiah gave the request pause.

"Ain't that against the rules? Leaving the job site except for injury?"

"Since when do you care about the rules?"

"Since always, sir. I ain't never broken a rule."

"But what you do here," Nate contemplated how to continue that line of thought.

"Never broke a rule, written or otherwise."

"The kids, they run off."

"I saw that," Jeremiah laughed. "So what? Let them go home, tell their stories."

"They ain't heading home."

"Well they're gonna be quite disappointed when they get to another camp and see it's just like this one."

"They ain't heading to another camp, they're going to The Enclaves."

Jeremiah stepped back, rubbed his chin, and used the bottom of his shirt to wipe his brow.

"Well I suppose you gotta go get them then."

"Can't go in alone."

"Got plenty of guards standing around here."

"I need someone I can trust."

"I'd love to help you," Jeremiah said as he tapped the red bracelet on his wrist, "but the moment we leave the perimeter they'll come for us."

"Ain't no one gonna come for you."

Jeremiah looked quizzically.

"These things track our every move, don't they?"

"They do."

"Then they'll know."

"You're asking the wrong question; you should be asking 'who's watching?'"

Jeremiah waited for the answer. "Who's watching?"

"No one. Not one soul in the normal, gives a shit, and we ain't got time, we have to go." Nate walked past him towards the truck. "Now."

"But, sir!"

"No one's watching, Caste! No one's watching and no one cares."

Jeremiah stood next to the wheelbarrow and felt the machines upset the earth. Heard the diesel engines, and the clanks, and the crunches, and the grunts. As he had for days, for months, for years. Spied the Plaids, and the guards, and his brothers, and with calm realism, took in the senses before that first step towards the truck that made the three closest guards gravitate.

"Boys!" Nate yelled to them in mid-entry to the truck, "it's alright!"

The guards heeded their boss' instructions and ceased their approach yet kept their hands on the batons. Just in case. Just in case. Jeremiah pulled the passenger door open, acknowledged the backseat arsenal, and set his large frame within the interior.

"You know what I really miss?" Nate asked with a serious tone as he pressed his forefinger on a fingerprint scanner embedded in the center console display.

"What?"

"Girls, I really miss girls," the screen filled with a menu, and Nate selected "Find a Company Vehicle" with his finger.

Maybe it was because he knew it was foolish to hope for such a thing, Jeremiah had forgotten he even had amorous feelings.

"Think I can get me some radioactive pussy down there?" Nate asked, then pressed *NME-CP1-PU1*.

Jeremiah thought about responding to keep alive the brotherly camaraderie but felt it unnecessary. They looked at each other, parsing the absurdity and the sensibility of the question posed as the GPS map flicked onto the screen, found their position, and their destination.

"Warning," a female voice echoed through the speakers, "this route may contain hazards and impassable roads. Proceed with caution. Warning, current traffic conditions unknown. Press 'accept' to continue."

Nate pressed accept with his finger and clicked the gear shifter into drive.

“Make a U-turn when possible.”

<h1 style="text-align:center">27</h1>

Carmen's left arm lay against the long edge of the pickup, his right against the tailgate. Both gripped hard through the bumps that elevated him from the bed as Michael sped through the camp. Through the rows of prisoner trailers. Through the empty path. Carmen looked back to see a guard in the distance, helping his fallen colleague. The prisoners who witnessed yet still kept their distance.

A sly grin across his face, across Alice's, and across Michael's as he slid into a right turn, then a left and out of the camp. Drove with steady confidence as, to the moment, something had gone right. He pulled over near the entrance for a subdivision and Carmen hopped from the bed and pulled open the passenger door, where Alice slid over to provide him space.

"Holy shit!" Carmen exclaimed as he reached behind Alice and tousled Michael's hair.

"Hell ya!" Michael responded, shoved his foot down on the gas pedal, and guided the truck out of the pebbled shoulder and back onto the cracked pavement.

He drove straight when he could, the tires on each side of the faded white centerline. Navigated around the buckled pavement where necessary and used the truck's high frame to mount others.

Alice reached over Carmen and rolled down the window. "Hey!" she yelled out the passenger window. "Hey you! Yeah, I see you! Screw you!" The small group of boars sunning on the front lawn ignored her insults, ignored her middle finger.

The subdivisions, single homes, and the mostly unobstructed road gave way under the 'Camp Andersonville' sign, backwards but the thick spray paint showed through the cloth. Ragged American flags. The debris that wafted through the felled stop lights. The skeletal automobiles and their abandoned Toyota.

Michael drove slow past the cemetery cinema, each remembering at once the scene as if the marquee letters were code only they knew. Slow, but he did not stop, nor did either passenger question the route or the destination. Not yet. Through the town. Around jutted pavement and over soiled mattresses. Partial business names on glass shard remnants through windows where racoons slunk with noses to the ground.

Out through the 'Harvest Days' and painted cornstalks. The outlier buildings that fit neither Main Street nor the country beyond. That one home that predated everything and out of place. Through a slanted stop sign and into the wild road. Over the reeds and tall grass that encroached on the concrete and the dandelions that shot through the cracks.

Michael slowed the truck until it settled and *click, click* into park. His finger floated in front of the navigation screen before settling on the 'System On' button. The screen flashed to life. "Welcome," a female voice sounded through the speakers, "enter bio-ID now."

"Huh," Michael muttered as Michael and Carmen alternated between looking at him and the screen which echoed the female voice in white text over black. He placed his finger on the square with the fingerprint icon.

"Not recognized," the female voice responded. Michael tried again. "Not recognized."

Carmen pulled open the glove box but found only the owner's manual for the truck. He pushed and it clicked securely. A gentle tug of the door handle and he was out, and he hopped into the bed. Scanned the horizon, down the road overgrown with branches that swayed tenderly with each breezy pass. To his left, paint-peeled wooden homes behind the oak canvas and to his right, the dilapidated silo that started its deterioration before any of this.

"South," he said confidently, as if at the helm of a ship, "south and west."

Michael looked back through the rear window as Alice slid it open to better hear him.

"South and west," Carmen repeated as he crouched down to reach into the duffel. He unscrewed the cap of a half-full water bottle and took a sip. "Right?" as he passed it through the window.

"Gotta be," Michael concurred, then turned around to look straight ahead. Then left, then right. "Which way is that?"

Carmen stood back up and circled in place where he stood. "I don't know."

"Mother fucker!" Michael yelled.

"Hey genius," Alice said to him as she pointed to the rearview mirror, "see where it says 'W'? That means 'west.' And I bet if you turn a different direction, it'll give you that direction too."

"Oh," Michael muttered, embarrassed. "Well I never had a car that had that."

"You're 12, you've never had a car. Or money, or good looks," she added the last two teasingly, but he took it as an insult. "Hey," she said sweetly while pulling on his neck, "I'm just messing with you, alright?"

He looked at her expressionless and then straight ahead, satisfied but unwilling to show her. Carmen hopped out of the bed and climbed into the cab. "Think they're coming after us?" he asked them as he shut the door.

"We ran over one of them and stole a truck," Alice said, "what do you think?"

"They better," Michael said when Carmen didn't answer, "depending on how far we're going we ain't got enough gas to get back home." He threw the truck into drive and gunned it down the road.

"How far can we get," Alice said with her voice raised over the revving engine and wind through the windows, "before we have to turn back?"

Michael took into consideration the remaining miles indicated on the dash, the distance from the camp and then further home. "Hundred, maybe a little more, after that we probably have to turn back."

Alice thought about asking him if he knew how to get home, but since she herself didn't, she refrained, for she didn't want to know the answer. She stared out the windshield as the ground rushed past and unconsciously touched her sutured cheek lightly. She examined the rusting automobiles that appeared on occasion, and as Michael maneuvered around them, she imagined the lives that once inhabited their cabins. A pickup truck, early Sunday fishing with his father before his mother insisted on church. An obese woman with her cackle of children, feasting on fast-food in the minivan. Their first date in his father's Wrangler, with cheap beer because she enjoys wine and he spent the majority of his meager earnings to satisfy her in the hopes that she'd later satisfy him.

The subdivisions devoid of humanity. Which had once emanated the aromas of meals over stoves and barbeques. Freshly mown grass. Had once announced said humanity with televisions. Children's glee and children's despair. Raised voices in the kitchens. In the bedrooms. Newborn beginnings in the American hope, and violent endings in the American ironies.

Gas stations devoid of fuel, and beef jerky, and soda next to strip malls more appropriate in their decay. The deer's steady gate across the parking lot. The bird's flutter as it emerged from the darkened interior through a broken window, and every few moments she felt selfish as she imagined her mother and father in panic. Soon, she reassured herself, she would be home, but this was too important to give up.

West, they went. Then south. Again, west. Each an arbitrary decision Michael had taken it upon himself to make. Steady on the accelerator. Easy on the brakes. He felt Alice's presence next to him and, through her, Carmen. Suddenly, he had trouble swallowing, as if his throat constricted. His shoulders shuddered with each sniffle which preceded a tear down his left cheek, then another down his right. This was the first time he felt that anyone truly cared. That he was connected, that he had reached out and someone had reached back. That this wasn't a setup, that there wasn't a belt waiting for him for some perceived slight or spit wads aimed his way from the mouths of football jocks. No one here was going to spew names at him in school hallways or from car windows. No one was going to grab him and shove him headfirst into a garbage can or pull his pants down and kick him into the girl's bathroom.

Alice noticed his tears. Carmen noticed, but neither said a word, for Michael was correct in his assessment. And Carmen stared out the passenger window and thought about his brother holding his mother tight, telling her that he's alright, that he'll be home soon. Espousing God's greatness at set intervals. Carmen's anxiety was far greater than Alice's, and it took more courage for him to hold it down, set it aside, and not say a word in reference. Further still, he felt the imbalance of his courage and cowardice. The fear that froze his legs on the bridge and that put them in motion on Main Street. His mother, he thought, could fret a little while longer if it meant her boy would return a man.

West, and they arrived in another town with its own festival. Its own boutique shops and diners, optometrists next to dentists below second-floor insurance offices. American chains with their Arabica coffee and low-carbohydrate burrito bowls and non-GMO sandwiches. Award programs managed on iPhones, and Androids scanned at registers and kiosks.

Parking meters sated with quarters at the curbs of diagonal parking spaces where three wild dogs ripped the flesh off a wild boar. A row of crows set above them on a metal bar, the remnants of a blue and white striped awning, cawed and waited.

South for miles through the thicket, the tree branches with lush leaves that tapped against the metal frame and encroached through the window. Deep, sated breaths brought by carbon intake. The roots. The thick hale trunks and veiny leaves.

West and Michael felt it first, a subtle change in the air. It was the metallic taste on the tongue, though he didn't surmise as such. All he knew was that something was different. Alice pressed her tongue against the roof of her mouth. Carmen stuck his out slightly and then back.

He stared at the leaves as they slipped inside, their emerald brilliance now mossy green and they exited. He thought maybe it was the position of the sun. Several miles and mossy green, and a mile further, olive. Wilted, frail, and once buoyant foliage stripped from their branches. Broke from their connections, littered the pavement behind them, and the twigs that grazed the truck snapped. Fell into the cab until Michael and Carmen were sufficiently covered in brittle green-black leaves mottled with brown, circular imperfections.

Windows up, and Carmen coughed in the acidic air. Michael adjusted his relaxed posture to match the newness. Straight, at attention with eyes alert. Alice pushed back into the bench and put on her seatbelt, and the audible click caused the boys to mimic her action.

South, and within a mile, the last remaining leaf had fallen. Trunks devoid of bark. Brittle, barren branches and morose twigs that hung over beds of decaying leaves. Grasses brown and stunted, either flat against the soil or bent over against his neighbor where they held each other those years ago. Homes, hidden for the miles before behind the rebirth now exposed. Caved in. Felled over. Shutters that dangled from rusty, recalcitrant nails. Flat tires on pickups. ATVs, Barbie bicycles, and RVs. Pool noodles still on the putrid water of an above-ground swimming pool. All exposed, laid bare in the chemical air.

Carmen took a swig of water, and Alice greedily grabbed it before handing the last sip to Michael. The salted forest enveloped them for several miles further until a slow grade led them up and over the tree line. Michael stopped the truck where the black tar ceased at the bridge's beginning.

The southern lanes, their edifice separate from the northern, had failed. Thick slabs of concrete that forced the silty water below into rapids. Worn smooth below the waterline where the river had made the trespass its own, though sharp angles remained where the dimpled construction stayed exposed to the air.

Divine intervention, or the accidental preciseness of the pylons struck deep into the soft riverbed, had kept the northern lanes aloft. Michael turned and looked to Carmen for guidance, then to Alice.

"Do it," Carmen mumbled and then swallowed hard, to which Alice did not object.

Michael released his foot from the brake and turned the wheel left for the approach. Steady, with the speedometer fluctuating between ten and fifteen miles per hour.

"There it is," Alice said with muted excitement and pointed out the window, her arm extended in front of Carmen's face, "it's real."

Michael set the brakes near the apex and Carmen opened his door without thought, exposing the truck interior to the elements unfiltered.

"Should we put the masks on?" Alice asked, yet neither boy answered. Their gazes fixed towards the eastern horizon. To the river's perceived end before the rolling hills where the stripped trees seemed so small, they could be held in their palms if they just wished hard enough. In its presence, Carmen's acrophobia wilted, and Alice forgot the air.

The sun behind haze still glinted off the metal panels that covered the arched structure. An artificial cocoon, half-finished and rising high above the failed landscape. It resembled an airplane hangar, though the roof was higher and the angle more acute. A construction crane of crisscrossed metalworks remained vertical near the opening, as if a flag while its counterparts had succumbed to the gravity, and the particles, and the tremors.

From their vantage point upon the bridge, they could see NME Reactor 3 clearly, and even with the distance and in shadow, the concave concrete towers within the exterior structure.

Where once the curves had been along the center of the cooling towers and then angled out at the top, they now terminated at the curvatures. Uneven and jagged at the canopy. Eerier without the steam bellowing from the openings atop. Supernatural in the silent dead forest. In the imperceptible toxicity.

"Jesus," Michael said with an emphasis on the first syllable.

"Why isn't it finished yet?" Carmen questioned.

"Shouldn't we be wearing the masks?" Alice asked.

"Maybe there ain't no one that wants to finish it." Michael said.

"Or maybe they just gave up," Carmen added, and for several moments more they stood at the precipice and stared.

28

"So," and Jeremiah cleared his throat, "how's your morning?"

A subtle smirk lifted the corner of Nate's mouth as he turned the wheel, letting his grip loosen to let the truck straighten. He drove with an eye on the road and the other on the console screen. Slow through the subdivision as to not arouse suspicion further than he already had. He gave a wide berth to a dump truck that hurled dust and pebbles and a simple nod accompanied a friendly wave.

He turned away from the camp at the subdivision's entrance, and as he headed into the wild, he felt a warmth flow through him. It started at his toes, tingled, and ran up through his legs, his thighs and coursed up his groin.

After his torso, the warmth flooded his head and garnered a deep sigh and unstoppable grin. He opened the windows and took in the aroma. All of it, all that scented life that was not in camp, or the bus route enveloped in crisp, unnatural air conditioning that filled the whole bus. That was not the train station that, when the air was right, festered with the fast-food drive-thrus that excised grease-laden processes through industrial vents.

Here, there was something sweet as the leaves left their scents on his shoulder. Jeremiah, too, felt the leaves, yet his mind went to the auditory and the ocular. Absent the machinery, the buzz of intermittent electricity. It had only been moments, yet the red lights and bells that announced the ground shakes seemed so distant. The murmurs and prayers through open windows that traveled between trailers set too close. The arguments between roommates in words and physicality, the unnerving beat of male masturbation that would echo off siding.

"So," Jeremiah said to shudder away his last thought as Nate maneuvered over the misshapen pavement, "you said no one's watching?"

"Yup."

"So I could, any of us, could just run off and that'd be that?"

"Well," Nate elongated the syllable, "yes and no. I mean you run off from camp and don't go near civilization, the normal, then no, no one's watching and ain't no one giving a shit. Hell we could drive all over this shithole and you don't gotta worry."

"But if I get near a town, or a city..."

"Yeah, you git within ten miles and you'd be triggered right off. Your little jewelry right there would start beeping and glowing and shit and you, you'd know you're straight-A, one hundred percent screwed."

"So why lie? Why tell all of us that our every step is being monitored?"

"Why do we gotta take our shoes off at the airport? Why do they make you sign a receipt at a supermarket? No one's got a bomb in their socks and no one reads your signature. What you gotta learn, Caste, is that it's all an illusion."

"That's crazy."

"It's not crazy. You think 'that guy's doing his job' and 'this signature keeps me safe' and 'if I run off, they'll know.' It'd be crazy if it didn't work."

"I guess."

The going was slow. The road, and therefore obstacles, were obstructed by the overgrowth and the deceptions brought by weeds and saplings that had broken through the concrete. Yet he pushed the speed where he could, determined to close the distance between the two trucks.

"Strawberry pie."

"What?" Nate asked.

"You asked me if I missed, um, relations. Me, I miss strawberry pie."

"We got pie at the camp."

"No, no sir, we do not have pie at the camp. Not my grandmomma's pie. The ripest strawberries. That sweetness. The crust, it was like it was so crisp like if she wasn't making it, it would burn up in the oven, but God wouldn't allow that. No, not for grandmomma. That's what I miss most, I miss that strawberry pie."

"At the next intersection," the female voice echoed, "turn left."

"Pie don't compare to pussy, Caste." Nate said confidently.

"Never said it did, just said what I missed."

"Guess you would go to food first," as he looked over Jeremiah's frame filled in the seat.

Jeremiah didn't respond and Nate quickly looked away embarrassed, his words had slipped without the thought. He focused on the road ahead, the GPS map and the homes set back and the spray paint that had normalized. The abandoned subdivision entrances that the truck ahead had already explored.

"Jeremiah," Caste said.

"What's that?"

"You keep callin' me 'Caste,' that's my last name. I'm Jeremiah."

"Are we on a first name basis now?" with a tone that implied a subtle authority.

"Well, I don't know, sir."

"Nate," Nate finally said to break the tension after a quarter mile, "I fucking hate 'sir.'"

Jeremiah looked over at him slyly and then returned to the window. "After a while," he said, "it all looks normal, don't it?"

"Yeah, yeah it does. But we're about to leave all that, and I ain't just saying that for the benefit of fear."

29

Clunk, clunk, clunk into park. Michael pulled on the door handle and stepped to the road. Carmen repeated the action on the opposite side, and Alice slid out to follow him.

The chemical tinge had gone from the air and the foliage had returned, yet the leaves had a yellowish pigment that meshed with the green. The twitters and tweets of songbirds, a far-off yelp that was returned.

In front of them, a steel gate blocked the road. Rusted at the top, brown and gray flakes on the rolled metal. From its edges, a chain link fence stretched to the horizon, or, at least, to their visual limits. Beyond it they saw nothing of consequence. Trees that whispered. The familiar design of a Taco Bell. The reassuring

Arches, albeit on a fallen pole rested on the building. The strip of nondescript businesses. The dry cleaners, the coffee shop, and the realtor's office. All recognizable yet partially hidden behind the freed nature.

The truck's idling engine was present behind them, and each sign bolted to the gate bounced in the gentle constant wind, the thin metal clang against thicker, hollow metal. Each faded with cracked lettering. The first, "Restricted Area," in white lettering against a red background. Below that text 'Authorized personnel only,' in black against white. The second followed the same design, 'Danger, do not enter,' and was accented with an exclamation point within a triangle.

It was third that gave them pause, that illuminated their distance from home, in miles multiplied by uncertainty, in unfamiliarity that contradicted the Arches. Weathered yellow with, ironically, the least aggressive warning. "Caution," then a black circle encircled by three black triangles, each with inner and outer lines curved out to match the centered oval. 'Caution,' it read, 'Radiation Area.'

They had arrived at the border, across which was the irradiated, deceitful pure land on which the Frog People had taken refuge. Too proud or too stupid to evacuate. Shrouded in their conspiracies and belief—further engrained than that of Jesus, that the government was, is, and will forever be out to get them.

"Shouldn't take too long to pick," Michael said as he tugged on the rusted lock that dangled from the rusted chain connected to the pole on the side of the road. He pondered if they would be received as gods or devils.

Carmen leaned over the gate on the opposite side and wondered if his upper body was being irradiated. He felt his nerves creep and silently subverted the cowardice.

Alice was centered in the road. She looked left at Carmen, his legs aloft with his stomach resting on the gate. Right at Michael as he fixated on the lock, and then the road behind them. She walked on the precipice of a run back to the truck, climbed into the driver's seat and thrust the shifter into "drive." The tires caught quickly; the truck lurched forward then caught traction.

Carmen and Michael turned and watched the truck rush towards them, Alice's eyes barely visible in the windshield.

"Oh shit!" Carmen yelled as he leapt off and to the side of the road.

Michael watched agape and took two steps away from the road. The truck went mostly straight and struck the gate flush. It careened off its anchors, stuck to the front end until she found the brake and it fell with a thud to the road.

The brake lights disappeared, and she jumped from the cab.

"Let's go boys!" she yelled from the distance. "Almost there, and I'm not gonna let some peg-leg stop us!"

Carmen lifted himself from the prickly brush, while Michael took two steps back to the road as Alice hoisted herself up and into the bed. She unzipped the duffel bag, cracked the seal on a water bottle, and took deep gulps before handing it over the side to Carmen, who, once sated, passed it to Michael.

"That's the last time you're drivin'," Carmen said.

"Aww," she responded, "I thought I did good."

"Yeah, but I got a longer track record of not killing us," Michael asserted.

A flock of sparrows above them shrieked within the tangled branches at the distant thunder, although above them remained a cloudless sky. Before Alice were the gas masks, each secure in its clear plastic packaging. Sharp, reflective black molded rubber with two large circular cutouts for eyesight. An elongated snout of matching black that terminated with an opening threaded on its interior. Thick straps that secured the device flush against the face, two horizontal and one vertical.

She unsealed the three accompanying filters, silver cylinders reminiscent of antique film canisters yet smaller and fatter. She took care to line the shafts correctly against the mask and slowly turned each until all three were prepared.

"Do these things really work?" Carmen asked as she handed his to him.

"Who knows," she said while handing Michael his, "but it's better than nothing."

All three inspected the devices, felt their material, and pulled on the straps. Michael was the first to put his on. It slipped snug onto his face and he reached to the back of his head to tighten the straps, yet he couldn't find the right angle.

"Hey Alice," he said muffled and deep through the mask.

"What?" she asked.

"Alice, I can't do it," as he pointed to the back of his head.

"Turn around," she told him and slid to the edge of the bed. He backed up until his back hit the truck. She tugged on the horizontal straps and then the vertical.

"Okay," he yelled, still muffled, "that's good."

Carmen pulled down on his mask, then again, and once more. His thick hair was preventing it from sealing against his face.

Michael laughed at his attempts, "had to look cool, right? Now look where it's got ya."

"What?" Carmen asked, as he could not understand the muted, deep delivery. He looked up at Alice who offered nothing further than a shrug.

"C'mere," she beckoned Carmen, "and turn around."

He followed her instructions and handed the mask to her. She placed it atop his head and every time she pulled down it sprung back up, recoiled by his full coif. She pushed harder, and with her elbow kept it down while he winced, and her free hand pulled hard on the straps.

"Is it good?" she asked.

He moved the mask by the snout to the left and then the right and seemed to be stuck in place. "It's good."

"Huh?"

He gave her a thumbs-up which set her to place the remaining mask on her head and tighten the straps.

"Like a pro!" Michael yelled with annunciation.

"I'm a natural," she responded with the same care.

"This feels weird," Carmen said.

They looked around, feeling out their new vision, or lack thereof. The road in, the charcoal clouds encroaching. The mottled trees and the sparrows that squawked, then took flight from their perches and into the sky. They knew, they always knew, and the ground began to shake, and Carmen tried to grasp the side of the truck and on his third wild try succeeded. Michael did the same as his knees bounced to match the fluctuating earth. He too was successful, yet the attempts were more comical than Carmen's, which made Alice laugh behind the black rubber as she swayed with her hands on the rails of the truck bed.

30

"I'm going to hell," Jeremiah said somberly while watching the trees clunk against the truck.

"No you ain't."

"Yeah, I am."

"Why's that?"

"Cause of the things I've done."

"There's a difference between who you are and what a place makes you."

"In the eyes of God?"

Nate kept his foot hard on the gas where he could. Elsewhere he reverted to a more subtle touch over the stuttered concrete hidden under aged branches and dead leaves collected by the winds. Trees hanging low by their apples that bounced off the truck's exterior.

Jeremiah sat quiet in the cab and waited for Nate to respond. He listened to the apples, and the twigs, and the rocks below connect, clanking the metal frame. His eyes set on the endless growth that spread beyond his vision.

"I used to go to church," Nate began while making adjustments on the steering wheel. "I went because she said we should go. I'd say 'we ain't gotta go to church, that's for married folk, folk with little kids that run 'round being little shits' and she'd say 'Jesus don't mind none of that... we's sinners so we go to church.' It was precisely cause of that sin we shouldn't go, I said. God ain't a vocal judger, but these people are. I shoulda said that, but I didn't, so we went to church on Sundays."

Red-tailed hawks soared over herds of deer on alert as tongues lapped at the quaint ponds half-hidden from the road. Squirrels, the black and the burnt orange, skittered from tree to tree. Dog packs, their pureness rectified over years of natural breeding, protected the porches of the abandoned homes set back and yelped over territory and trespass.

"It was one mile," Nate continued. "One mile that separated us from the meltdown that got you with the quick death. We watched them drive, a caravan of those dark green trucks with the canvas all around them and you could see as they passed by the soldiers through the flaps with their gas masks on. See I ain't got no kids, so I don't really know what it's like to worry like that. That fear, that primal, gut-turning fear, I mean you could see it in their eyes. With the mothers and the fathers and the earth had just shook so violently and it just kept going and the smell in the air and the sirens and you could see it, man. Shit, you could feel it." Then softly, "you could just feel it."

The foliage began to falter as they neared the fracking field. The saturation muted and compounded by the storm clouds behind them. Nate fished out the flask and took a long, hard sip, then held it out for Jeremiah, who declined with indifference.

"I told her, I said this ain't no place to live. Secluded, isolated in this place. Got no power, no phones, no TV, nothing. She didn't want to leave, and I was dying, man. I mean, imagine you got all those things and then, bam, they're gone? Crazy, man, I was going crazy. So one night I just left, just up and left. Got lost and drunk and robbed and got with whores. I told her I'd never leave her. No matter what happened I promised her I'd always be there. A faithful steward, and now," he pointed to the truck screen centered on the dash, "it looks like I'm going back. We're all sinners, Jeremiah, it's a sliding scale, but we're all on it."

"You think those kids are in danger?" Jeremiah asked, unmoved by Nate's words. "I mean, with the D.O.C. clothes on?"

Nate inhaled, held it, then released through his nose. "Nah, they'll see they're just kids. Probably give them folks a start, but danger? They're good people down there, least that's how I remember it."

"How long's it been? Since you've been here?"

"Years."

"How'd they defeat the army?"

"Shit," Nate laughed, "ain't no one defeat no army, no marines, and hell if the navy run up the river, they ain't defeat them either. You think they gave a shit if they stayed or went? Who cares if a bunch a hillbillies wanna live in a radiated town? We didn't. We came, they said we don't want to leave and we left. Less of them to take care of, no resettling. I take that back, the loudest and dumbest said they don't want to leave. But if you tell the story that even the U.S. Army couldn't move them, well, that keeps any ol' asshole away, don't it?"

"Black folks down here?"

"Yeah, you ain't gotta worry," Nate reassured him as he slowed in reverence to the XL 1-Orange Pad out the passenger window. The corroded landscape with its varying shades of gray. He stopped at the entrance and examined its metal gate, which still offered some protection, yet there remained no threat. A "no-trespassing" sign and another sign, "New Madrid Energy, XL1-Orange Pad, Access Road Entrance." The seemingly random numbers, the instruction to call 9-1-1 in an emergency or the 800-number listed. The dead brush that surrounded the metal poles stuck into the ground and the two black mailboxes, one with its red flag raised.

He imagined all the times he had traveled that dirt road. The hazing of the roustabouts fresh from the trains and the whiskey that made the rounds. Determined minds at dawn and aching backs at dusk. The stories of wives and girlfriends, comfort and conquest from bunk beds dimly lit by portable LED lamps. The boys who sent their wages to the bar and their lust to the back rooms. The men who deposited their wages in the company bank and sent word of budgets for milk and schoolbooks and secret stashes of gin far afield.

The adventurous short bursts of moved earth along the plates. The nothing. The crack and reverb and they rode the steal gear like mechanical bulls with maniacal cackles. Those who fell and those who were crushed were them. Always them. They awoke in March and a "them" met his fate at then, yet not another until they found April and three 'thems' got theirs. Undeterred, and May brought the collapse and the explosion which took twenty-two 'thems.'

"Onward!" screamed the company. "Unsubstantiated!" growled the public relations team. "Anti-business!" cried the senators. "Elitists! No Proof! Rabble! Rabble! Rabble!" barked the keyboard warriors.

June came, and thousands of 'thems' would not wake. Beyond the exploding fracking pads, the quick death of mothers who held their children tight found under the rubble of homes and stores and high rises. The slow death in the shadow of Reactor One; those closest felt the deepest violence yet it did not last. Those further felt it too, softer, and it lingered for weeks until the last breath flowed.

"Overblown," the company went on record. "It is not the time for new laws. It is a time to grieve," wrote the PR representatives. "We will investigate," the senators crooned at the cameras. "False flag!" screamed the keyboard warriors.

31

Splat. Then a pause. *Splat, splat.* Michael let the prelude to the storm go without the wipers interrupting the introduction. The graying sky slipped quickly into an opaque blackness with a tinge of green and opened. Rain pounded the roof and slipped in sheets up the windshield. The headlamps turned themselves on, the dash illuminated blue.

The road had widened, no longer a two-lane enveloped in claustrophobic greenery. Two lanes each direction. The rubble outline of the McDonald's, the Taco Bell, and a strip mall ten tenants wide that left no clues. A winding sideroad that led to a parking lot. Through the cracks grew saplings, weeds, and thickets that had overcome the pavement and encroached on the immense building behind that had cracked yet still stood—its gray cinder-block façade and faded blue trim.

Click. A pause. *Click, click, click,* went the Geiger counter in Alice's hand as she watched the numbers. Over limbs and over rocks she bounced, centered in the cab, her left shoulder bumped against Michael's, then her right rubbed Carmen's. Faster, she assumed, was worse, yet she had no baseline reference, nor had she acclimated to the cylindrical eye holes in the mask, and each prolonged glance ended with a dizzying motion sickness.

Several miles still of the familiar in disrepair. Oil changes known by their three bays. Gas stations by corner locations and duplication at the streetlights resting on the road. Brick office parks behind the casual fast-food. Dental offices between donut shops and liquor stores that precipitated churches.

Michael kept in the left lane where he could. Shopping carts, abandoned vehicles, and dumpsters. Rotted trees from the grassy median and the tires crunched hundreds of plastic bottles collected and left stuck between the curbs.

At the end of the suburban expanse, the road narrowed again to two lanes. They watched through the quick wipers that worked to clear the hard rain. Through the circular eyelets. Click, click, click, in rapid succession in Alice's hand.

"Old Main Street" the sign read stuck in the tall grass curb, unseen through the torrent and still erect with an arrow forward. The headlamps caught glimpses of vehicles angled into the ditches where the metal sheen survived. White-knuckled on the steering wheel. White-knuckled on the Geiger counter and the same on the door handle.

Thunderclaps that coursed and lightning that split the ominous gray to make the horizon scream muted green. Michael's eyes fixed on the five-foot visibility. Felt the claustrophobia when he realized the angled cars were not accidental remains but set at the angles and each several inches closer to the center to the road. Front ends pointed forward; their corners pinched in on the truck as it went at a steady clip over clean concrete washed clean in the deluge.

White knuckles. Click, click, click. The wiper motor and the wet sheets across the windshield.

"Turn around!" Carmen screamed in his head. The camp, that was the story, there was no need to embellish. They had seen enough to walk the school halls as heroes. They were seeking ghosts in the reality of his worried mother. "Turn around!" yet his lips did not move, stuck between the pain he was causing and the cowardice that still lingered.

Death, a calm consciousness reminded Michael, is only a dream. Fate. Circumstantial victimhood, a driven purpose two clicks shy of suicide, and he parsed the undertaking it must have been to maneuver these hundred vehicles to the road and position them thusly. This had to be the way, to the Frog People, or at least, something.

Alice watched the counter and repeated the numbers in her head as they rose. Spiked. Relaxed. Rose. The world around her was fear, and what was the point of watching it, letting it in, when she knew its existence and purpose?

The vehicles ceased encroaching, still angled and in line but no longer pulled tighter. The rain softened, the wipers slowed, and Alice took the audible cue to take her eyes from the counter. Carmen's grip lessened as Michael's back, for many minutes stiff and at attention, relaxed. He found his groove between the cars and pushed the speed without obstacle. The slate sky transformed to a whispering white smoke and the rain continued steadily, as if to reassure that the worst had passed.

Michael followed the road as it curved to the right, and the sedans and minivans and SUVs on each side followed the arc. As the road returned true, he eased back on the gas pedal. As with the vehicles to the left and right, the semi tractor-trailer was placed with purpose. Perpendicular to their trajectory, faded white, cleansed in the falling rain and invigorated as the headlights neared.

"Eden," written in meticulous cursive, sky blue and a blackened arrow with lost luster and this spanned the middle third of the trailer. Bookended by cartoonish whimsy with purposeful brush strokes wherein there was time to meticulous intent. A rainbow kept true from red to violet, it descended left to a pot of gold and right to the outline of a puffy cloud. An apple tree in full summer doldrum bearing a single fruit ripe on a branch.

A hundred feet from the trailer they could see the opening in the direction of the arrows created by the absence of the last car to their right. Alice and Carmen's eyes were wide and alert, and if it were possible, would have filled the circular openings of their masks. The filters labored their breathing just enough to make the difference perceptible. She adjusted until her knees were bent and sat on her legs to better see through the rain splattered windshield. He leaned forward to make out what was to come beyond, what was hidden beyond the turn.

While he hid any hint of emotion, Michael pushed forward with an anxious heart and he felt it pulsing through the rubber against the arteries in his neck. Sweat amplified the connection and triggered him to look in the rearview mirror to confirm that there was no way to turn around. That they were to continue or reverse the mile to where the road was wider. Or was it two miles? Between the rain and the hypnotic lines of automobiles, he could not perceive the distance, nor had he any reason to spy the trip meter.

It was the gas pedal that brought him out of these thoughts, out of the possibilities and into the now. The soft tension that had pressed against his foot since the dawn had left. That difference sunk his stomach, which then transferred to Alice and Carmen in an instant. The warning lights on the dash that twinkled in randomness. The radio rushed on with static then cut out as the wipers stuck upright against the windshield. The blackened screen and silhouetted dashboard and muted dials. The rain minus the engine. The click of the Geiger counter. They were stuck in the unknown, the sickening bliss of uncertainty without the first understanding of where safe harbor was, let alone the way home. All that remained was the rain, and the clicks, and their compressed breaths that hinted at the unseeable dread behind the masks.

Part 3

32

The worn wooden stairs were almost vertical, eight rungs and held to the opening of the attic with curved metal hooks. The angled bottom had worn a rectangular pattern in the thin moss-colored carpet below, which covered the landing and, around it, a cracked white clothes hamper half full. Another overflowed with dust-covered toy trucks and plastic dolls and princess castles all wrapped securely, yet unintentionally, in Christmas tree lights. The floodlight cast from the tungsten bulb that originated in the shadeless 1970s lamp upon an end table pushed to the corner. Besides a bedroom door and opposite the staircase that led down to the main floor of the house.

Up into the attic, there was a floor of shifting plywood laid across the supporting boards and, in the corners, pink insulation poked through. The roof slanted sharply, which limited the usable space lit by a single bulb hung from its wire near the apex. The electrical prongs stuck into an extension cord halfway between the roof and the floor. From there, it ran along the plywood to a full surge protector at the structure's convergence.

The desk was an aggregate of two that extended the working surface along the workable wall—an acorn-stained antique that would have paired well with the landing lamp and a faux wood veneer fiberboard of utility born of a limited budget. Two metal file cabinets elongated further the right side of the workstation. One black, one pewter gray and raised with hard cover books to match the height of the former.

She picked up one of the computer keyboards and set it on several empty candy wrappers, which themselves were upon comic books distributed among pre-teen mystery novels and the 'Annotated History of American Serial Killers.' In front of a rectangular LCD computer monitor, which was centered between another of a different brand and one set vertical.

There, in the space she created, bookended by a variety of electronic gadgets haphazardly laid near the edges of the desk and piled below, she set the plastic bowl. A metal spoon, the Lucky Charms, and a roll of paper towels. The bottle of water on which the label had rubbed illegible and the small tin of condensed milk.

A faded purple t-shirt draped over the office chair; an azure training bra dangled from the plastic curve where the seat attached to the seatback. She leaned forward and tore two paper towels from the roll, set them on the desk, and poured the cereal onto one of the towels, then set the box aside. She plucked the exposed unicorn marshmallows between her thumb and forefinger, transitioned them to the other towel and they bounced when the floor-standing fan swiveled towards the desk. From there she dug deeper to reveal the hidden charms she deemed unfit for consumption.

Her chestnut hair transitioned to a fairer blond near the ends in a smooth, natural gradient. Pulled taut behind her head into a tight ponytail, yet several strands ran down each cheek and whispered. Pale hazel eyes accented with muted freckles on her cheekbones. Gentle lips of mellow pink that, when parted, revealed the tips of her dainty white teeth. Her ribbed white tank-top hung loose on her torso and the royal blue basketball shorts covered her knees. The last of the unicorns removed, she pulled two opposing corners of the paper towel toward the center and twisted the tips. Then she repeated the process with the remaining until the marshmallows were hidden within the paper sack. She set the contained unicorns on a stack of external hard drives and slid the bowl to center. Poured the water to fill halfway, removed the lid from the condensed milk and scooped the pearly powder into the liquid with the spoon and stirred. Satisfied, she added the cereal, pressed the morsels into the milk and began to eat.

"North," written with a silver marker at the top of the left monitor frame—left side. A camera feed from the top of the tractor trailer, set above the rainbow and the apple tree and focused down the center of the road condensed by the vehicles. Full definition yet it seemed grainy with the falling rain and several drops had landed on the lens, fell, and then replaced with others. "South" filled the right side of the monitor, then "East" and "West" on the next.

Each contained text set at the bottom of the frame; battery status, connection status, time stamp, and camera identification.

The third monitor, arranged vertically due to the limited space, had at the top of the screen a program that monitored road sensors and were linked to quarter-inch rubber tubes that ran across the roads near Eden's entrances. Route53 / Dexter. RedMaple / PleasantTrail. Route62 / SpringDale. Hoffman / Lombardi. Emerald-green rectangles with 'Normal' in white text within next to each.

Below that, a colorful word game in which she used the screen name 'EvaisAwesome1' and switched between different opponents. Mark32. Sherrybabe, LAhottie4, and Guest12a7244lq. She moved several tiles with the mouse to spell 'plant' and slurped another spoonful of cereal as high-pitched chimes reassured her choice from the computer speakers.

A drop of watery milk slipped down her chin and she wiped it away with her forearm. She giggled as LAhottie4 played 'run' on the board and as she went to counter with a word containing more than one syllable the Route53/Dexter's green rectangle turned red. 'Normal' was replaced with 'Warning.' Grating buzzer from the speakers. Spoon down. Chew. Chew. Swallow. Swivel left to the cameras and quick on the keyboard.

White pickup truck. Can't make out the occupants. How many? Zoom out. No other vehicles. Reset the focal length. Slow pace. Closer, two, maybe three?

"Damn rain," she said.

She swallowed hard and watched the truck make its slow approach to the perpendicular tractor-trailer. This was the first invader she had spotted since being tasked as a Watcher. Since being taught the software. How to manage the cameras and the sensors and the kill switches. The wariness brought about by the blue flame atop a half-circle of orange, a D.O.C. issued outfit. There had been friends and there had been foes, yet for the good of all, defectors were to be treated as the latter. All of them. For the good of all.

"Eva," she said into the walkie-talkie, but her voice was coarse and meek. She quickly released her thumb from the handset, cleared her throat and reset the radio back to her lips.

"Eva to Bobby, Eva to Bobby," she said with faux confidence and then waited.

When no response came, she checked the piece of scrap paper taped to the desk. 'Channel

5' and she verified on the radio. The LED readouts were alert and she twisted the volume knob left to its resistance and then back just to make sure.

"Eva to Bobby, Eva to Bobby," she called again.

"You ain't playin' again are ya, girl?" Bobby responded; his voice distorted through the small speaker.

"I ain't playin' and I never played on the radio."

"Yeah, you have."

"Never mind that. Got a bogey comin' in. Two, maybe three."

"Well, is it two or three?"

"Can't tell."

"How can you not tell?"

"Cause of the rain," she said, frustrated, and wished she could have added "you prick" to the end of the sentence.

"They armed?"

"I don't know."

"How you not know?"

"Because they're surrounded by a truck with doors and shit."

"Don't give me no lip."

"What a moron," she said aloud while ensuring her thumb was far from the button.

"Which entrance?"

"North, Route 53 and Dexter."

"Distance?"

"'Bout ten cars from the red ones."

"Age?"

"New truck. 'Newish'"

"Kill the vehicle," he commanded with his lips close to the microphone. "As soon as it passes the reds and confirm."

Eva set the walkie down and took hold of the mouse. She cycled through several programs until a simple software dashboard filled the screen. She selected 'Route53/Dexter' from a dropdown menu. Clicked 'Arm.' Status bar to 'Ready' and the mouse hovered over the button 'Deploy.'

She swiveled her head to the camera feed and watched the slow approach. Then back to the program. Turned again. The truck split the two red cars and she waited for the rear to clear the border. Click.

"Eva to Bobby, Eva to Bobby."

"Go for Bobby."

"Confirmed. Vehicle is dead."

33

"What happened?" Carmen said, his voice muffled through the mask. The truck stalled in front of the tractor-trailer sign for Eden.

No answer. Rain against the windshield.

"What do we do?" a muffled Alice.

No answer. A long low end of thunder.

"We get outta this truck," Michael said, "that's what we do."

No movement, then the frantic tug of the car doors and they tumbled out.

"Get the shit!" Carmen instructed Michael who hoisted himself up the truck bed and tossed the duffel with the food and the water down to the ground. Carmen scooped up the duffel and guided Alice between two of the cars that lined the road.

"The Frog People did this, I know they did," Alice exclaimed through the mask with the Geiger counter still in her hand. "They don't like intruders."

"So," Michael said as he crouched down next to them against a car, "fuck." A few seconds later he expanded upon his thought, "Fuck."

"We need to get out of here," Alice told them.

"I know," Michael responded.

"Wait," Carmen chimed excitedly, "you still got that thing?"

"What thing?"

"The thing, the thing that you can start cars with. The thing."

Michael unzipped the duffel bag, rifled through the water bottles and candy bars. "Shit."

"It ain't there?" Alice asked.

"No, they took our knives at the camp," he searched more, "and the Slim Jim." He removed the sputnik, held it up for them to see and without the need for explanation pulled open the car door from where he had been leaning. He slid to the driver's seat, extended the tool to the side of the steering wheel and leaned in. In lieu of a keyhole there was a push start button.

He opened the door and slinked to the next car. "What happened?" Alice asked as she and Carmen followed, still crouched.

"Push start, sputnik won't work," Michael answered as he tried the door for the next car. Locked, he moved on.

Condensation formed on the inside of the mask from his perspiration as he worked. He saw the sputnik through a fog which made the delicate work of aligning the pins in the ignition keyhole that much more challenging. Lithe fingers and slow progress against the metal that tested the nerves of the two exterior. The original key mimicked; he turned the sputnik away from his body. *Click.*

"Idiot!" he yelled out, and between the mask and the rain and the metal frame no one heard him. He found the hood release, pulled up on the lever then opened the door. He left it open so as to not disturb the delicacy of the tool still inserted in the ignition. Unzipped the duffel again and quickly set the connections for the portable battery charger. Flipped the switch and was met with a flashing symbol on the LCD readout.

His hands let loose and fell despondent to his sides, which made his already lengthy appendages seem comically long. He plodded the few steps to his friends who were on their knees observing with their heads just over the quarter panel to see into the hood. He looked down at them, and while his emotions were hidden by the mask, his inaction imparted what they had already deduced. Alice and Carmen slunk down against the side of the car and stared off into the distance. Unfocused on the giant elms along the berm as raindrops slid from the tips of their wide, veiny leaves. The parting clouds as the storm moved its exercise east. The remains of Maggie's Pancake House. Conoco. Rite-Aid, Siam Palace, and Sam's Quick Mart.

Michael took his place next to Alice and felt the wet pavement through the thin D.O.C. material on his butt. She reached out and touched his forearm, then followed his skin down to his wrist and grasped his hand in embrace. With her right she did the same to Carmen and felt both boys squeeze her hands in affirmation of the gesture.

The lull brought thirst. A thirst that could be sated in short order, yet that would require removing their masks. Alice watched the numbers dance on the counter, still unsure of what the digits meant. Carmen swallowed the dryness, still skeptical of his courage regardless of small victories. Michael knew that water in the radiated air was the precursor to death, at least he had read that somewhere. About something that he could not be sure was true.

"It's eerie any way you parse it," Nate informed Jeremiah as they looked out over the river to NME Reactor 3. Perched at the precipice of the northern lanes that rose over the water.

Nate's thoughts went to the causes, the ramifications, be it sociological or ecological, whereas Jeremiah's thoughts stayed rooted in the present. It was the proximity to survival that narrowed his philosophical intrigue to the moments. Keep a roof over his head, find sustenance, avoid the bullet, evade the badge. The goal, as it had been told and retold through generations parted by plexiglass through nicked payphone receivers, was always to make it to tomorrow. There were only so many allowed to elevate beyond, to have the leisure of time to philosophize, to speculate on beliefs or ask generally why. He would not, in this moment, reflect on his own life. The circumstances of his incarceration. His initiation into the liquidation of those deemed unworthy of life at Camp Andersonville as directed by some unknown force. Instructed by some white man in a suit surrounded by other white men in their suits on some day that had passed. It was what it was, and in those moments, he was someone, he mattered, and the reason why was never going to be in his control.

"It's in the air, it's in the trees," Nate continued, "an' it's in the water, and there ain't nothing we can do about it."

"How do you know black people down there? You haven't been there in years."

Nate stayed focused on the broken reactor for a few seconds, then turned to Jeremiah. "It ain't never been a sundown town, never been all about the flag."

"You sure?"

"I got you, ain't gonna let nothing happen to you."

"Oh you're my 'protector'?"

"It ain't like that. Look, let's stay focused on getting those kids, ain't nothing gonna happen to you I promise."

Jeremiah examined Nate's eyes and searched for a break in the connection. There was honesty behind the pupils, or, at least, he felt the implication of empathy. Satisfied, he turned and walked back to the truck idling on the bridge with Nate not far behind.

"They stopped," Nate told Jeremiah, who looked down at the center screen in the truck and saw the icon that represented their prey. He shifted the gears into drive and pressed on over the bridge.

"Is there," Jeremiah started, "what do you know about these people?"

"There are rumors, mind you, they are just rumors, yet more vivid and creative than what the boy told me about the 'Frog People.' That they had, for the first couple years, kept it together. Kept a society just like any other."

"Like ours, at the camp?"

"Like any normal society. Then it broke, as does anything living on the edge. With no support. And when it broke down, they started raiding the towns for food and supplies, the radiation poisonin' their bodies, poisonin; their minds. Rigged their remaining cars with the remaining gasoline like some Mad Max shit, but that's a little far-fetched for me."

"That they started raiding towns?"

"Nah, that they built them crazy cars. Seems like you go raiding you wanna be as subtle as possible. But, an' I must remind you that this is

319

all rumor, all conjecture. That, and this reinforces my belief in subtlety, that they would slip into young girl's bedrooms at night and kidnap them. Take them back and hold them as their sexual playthings."

"Shit."

"Take the society out of a man and he becomes feral, a slave to his inner thoughts that were once suppressed. Still, he's withdrawn. Take the society out of group of people, and they become crazed. Why you get the stories that come outta war. The raping, the pillaging, the mothers watchin' their children murdered in front of their eyes. This ain't rumor. They are a feral people who bounce the insanity off each other till it reaches a fever pitch. We must assume it has reached its apex, and we must be prepared for such."

Nate reached back over the seat and handed a handgun to Jeremiah. He held it with a reverence, a responsibility he was not prepared to take on. There was no pageantry in this potential murder. No sanctity. "I never shot a gun before."

"Never?" Nate asked with a whiff of disbelief.

"Never."

"Well if there ever was a time. Mind the trees. Mind your steps. Think the worst of feces-tipped spikes set at the bottom of pits. Trip wires, anything meant to inflict pain over and beyond protecting them. The feral, they ain't got no sense of fair play, no sense of decorum." Nate set his hand on the gun and removed the safety. "This way you don't have to wonder if it's ready to go when you point it at an animal."

34

"Stand the fuck up!" Bobby yelled as he revealed himself from behind family sedans and minivans parked at Maggie's Pancake house and before the elms that created a barrier between himself and the kids. His short stature made the rifle—elevated and aimed—seem more imposing, more prominent in the distance between. Thin, dirty blond hair hung down to his shoulders and lay upon his freckled shoulders exposed from a blue and white striped tank top. Taut, pale skin along ridged cheekbones and hard eyes. Khaki cargo shorts, the hem ripped down the right side. The pockets along his left thigh protruded from the walkie talkie; the black antenna stuck out, and an earpiece ran up his torso to his ear. Dirt-dyed white sneakers over bare feet.

Another man emerged, tall and rotund, his white t-shirt wet with sweat, pooled in the crevasse between his belly and his chest. A heavy head of deep black hair haphazard and lacking at the top of his forehead. Rotund cheeks pockmarked; his upper lip hidden by a bushy, unkempt mustache. The kids deduced, without previous experience, this man was uncomfortable holding a firearm, simply from his posture.

The third, a young woman, materialized from the rear of a minivan set to the side as if to block the way from which the kids had come. Her copper hair was held back with a pink band. Her features were fair, and her persuasive green eyes drew Alice in while her seductive soft lips sang sirens to the boys. They could not rectify her looks, the form she presented with her nipples outlined through the tight tank top with the shotgun aimed at them. Instead, they focused on Bobby, the "true" danger as perceived.

"Get up!" Bobby commanded again as his counterparts walked to his side. Carmen raised his hands over his head and used the car against his back to rise. Alice followed, then Michael.

"Walk forward!"

There was a hesitance, though short, that bothered Bobby.

"Now!"

In unison the kids took that first step, then another.

"Stop!" Bobby ordered as they reached the halfway point between the cars and the ones with the guns.

Alice and Michael stopped while Carmen stuttered before ceasing his movement forward. Three abreast in matching white outfits, D.O.C. emblemed and their faces obscured by the gas masks.

"Check em," Bobby said as his eyes focused on Carmen for the transgression. "Arm's out to your sides!"

The large man set his rifle against an elm and walked with wide steps to the kids, accommodating his frame. He started with Carmen, who flinched as the man's palms set against his shoulders. He swallowed through a constricted throat and felt clenched and that queasy feeling of vomiting as the man's hands traveled down his arms. Around his waist.

Down his pant leg, up to his groin and then back down.

He side-stepped to Alice and could feel her pulse through her shoulders. Down her arms, across her chest and he felt her small breasts and released immediately as he realized that this was a girl. He cleared his throat as if to shake off the embarrassment and, as if to rectify the trespass, barely touched her legs before moving on to Michael.

There were no nonverbal cues that Michael communicated as the man stroked his arms, squeezed his biceps to confirm his gender. His heart did not race, his stomach felt fine, and his skin did not sweat.

"They're clean," the man yelled to Bobby.

"Take off the masks."

The man inspected the masks from various angles. "I don't know how."

"Take off your masks!" Bobby barked with the gun pointed.

Michael reached first, followed by Alice and then Carmen. Bobby stood alert, his female companion did the same, and the obese man took several steps back. As each mask came to rest at their sides, Bobby came to realize the small size of their hands. Michael's boyish features that belied his height. Carmen's chubby cheeks that fought the change and Alice's linear hips.

"They're just kids," Bobby said softly and lowered his rifle. The woman followed his lead and walked with a quickness to the kids.

"You poor thing," she said to Alice as she turned her head to inspect the bandaged gash along her cheek and immediately felt the statement aged her.

Bobby approached them and, starting with Michael, inspected each as he walked to his right. The uncertainty in their eyes. The dirt stuck to their cheeks, stayed from sweat that had passed. The matching ensembles and the absurdity of size as the short sleeves fell to three-quarters upon Alice and Carmen's arms, whereas Michael's seemed only somewhat off. The clutch of the gas masks and the Geiger counter in Alice's petite hand. The portable jumper cables that dangled from the engine compartment behind them. The black duffel bag.

He walked over to the bag, crouched down, pulled the zipper, and stretched the sides to expose the contents. He rummaged through the water bottles and the candy bars and the flashlights, grabbed the Sputnik, the bump keys. He stood up, returned to the kids and this time started with Carmen, his fingers running along the tools in his hands. For a few seconds he stared at Carmen, then took a step to Alice and repeated. At Michael he delayed, waited for his eyes to betray him and look down at the tools.

"You did this," Bobby told Michael with a smile, "you got you here."

Michael, still unsure, didn't respond.

"Don't be shy, y'all are here, because of you, ain't you?"

Michael slowly nodded in affirmation.

Bobby looked at the Sputnik, the jumper cables and thought of the distance and obstacles between Eden and the real world. He took a step towards Michael and put his hand on his shoulder.

"Damn son," he said with beaming adulation, "why are you wasting your talents in the real world?"

He released Michael's shoulder and took a step back. "Ricky, grab them waters from the bag. Tessa, radio in, let them know there ain't no threat."

"Tessa to Eva," she said while pressing the button on her walkie-talkie as Ricky handed each of the kids a bottle of water.

"Drink," he said, "rehydrate yourselves."

"We got kids here," Tessa said into the microphone, "bringing them back." She then walked up to Alice and gently took the Geiger counter from her hand. "You don't need this anymore," she said softly, "you're in God's land now."

35

Main Street—again, akin to the many they had traveled through on their way to the camp and beyond. Yet here there was care taken with the thoroughfare. Although the pavement was cracked through the weathered years, it was swept and devoid of the automobile shells that had littered the preceding towns. The sidewalks, too, were cared for, darkened by the storm that had passed through. The cracks that ran up the buildings and split, originating from the tremors, were patched. Filled with cement within the bricks or covered by two-by-fours for the wooden structures. Most of the glass windows were replaced with a patchwork of plexiglass or simple plastic wrap layered to give at least the illusion of strength. For others, the glass was never replaced, and rudimentary shutters enclosed the openings.

Word had spread, from Eva and from walkie-talkies set to channel 5 on kitchen tables, on nightstands, and in backyard gardens. Mothers, some in summer dresses and others in t-shirts and jean shorts brought their sons in buggies. Daughters pressed against their fathers' knees for protection. The teenagers congregated in front of a narrow walkway where the buildings paused before continuing, and the pre-teens positioned themselves near them but not close enough to be intruding on the hierarchy.

The entire population had come to witness the foreign children. The Caucasian majority interspersed with Asians, African Americans, Hispanics. Under elms and oaks that swayed in the post-storm freshness and from which a wayward water droplet would fall to a shoulder. In front of the barbershop. The general store, the clinic, the bar, and the butcher shop.

They were hidden at first, with the distance and the bodies that led them towards the waiting crowd. Eva stepped from her pre-teen peers to the edge of the sidewalk to get a better view.

"Lose some fucking weight, Randy," she said to herself as he blocked their angle more than Tessa or Bobby who had slung the duffel over his shoulder.

Down the middle of the noiseless and empty street, the kids marched. Spied out their peripherals at the onlookers, saw the pity and concern from the mothers and fathers—those old enough to remember the normal. The curiosity and hesitancy educed from those younger. The coordinating outfits, the gas masks grasped, and the discernible looks of trials experienced.

They marched. The quiet broken only by the elders' reflexive throat clearing and sideways coughs. Past the few hardened and nearest, armed though the barrels pointed either towards the ground or skyward. Then into the gauntlet, and the crowds on either side of the street drew in. They encircled the travelers and their escorts yet gave the circle breathing room.

She emerged from the throng as if she had never been there. As if she had simply appeared in front of the kids, as if elevated from commoners and at over six feet and she had always had a sense of levitation. Her hair was pulled into a tight bun, natural highlights that flowed between the tan of an acorn body and the brown of the cap. The lines had started to form near her eyes from middle age, and the sun, and burdens, though her eyes remained brilliant and sharp. She commanded respect and attention without a word and softened that innate response with a tempered wardrobe. An azure t-shirt imprinted with a brilliant yellow hibiscus over one breast and a luminous pink plumeria over the other. "Hawaii" written in a tropical font between them. Black denim shorts that settled just above her knee. White ankle socks with gray poms that hung just above her navy-blue sneakers.

"My name," she said as she inspected their appearance in much the same way as Bobby had and then squatted to reduce her height, "is Miss Valerie." There was a slight elongation to her pronunciations, as if she restrained origins more conspicuous.

Valerie had set herself in the middle of the three, directly in front of Alice. "What's your name?" she asked.

Alice looked at her, then at the crowd of people and their inquisitive eyes that made her squirm.

"It's okay," Valerie continued, "no one's going to hurt you here, we're just naturally curious about you being here. You can understand that, right?"

"Alice," she said in a volume only Valerie and those closest could hear.

"Alice," Valerie repeated, "that's a pretty name."

She stood up, sidestepped to Michael, and again squatted. "And you?"

"Michael."

"Nice to meet you, Michael."

Again, she repositioned, but this time simply waited for a response.

"Carmen."

"Carmen," she echoed, "do you know what your name means in Latin?"

"No, ma'am."

"It means 'poem,' and poets are thinkers. Are you a 'thinker' Carmen?"

Carmen parsed the question for a time, "I don't know. Michael's the one who reads a lot."

Valerie smiled as she arose then looked them over again.

"Aren't you afraid?" Alice asked Valerie and immediately felt her nerves elevate.

"Afraid of what, dear?"

Alice swallowed hard; she was inquisitive yet afraid to offend. "Of the air, of the water, the wild animals. The-the poison?"

Valerie contextualized the question before answering. Alice's own fear, her bandaged cheek, the exhaustion she was trying to hide, and the gas mask still gripped tight.

"This is all God's will. Everything is God's will," she said with a calming tone through a slight smile, "there is nothing to be afraid of."

◆◆◆

Nate took point as they walked towards the tractor trailer sprayed with "Eden." Hugged the cars as if danger would at any moment pierce the quiet. "Careful not to touch the cars," Nate whispered. "Don't want a rusty surprise." The direction made Jeremiah awkward in his hunched, squatted stance as he walked. His inexperience with the gun was amplified by Nate's proficiency, and he swung it around each hidden with precision and intent. Leveled at the presumed chest of enemies and angled towards the treetops. They advanced beyond the trailer and into a narrow inlet, the walls made of cars placed on cars and covered by corrugated sheet metal which drew darkness around them. "Slow," Nate commanded,."Slooow." They approached a break in the cars where the sunlight slipped through vertically. Offset, the sunlight came through first on the left, then the right. There was a reason for this, Nate thought, and slowed further then stopped. It was luck that his fully formed leg led at this moment rather than the unfeeling prosthetic. The just noticeable difference against his pants that he felt tickle the hairs on his leg. "Stop," he barked. "Don't move." Jeremiah stood still behind Nate as he lowered his body to the ground and ran his forefinger across the invisible fishing line. Pull, and the contraption could rouse the feral and bring them this way. Step over, and a misstep would mean death, or worse, maiming—and then death. They could turn back and go through the parking lot, but snipers, he assumed, were surely about with the kids' intrusion. "Stand back, I'm gonna pull it." Jeremiah obeyed, with oversized steps opposite Nate who waited until he felt his companion was far enough arear. He pulled, first just enough for movement. Nothing. Harder. Nothing. With held breath he tugged again which returned no action.

"Maybe you have to push it," Jeremiah offered.

"It ain't like that, I've seen plenty of these and push, pull, it doesn't matter," and at that moment he set the wire against his palm and pushed it away. "See?" he reassured and before Jeremiah could acquiesce to the proof the whoosh of air in front of them that echoed left and echoed right. A split second and the metal tips of the arrows, twenty or thirty, bit into the compromised rust of the walls made of cars. They shattered the windows that remained. Their origins unknown, the contraptions hidden within the walls. "Jesus," Nate elongated, paused, "H," paused, "Christ. I told you, feral is crazy." He stepped over the wire and pulled an arrow from a car door, "Lord of the Flies shit."

"If this is the beginning," Jeremiah said and then stopped, not wanting to vocalize his regret of joining Nate. How he had thought it had to be better than the camp, how he would enjoy the change of scenery. There was no need to let his fear be known.

"C'mon," Nate said, "let's go," and he walked through the manmade tunnel and hopped over a puddle into the open air. Jeremiah followed; his gun pointed at any perceived threat—all imaginary.

36

"It don't make sense," Nate whispered to Jeremiah crouched within the overgrown patch of land left untended along Main Street. His face peeked through the whispering tall grass and Jeremiah's joined his. They could see the inhabitants of Eden, the kids surrounded yet not in danger.

"No?"

"My imaginations of this place are not setting with what I'm seeing."

"But there are guns."

"That are pointed this way, and the other way."

"What does that mean?"

"They don't feel threatened by those who have arrived."

"Then why the guns?"

"Because there's been a disruption, they're on edge."

"What do we do?"

"Have to get the children," and Nate stuck his gun down his pants. "Put your gun away." Jeremiah tossed the gun and it disappeared into the grass. "I meant in your pants."

"Do you want me to go get it?"

Nate scowled at the stupidity that Jeremiah had displayed, "no, I don't want you to go get it."

"Okay," and he was content letting Nate find his action foolish, for he was looking for any opportunity to rid himself of the weapon as he dreaded the thought of using it. "What now?"

"We start walking," Nate said as he stood, "and the rest will come naturally."

The murmur within the enclosed crowd started with a whisper. It started with the first to feel the intrusion from where the parade had originated and crane their neck. It spread to his neighbor, then the next, until it reached the first who was armed.

"Stop!" he yelled with an instinctive pump of the shotgun and a deliberate lowering of his vocals as he was barely a man.

Jeremiah, for his experiences, stopped immediately, with even his breaths imperceptible. Nate, rather, in his pedestrian clothes, took that extra step that Jeremiah had seen produce the pull of a trigger and he braced for the decibels that preceded the screams. It did not come, and he processed that there was a difference in the threat perceived.

"I said stop!"

Nate finally came to a complete stop and steadied himself on the prosthetic.

"Hands up!"

Both the men did as instructed, and the gun Nate had concealed within his pants was exposed.

"Gun!" an armed man yelled.

"Gun!" echoed male.

"Gun!" echoed female.

Tessa broke ranks from the crowd and removed the gun while Bobby and Randy joined her several feet from Nate and Jeremiah, weapons aimed. The circle spread out into a line three to four deep. Eva pushed her way to the front of the general community and Valerie repositioned herself in front of the kids now facing Nate and Jeremiah.

"On your knees!" Tessa ordered.

"They're with us," Alice yelled to Tessa, "they're not a threat." Unswayed, she kept the gun pointed in their direction.

"Now!"

Jeremiah dropped, lithely, having been in this position before, though Nate stayed standing.

"Did you hear me! I said, on your knees!"

"Miss," Nate responded calmly, "I can't."

"And why not?"

He extended his right leg, which pushed the prosthetic leg further from under his pant leg so she could see it.

"See I got a prosthetic leg, and I'm afraid, if I am to do what you ask, with my hands over my head, in the position that my colleague is now in, that I might fall over. Miss."

She adjusted her hands on the barrel which allowed her those moments of thought.

"Randy, check 'em standing. You try anything and I'll shoot off your other leg."

"Understood."

"Bobby, can you check the other one?"

Randy waddled over to Nate and ran his hands over his shoulders. Down his arms. Around his stomach and against his back. Up his fake leg to his groin and back down. He was surprised to be relieved at the normalcy that skin and muscle and bone. As he rose up, he saw the outline of a wallet on Nate's back pocket. He pulled it from the denim and handed it to Valerie who had walked calmly to the front of the crowd.

With slight emasculation, Bobby did a cursory pat down of Jeremiah, as the D.O.C. uniforms were deliberately designed to show any bulges or hidden items. He was more interested in Jeremiah's red bracelet, grasped his wrist and turned it to examine it further.

'#20991. 995 – Attempted Burglary. 707 – Child Support NonPay. 447 – ParolViol.'

"Is he clean?" Tessa asked Bobby as he lingered on the bracelet.

"Yeah, he ain't got nothing."

Valerie walked calmly, deliberately as Bobby and Randy retreated and stood next to Tessa.

"Please, stand up." she said to Jeremiah while standing close enough to reach out and touch him. Jeremiah hesitated, then slowly stood.

"My apologies for our vigilance, but I can be sure you understand. My name is Valerie," she said softly.

"Caste, ma'am, Jeremiah Caste."

"It's a pleasure to meet you, Jeremiah," and she extended her arm. He reciprocated, and her hand disappeared into the gentle, giant pressure of his. "Welcome to Eden." She pulled her hand from his grip and took a step back. She held her gaze on Jeremiah as the ground rolled, which allowed her more time to collect her thoughts and act appropriately to the other man. The crowd, however, felt the tremor a cruel delay.

The earth finally subsided, although those present still felt the roll, like a phantom limb, and Valerie stepped in front of Nate. Her height, several inches taller than his, caused him to look up to meet her eyes.

"You can relax your arms," she said, and Nate lowered his arms.

"And you are?"

"Nate, ma'am."

"Nate. What is that short for, Nathaniel? Nathan?"

"Nathaniel."

"Well, Nathaniel, may I assume that you're the one in charge here, in your band of two?"

"I am."

"Wonderful. And I can assume by their attire that you've previously encountered them?"

Nate nodded in the affirmative.

"And if, if, they were to be in your possession, what are your plans with them?"

"Jus' want to take them home, ma'am."

"I see," she stepped back and opened his wallet. "I see," she repeated as she removed his driver's license from one of the pockets. "Nathaniel. Abner. Jones," she said with a scold "Were you aware that this license is expired?"

He was ready to respond yet she had moved on, set the license back in the wallet and took out another card. "Operations Manager, I have the kids, they're fine. My, my, that is a fancy title."

She returned the second, folded the wallet and handed it to him.

"So, here we are," she said as he placed the wallet back in his pocket. "And I'm afraid that these will remain in my care until I am comfortable, extremely comfortable, that I can trust an Operations Manager and his traveling companion. Until that time, you are our guests conditionally. Do you understand?"

"Yes ma'am."

She slid over to Jeremiah. "Do you trust this man? Do you trust Nathaniel, Abner, Jones?"

"I do."

"Well that's a good start."

37

"Where are you from?" Eva asked.

She sat on the taupe sofa in a den with walls adorned with faux, dark wood paneling. Two her age sat to her left, another two to her right. Three more pre-teens sat on the matted carpet with their backs against the sofa. All seven ignored the discomfort of such close quarters and set their eyes on the three newcomers. Tessa stood against the back wall, her thoughts concentrated on the doorway opposite the room. Her hands were tight against the long gun, although she was as interested in the conversation as she was any threat.

The newcomers, for their part, were equally uncomfortable on a short loveseat, frayed at the arms with faded stripes of seaweed green and mustard yellow. Their prison clothes had been discarded, and Michael had acquired a royal blue t-shirt that read 'BG's Mongolian Grill—We do it on a Grill' in cursive lettering. Gray sweatpants with a thick white drawstring that were darker around the knees from age. Alice, who again was between the two boys, had been given Eva's attire—a tight lavender tank top and Nike basketball shorts. The girls noticed and dismissed the similarities in their dress. Carmen's shirt read 'Smith Family Reunion—It's all apples, baby!' White with big, red, block lettering and the outline of an apple above the script. Acid-washed jeans with a rip through the left knee and a half-size too small, which made it uncomfortable to sit forward on the loveseat.

"Where are you from?" Eva inquired again when none of the kids answered.

"Marysville," Carmen answered.

"Never heard of it," a kid answered from the carpet.

"It's in The Normal," someone chimed.

"How'd you get here?" came a query from the sofa.

"Drove," Carmen answered again, having become the de facto relator of events.

"Nah, she means how'd you find this place," chimed in another as each inquisitor followed the line of questioning.

"We didn't mean to."

"What you mean you 'didn't mean to'?"

"I mean we just drove."

"But you was wearing them outfits."

"Yeah."

"How'd you get those?"

"Got them at a prison camp."

"You been there?!" a kid said excitedly, to which Eva tempered their excitement with a glare.

"Yeah, we've been to a camp."

"What's it like?"

"It's a prison camp, what do you think it's like?"

"But how'd you get out of The Normal?"

"Crawled under a fence."

"But how'd you get here?"

"In a truck."

"Who drove?"

"He did."

They looked at Michael, studied his long frame and accepted the answer.

"How'd you get a truck?"

"Took it from the camp."

"But how did you get to the camp?"

"We drove."

"But then how'd you get to the camp?"

"We drove."

"What happened to your face?"

"She cut it."

"Can we, can we see it?"

"No."

"Why are you here?" Eva asked, and the directness hushed the audience. That, and the fact that the *why* was more important than the *how*.

"We're here to see you," Alice said when Carmen stayed silent.

"Us?" Eva questioned. "You don't even know us."

"We've heard of you."

"How?"

"Cause we all know about you."

"And what have you heard?"

Alice knew that their nickname was a slight and was hesitant to repeat it in their presence.

"Well, we've heard there were people who didn't want to leave when the ground shook. That you live near the nuclear plant that melted down."

The accuracy of Alice's description kept them without further questions. Set a pall over what had been a stream of consciousness, which made them all squirm a bit on the sofas, on the carpet. There was no television to turn to, no electronic hum to tune into, nor the hope of a telephone—be it ring or vibration.

"You're the 'Frog People,'" Michael said. Alice knew he shouldn't have and slunk down into the loveseat. Carmen followed in a fraction of a second.

"Excuse me?" Eva asked.

"You're all infected with the radiation." He pointed to his throat, "got the cancer growin' in you till you look like a frog."

Eva's eyes tightened as she stared at Michael, her lips pressed tight and her breaths short. She held in the fury, the hatred where she had only curiosity before he spoke. Imagined herself leaping from the sofa and punching him in the face. Over, and over, and over again. Yet this check on her contempt enabled another reaction and the tears followed and fell down her cheeks. Sniffles which forced her mouth open and made her vulnerable. Uncontrollable. All eyes on her. She tried to contain it, but it was too aggressive. Quickly she stood, walked with her head down and shoved the back door open. It clanged, clanged again, then settled. All eyes on Michael, and he knew he had said something very wrong.

The ecru shades floated with the breeze through the open window above the sink. Pulled open, the rose petal patterns bent into the seams and let the earthy aroma of the garden into the kitchen. The tomatoes and zucchini and peppers and the strawberries.

Valerie listened to the interrogation occurring in the back room, but the distance made the words indiscernible. She poured water from a clear pitcher into a silver tea kettle and set it on the camping stove. She primed the kerosene pump, turned the knob to allow the gas to flow and set the match to the burner which flicked the fire around black iron. Pulled back the plastic lid from a coffee tin, its logo long since faded and scooped several spoonfuls of ground coffee into the French Press. She took three white mugs from the drying rack next to the sink. Then set one on the kitchen table in front of Nate and the other two on placemats set at empty seats.

Bobby watched her every movement as he leaned against the cabinets, more alert any time the distance between her and the stranger closed. It was her job, he felt, to make a stranger in a strange land feel comfortable. It was her nature, and the nature of any good person. It was his job, he knew, to ensure that this civility continued without confrontation, and he was prepared to do what was necessary to keep her safe.

The kettle, still a minute or two off from whistling, began to gurgle and she busied herself with returning clean and dry dishes to their proper places in the cabinets. A potholder on the counter. The pull of the press plunger to ready its placement and the whistle came and the steam escaped and she turned the dial left on the stove. Poured the hot water into the press and set the top with the rubber around the plunger flush against the glass interior.

"All we want to do is get those kids back," Nate started.

"It ain't time yet," she responded curtly yet reassuringly, his sentence barely finished, "and besides, it's too late in the day for an adventure."

"It's real important that I get them back, now."

"It ain't time yet."

She set the French Press down next to her mug, pulled the chair out slightly and sat down across from him. She stared at him without an additional word. Nate would have welcomed a ticking clock or the ability to understand the words in the den. Anything to alleviate the silence that cocooned the kitchen.

Finally, after tortured minutes she pushed the plunger down into the press which forced the coffee grounds to the bottom of the cylinder. Extended her arm to fill his mug then retracted to fill hers. She set the press at the center of the table then nodded to affirm their conversation could commence.

"Here's the thing," Nate started, "and it ain't a big thing but it's gonna bother me. My middle name."

"Abner."

"Yeah, you see I've never been too keen on it, and if, out of common courtesy, you could refrain from speaking it again, I would greatly appreciate it."

"You don't like it?"

"Like nails on a chalkboard."

"I will do you this favor," she paused to take a sip from her mug, "since you have made a good first impression."

"Actually," Nate responded after his own sip, "this ain't the first time we've met."

"No?"

"No ma'am, I met you years ago. Nine, to be exact."

"Did you, now?"

"I did, but I can understand if you don't recall as I had both legs at that time."

He smirked, letting her in on the joke, and she reciprocated. It was then that he realized that it had been some time since he had spoken to a woman. Truly spoken, not just in passing. And she continued to smile, content in speaking to someone who's reactions and tendencies she did not know.

"But you will remember the situation, I'm sure. The canvas covered trucks and all the soldiers that jumped out of them in camouflage and guns with gas masks."

"You were there the day they came. You were 'they.'"

"One of 'em, just a soldier, had no real authority on the matter."

"Just following orders."

"Just going where they told me to go an' standing where they told me to stand."

"And shoot who they tell you who to shoot."

"If it had come to that, yeah."

"Would you?"

"Would I have shot anybody?"

"Yes."

"Never thought about it, ain't come close to that that day."

"But you did have a gun."

"I always had a gun, at that time. You forget the gun and you're one with the gun."

"I see."

"You understand that?"

"Not entirely, but I accept it."

"Where's Jeremiah?"

"Aww, are you worried about your friend?" she asked as if speaking to a child.

Nate was taken aback by the slight, and she felt it.

"He went with Randy, Randy being the only one here to match your friend's, let's say 'stature,' to get a change of clothes. No need for the children to see the overt reality of a prisoner in their home. Randy, being of, 'stature,' does not move fast, nor I assume does your friend. Combine that with the distance to Randy's house and you've got me and you for a bit longer."

Satisfied, and after another sip, Nate continued, "did you think we were going to shoot you?"

"Was there time to think back then? Hmmm? Only time to react to what's in front of you. Our world was turned upside down. Shook, literally. And here comes soldiers hidden behind gas masks and the first thought is why don't we have gas masks? Should we?"

"So you see all that, and your town is shaking, and you don't think to leave? That maybe leaving's a good idea?"

She sat back in her chair before responding, unsure how much to divulge to one she still didn't fully trust.

"Have you ever thought that maybe there's more to it?"

"More to what? To a destroyed town? Got no water, got no food or at least running out. I mean you can't see the radiation but you could see that, right?"

"In hindsight, Nathaniel, were those fears overblown?"

He thought for a second. "In some ways, yeah, but in other ways, no. But you gotta understand something, at some point they're gonna come for your town."

"The army?"

"The company."

"New Madrid?"

"Yes."

"For what reason? I know you're rebuilding all around here. We've already rebuilt."

"Looks to me like you've put a Band-Aid on it."

"Well it works for us."

"But we ain't rebuilding, we're clearing."

"Clearing for what?"

"For the company."

"For the company?"

"For what's below your town."

"Well, they're certainly taking their sweet time."

"They hoping the ground will eventually stop shaking. And, for all those that did leave, it's easier to say you ain't going home when the memory has faded. But for you, they gonna come back and they ain't going to give you a choice when they do."

"Well then, that is something we will have to prepare for."

Valerie picked up the French Press, refilled her mug and motioned to Nate.

"No thank you. Kindly."

"We had created an Eden before it was 'Eden.'"

She set the press back down and took a sip from the refreshed mug.

"A community that welcomed all, not just on a sign at the border but truly, truly welcomed. Expelled any and all that felt different. But try as we might, we could not keep out all the negative influences. Those who had left by force found their revenge through the keyboard. Put our names, our addresses on websites. Told the unstable who frequented those websites where we live and what terrible things, all in hypotheticals, mind you, should be done to us. Told them about these 'nigger-loving white folks' who had, for whatever it's worth, a backwards utopia where 'spics roam free' and 'Jews spread like rats.' Our 'utopia,' to them, was a dystopia bent on destroying the white race. And they found our kids on social media and threatened them. Told them they were going to kill them."

"There's always crazies in this world," Nate empathized. "Always were, always will be, you just gotta tune them out."

"They said it," Valerie continued, ignoring his advice. "Again and again. Louder and louder. There wasn't any difference between our town and any other, you see. They just needed an enemy. And one day," she continued without acknowledging his advice, "a young man we kicked out did return. He pressed record and it started and he turned the phone to his face, hidden behind a gas mask. Said 'this is for the white race' then taped his phone to his chest so all his newfound friends on the internet could watch what he was doing as he did it. He looked like you did when you were here those years ago. A soldier. Face hidden behind a mask. He walked into the elementary school and took the butt of his AR-15 and shattered the glass to the office and threw a canister of tear gas into the room behind the desks. Luckily, she was able to hit the alarm before the gas overcame her. She crawled out from behind the desk to get away from the gas and he shot her in the head. Mary Collins," she added to humanize the story.

"He walked into the main hallway," she continued, "and you could hear the doors slamming shut between the sound of the alarm. He tried a door to a classroom, but it was locked. Went to the next one, same thing. The third, locked. But this time he kicked the door. Again, kicked the door. And finally he kicked it open. And there, at the back of the room along the windows there was a teacher picking up the children and dropping them through a window. And you could see his arm come up and block the camera in the corner of it and the teacher didn't turn around. He didn't stop, just kept lifting the children from behind the desk and the chairs they had put up in the corner to give them at least some protection, for whatever that was worth. *Pop. Pop. Pop.* And the teacher fell to the ground and he lost his grip on the child, Charlotte, and she fell through the open window." She paused as she recalled Charlotte's face.

"And the young man walked slowly to where the desk was, and you could hear the children crying. You could hear it, Nathaniel. Have you ever heard a child cry knowing death was coming but not quite understanding what that meant?"

Nate cleared his throat before answering softly. "No."

"You and me, we get it, we get what a gun pointed in our direction means. What it can mean. But a child? It's-it's like this combination of fear and confusion, and once you've seen it, you can never unsee it."

She paused for a moment, ran her index finger along the rim of the mug, and then took another sip.

"And he saw it, but he wanted to see more of it. 'Look at me!' he yelled at them through the mask. None did. 'Look at me!' he ordered again. But they didn't look, and do you know why?"

"I don't," he whispered.

"Because, to a child, to anybody, if you don't look at the devil, the devil ain't there. He shot his gun in the air and repeated 'look at me!' and slowly the first boy did. Nathaniel, just like you. Then the next, until all of them were looking at the man. The boy. And you could see his arm come up and point that gun at them and they watched. And then, do you know what happened?"

"No ma'am."

"You do, because you remember the day. It was one of those 'where you when' days. When the ground opened up with vengeance. When the faults went. That was the day it happened. And for us, for our families, it happened just as a deranged, piece of shit, was pointing an assault rifle at our children. The children, those cowering behind the desk, looking up at him, fell about the floor. The boy fell too, and he tried to stand back up, but you know the ground did not allow that. Not that day. So he stayed on the floor. Near the teacher, near the children who crawled underneath the desk and held each other. And then the windows broke and the roof collapsed and the classroom was covered in debris and the teacher's eyes shot open and he gasped. Shot, bleeding, he reached out for gun and grabbed onto the barrel. He was able to get his foot on the boy's stomach and push him away and with the gun he pulled the trigger as many times as he could and when he was done the boy didn't move."

"So..." Nate started.

"So, the tragedy that you see, that everyone else sees, to us, was a miracle. Who are we to deny it?"

"But the teacher…"

"Yes, my husband did die. A martyr if there ever was one."

Nate sat back in his chair and parsed the story.

"That don't change the fact that they will come."

"Let them come."

"If those kids ain't back home they'll come quicker than you'll want."

"We are prepared for that."

"Do you know what they call you? Out there, in The Normal?"

"'The Normal'?"

"The Normal, everywhere but here, where you live. Where I live. Which, no matter what stories you tell them, how normal you think you are, makes you abnormal by default. Backwards hillbillies too stupid to know what's good for ya. Which means, when they come, they ain't treating you as equals. Ain't no civil conversation over coffee."

It was Valerie's turn to try and understand something foreign.

"So what do they call us?"

"They call you the 'Frog People.'"

"The 'Frog People?'"

"Yeah, it made me giggle when they told me I'm ashamed to admit. A bunch of people mutated from the radiation with extra toes, extra fingers, tumors comin' out their necks so they look like frogs. Got their own language cause the deformities make it hard to talk."

"That's insane."

"Is it?"

"Yes, it is."

"And they also think you took on the whole damn army and won. And just a minute ago you expected me to believe that the tragedy of that day was simply a miracle that come down from heaven to save your children."

"It was."

"Well it wasn't for my family. For my wife. For my daughter."

She paused before responding. "Well, I am certainly sad to hear that."

"At a certain point, soon," Nate said while holding up the green bracelet around his wrist, "they're going to turn their attention from The Normal, turn their attention south for these kids, and when they do someone is gonna know where I am. Where Jeremiah is, and they're gonna come here. Fast. This 'Eden,' 'utopia,' whatever, will have some problems if I don't get them back. And you've been hidden so long you ain't human to them no more. Just a problem they've been puttin' off and might as well solve it now. You're something 'other' and 'other' is unpredictable. 'Other,' Valerie, is easier to kill."

She stood up and walked to the sink. Slowly, deliberately, poured the remainder of her coffee from the mug into the drain then pulled up on the handle for the faucet. Bobby watched her with curiosity and when no water fell from the spicket her laugh started slowly then built.

"We already have problems, Nathaniel." She felt herself becoming vulnerable and recomposed. "When do you want to take them home?"

"As soon as possible."

"Can I feed them supper before you go? I would like to send them home full. Let their parents know they were cared for at least."

Nate relaxed in his chair, exhaled, and as he started to respond the screen door to the kitchen opened. The afternoon sun was temporarily blocked by Randy as he stepped up into the room. It continued to be blocked as Jeremiah followed, now wearing a crimson t-shirt with the Nike 'swoosh' across the chest and navy-blue sweatpants that had been cut at the knees.

"What'd I miss?" Randy asked through short breaths, which drew a sneer from Bobby and took Valerie by surprise.

"We were just discussing supper," she said, and thought to herself, you know, your favorite subject. Yet it was not in her nature to vocalize insults, however apt.

"Supper?" he asked.

"Yes, Randall. We will be treating our guests before sending them on their way." She turned to Nate, "I insist." Then to Jeremiah, "please, sit, have some coffee," and Bobby lowered the gun barrel to an angle above their heads to emphasize the point.

38

Michael reluctantly followed the boy and they turned from the overgrowth that covered the cracked sidewalk. Navigated the rusted cars and high grass that made it difficult to know where the driveway ended, and the yard began. Yet from the unkempt lawn rose three large solar panels, their metallic squared cells inconspicuously rotating to collect the sun.

He didn't enjoy being escorted, as if he was a threat, let alone by someone he assumed was younger than him. He didn't relish the feeling that the boy would prevail in a physical confrontation. He had a solid frame and the demeanor of one who had fought before. Most of all, he didn't feel that he had anything to apologize for, but he lost the vote.

The boy led him up the soft wood steps, browned and blackened where the rains had intruded. They stepped high to avoid the missing second step and onto the porch with plywood laid to fill in the gaps.

It was a modest house. Single-story, the windows replaced with plexiglass and plastic wrap as they were on Main Street. The walnut blinds pulled shut except in several places where the sides were broken. The beige paint on the siding either cracked or peeling where it was still noticeable.

"What's her name again?" Michael asked as the boy pushed the door open and he stopped.

"Eva," he answered sharply. He kept the door slightly ajar, "I don't trust you."

They stared and the boy held the door until Michael was noticeably uncomfortable, then pushed it open. There was a staleness in the air which complemented the antiquated furniture. Besides the sunlight that crept through the broken blinds, the only light came from a floor lamp of equal antiquation.

"Eva?" Michael yelled while attempting not to yell. "It's Michael. Um, one of the people, the kids, that came here today."

The boy fell into a brown recliner and the force pushed the backrest into the wall, vibrating the structure enough to make Michael take notice.

"Eva?" he repeated louder. "I just wanted to say I'm sorry," he continued to the back of the house, unsure if she was even there. "You know, I didn't mean it."

"Get outta here!" she yelled from the back of the house, her voice echoing, which made it impossible for Michael to know from where.

"Well," the boy said as he stood up, "time to go."

Michael ignored him and took several steps towards the logical source of her voice.

"I really am sorry. Sometimes I say stupid shit, I didn't mean no offense."

"Go away."

"Can I at least say I'm sorry?"

"Fine, you're sorry. Now go back to where you came from."

Michael waited for more, but nothing came. He turned and took a step towards the front door.

"Know what? I ain't sorry. You are the "Frog People." That's why the counter went off when we got close to here and that's why you hiding. You're freaks. It was stupid of us to come here."

The boy stepped hard as he closed the distance fast, grabbed Michael at his armpits and shoved him against the wall. Michael struggled to free himself but couldn't. The boy swung him around, flung him across the room. Michael staggered backwards and he let out a howl as his lower back hit flush against the edge of a table. The boy pressed, then ran his knee into Michael's stomach which brought him to the ground.

"Nick!"

The boy froze, his leg bent back and aimed at Michael's head. He turned towards the cluttered hallway between the two-bedroom doors and Eva, who steadied herself in front of the ladder.

"Go home."

Nick put his leg down.

"But," he answered through adrenaline, "I can't leave you here alone with an outsider."

"I said go home."

"I ain't going."

"Yeah, you are."

"Fine, then you explain it to Miss Valerie."

"Fine," Eva relented, "then sit your ass down and don't say another word."

He stepped back from Michael and motioned his acquiescence with his index finger over his lips. She leered at him until he retreated further, returning to the recliner with the thud.

Michael set his palms on the floor, pushed himself to his knees and struggled to regain normalcy in his lungs. Eva waited in the doorway patiently for his composure to return.

"C'mon," she said to him.

Her words were still an echo, just as her conversation had been whilst he laid prone on the floor.

"C'mon," she repeated.

From his knees, he slowly looked up at her. Somber, although he did not discern sympathy upon her face. With the help of the table edge, he came to his feet, keeled over, then leveled himself almost upright for good. As he started towards her, she disappeared up the ladder, removing the security of her being. He looked back to where Nick had sat but the recliner was hidden behind the clutter and the exterior of a bedroom wall. He walked towards the ladder. The jumble of toys and clothes entangled in the Christmas tree lights lit sadly by the yellowed, bare bulb that stuck out from the lamp. He felt a pang in his ribs as he reached for the first rung, then continued with the pain expected.

Eva was already sitting when his head emerged through the rectangular opening in the attic floor. He inspected his new surroundings, suspicious of the confined space and her antipathy he felt, rightly so, towards him. The singular bulb. The desks married together. A box of Lucky Charms and the book of serial killers. Yet what drew him near her was the technology. The computer monitors and gadgets and the walkie-talkie, of which he perceived only people of importance possessed. It reminded him of his shed in the backyard, the safety of it and the similarities—all of which, and the distance from Nick, put him at ease.

She clicked on the walkie-talkie as he looked over her shoulder at the monitors.

"That's the truck," he said with muted excitement as he looked at the camera feeds.

"Yeah," she responded, "and that's your friend's truck behind it."

"So you watched us?"

"Yup."

"Why did the truck stop?"

"I did that."

"How?"

"Electromagnetic pulse, fries your computers, got 'em hidden in the cars. Only works on newer cars, can't be no antique."

"Why?"

"Ain't got computers."

"What do you do then?"

"Never come up."

"You should be prepared for all possibilities."

"What, like you were?"

Michael felt the sting and decided to hold off on any further advice.

"There's a folding chair in the corner."

He looked to the corner and saw a wooden chair collapsed under a stack of dog-eared books. With deliberate precision he removed the books and set them to the side, resting on the exposed insulation. As he reached for the chair, he noticed a book he recognized and brought it with the chair.

"I got this book," he told her as he sat down on the chair. "'When all the world recognizes beauty as beauty, this in itself is ugliness. When all the world recognizes good as good, this in itself is evil.'"

"Did you come up here to read me a story?"

"No, I just," he paused, then set the book on the desk.

"So," Eva continued, "you want to keep yelling at me or really apologize?"

"I came up here cause you told me to."

"You didn't have to."

Michael turned his attention to the monitors, unsure of how to continue the conversation.

"Why did you come here?" she asked.

"Cause I said something mean."

"And you decided to come say you're sorry?"

"Yes," he said, although it was a lie, he had no choice in the matter. "What do you do if you see something?"

"Nothing."

"Nothing?"

"It's not my shift."

"Oh."

Eva pointed to a piece of copy paper taped to the desk. The days and nights sectioned into eight-hour blocks and a name written within each block.

"If it was your shift?"

"Call someone. Tell them who, tell them where."

"So you just come up here when it's your shift?"

The question caused her to look at him, as she wondered if she should divulge more personal information or ignore the query.

"I like being up here. Everyone else got their setups in their rooms."

"What's that?" he asked, pointing to another monitor.

"Road sensors."

He wanted to ask what the protocol was if intruders entered somewhere other than the roads but refrained.

"How many people you stopped?"

"Besides you?"

"Yeah."

"And those guys?"

"Yeah."

"Um," she muttered to extend her time, "no one."

"No one?"

"Nope. But we practice all the time."

"That's got to get kinda boring, watchin' a screen that never does nothing."

She didn't understand the sentiment, this was something that no one questioned.

"Do you like it here?"

"As opposed to other places or am I happy?"

"I guess as opposed to other places."

"I don't know."

"You don't know?"

"It's all I know."

"We're going home soon, after dinner."

She feigned indifference.

"I like it here."

"You only been here a couple hours."

"Yeah."

"And some of that time you had a gun on you."

"Yeah, but no one called me any names."

"I called you an 'asshole' a bunch of times today."

Michael tried to contain the chuckle.

"Why's that funny?"

"Cause I don't mind being called an 'asshole'."

"Asshole."

He laughed harder.

"So what'd they call you?" Eva asked once the attic had gone quiet again.

"I don't wanna say."

She looked at him without a word and decided not to push the issue.

"Stink Boy," he said in a whisper and waited for Eva's reaction of which there was none.

"Stink Ass," a beat, "Swamp Thing. I don't wanna go home."

She took a second before responding, "you have to."

"I want to stay here."

"You can't stay here."

"I'm sick of gettin' beat. I'm sick of not having no friends."

"You got friends."

"No, I don't."

"Then who are those two you came with?"

"They ain't my friends, they just tolerate me. They needed me to get here."

"They used you?"

"Yeah, they used me."

"I'm sorry."

"Why can't I stay here?"

"Cause we don't know you."

Michael knew it was futile. He was an outsider once again, yet this time, there was logic behind the situation. He was sure he had found a kindred spirit. Hidden in an attic just as he hid in the shed. Surrounded by widgets and tech and books about philosophy and the murderers. He arrived somewhere he felt accepted, without any evidence to solidify this feeling, and that inference was impossible to verify before he'd be forced to leave.

"How'd you get these?" he asked as he picked up the box of Lucky Charms.

"What do you mean?"

"There's no stores here."

"We go out."

"You go out?"

"Well, I don't. But people do. Go and get things. From other towns, places that have stores."

"You leave here?"

"Some do."

"Have you ever left?"

Eva turned her attention back to the monitors. "No, I've never left." She poked at random keys, flipped between programs arbitrarily before she stood up. "C'mon, I want to show you something." She walked to the opening in the floor, set her stomach against the plywood and slid her body down onto the ladder.

39

The kitchen buzzed. A young woman sat next to Jeremiah at the table and picked potatoes from a water-filled plastic bin normally used for storage as she rebuffed his offers to assist. She peeled each then transferred them one by one to a milky, opaque cutting board and sliced them into pieces before placing them in a bin opposite the first. Nearest Nate, a middle-aged man kneaded dough, the flour falling from the edges of the wooden board. The activities continued upon the countertops. Huge cuts of meat cleaved smaller, set on platters and carried outside. Cucumbers sliced. Carrots scrubbed. Onions peeled. Mushrooms cleared of the dirt remaining against their bases.

Bobby had moved to the opposite side of the room as to not get in the way while still being able to watch the strangers. He kept repeating the actions he would take if the situation would arise. He had exhausted all the *ifs*—they run away, they attack someone, they try to take his gun. He felt confident in his abilities and at the same time wished it was Tessa next to him instead of Randy.

Valerie walked slowly behind each person at the counters and looked over their shoulder, inspecting their work. Between each analysis she stole a glance back to the table, to Nate and Jeremiah. They both had met her eyes the first two times she did, but felt it uncomfortable to continue after that. Once she had reached the end of the counters nearest the door, she reversed direction. Halfway on the return trip she turned towards the table, froze in the movements around her and stared at Nate. Jeremiah had worn down the young woman with his insistence and she handed him the knife.

"No!" Bobby yelled, Jeremiah froze, and all activity ceased. "You cut; he peels."

He set the knife down gently on the table and slid it back to her. As deftly as she had handed the knife, she handed him the peeler. Bobby relaxed, proud that he had headed off a possible disaster. Jeremiah picked up a potato which at first disappeared within his grasp then set the peeler against the brown skin.

"May I speak with you?" Valerie requested in a whisper crouched next to Nate's chair.

Her face was close enough where he could feel the wisps of breath from her mouth. Perhaps it was the domesticated activities that made him see her now in attraction, that made him swallow hard at the proximity of her lips. He nodded in agreement, and it was all he could muster in the swell of desire left idle for so many years. She turned towards the hallway, and he stood to follow her.

"You stay on him," Bobby directed Randy, then followed Nate into the hallway.

"Bobby," Valerie said as she set her hand on a bedroom doorknob, "I'd like to speak with our guest alone."

"But, Miss Valerie."

"Please," as she put her hand on his shoulder. "Please, Bobby."

"I'll be right outside this door," he said and stepped back from the doorway to give her some space.

"I'd prefer it if you go back to your place in the kitchen."

"But protocol."

"But nothing, Robert."

They stared at each other while Nate looked away, he had no say in this and listened to the noises from the kitchen. She waited to turn the knob until he had disappeared from their view.

"So," Valerie asked, "what does an 'Operations Manager' do?"

"Huh?" Nate asked, lost in his own thoughts and standing inside the doorway, giving just enough to allow her to close the door behind him.

"That's what you do at the camp, right?"

"Uh, yes ma'am."

"Then what does your title mean?" she continued as she stepped to the window in the darkened room and released the shudders. The new sun painted leafy patterns on the wall through the western window.

"It means I'm in charge of the camp."

"Which one?" She looked out the window as the conversation continued and could see the smoke from the grills rise and the wind push it over the garden.

"Camp A."

"That's not very original."

"Well they call it 'Andersonville.'"

"Who does?"

"The prisoners."

She chuckled to herself for a second. "I see. And are you?"

"Am I what?"

"Are you in charge?"

Nate had never thought to ask himself that question and an involuntary truth came out. "No."

"No?"

"I mean, I'm in charge of picking up new prisoners and telling them where to live. Where to go on a given day."

"How's the food?"

"The food?"

"Yes, you have to eat, don't you?"

"It's food. I guess."

"And how do you feel? How do you feel when you close your eyes at night? Do you feel you're making a difference? That you're doing right? Do you feel like your life is worth it?"

Here he had assumed that he was, that it was. Or maybe someone had told him somewhere that he was making a difference. Either way, he had never examined the thought himself. She sat down at the corner of the bed, which gave him time to examine the room. Simple wood stained dark. Diecast cars set on the dresser. Books stacked upon the far nightstand, the top a children's book about baseball. The bed made perfectly with two pillows against the headboard.

"I only ask," she continued, "because that's all I can think about right now. Am I doing right? Is it worth it?"

"Those are common thoughts to have," he empathized after a long pause.

"You see I don't doubt that it was God who saved our children that day, but, I'm afraid that it's me who's killing them now."

"I don't understand."

"This was John's room," she said as she ran her palm back and forth across the quilt. "He passed two days ago. There are others, and there are others who are dying. Right now. As we speak. I've tried, we've tried to make it stop. All this, everything here, is on me, it's on me Nathaniel, and I can't take it one minute more."

"I'm sorry to hear that, really," Nate said quietly without offering anything more.

"Why'd you come here?"

"To get them kids. Take them home."

"Is that all?"

"Yeah."

"Who brought you here?"

"I did."

"And what are you going to do after you've got those kids home?"

"Go back to the camp."

"What if you could do more?"

"I'm doing all I want to be doing. Look, ma'am, Valerie, I appreciate, very much, your hospitality here and all, but I gotta get them kids back. I've got to get back to the camp. I've agreed we'll eat here and I ain't backin' out from that, but after that we have to be going." He let go a superficial smile.

"This is our chance, our one chance that's come along in all these years."

"With all due respect, I don't believe that."

"For all these years I've told them that this is a paradise. Do you think anyone would have left even if I told them to? Even if I demanded it? Leave all they've known for some of them? For others, the memory has faded beyond recognition that they wouldn't even know how to act anywhere else. And now, when God is taking our people, our children, you just happen upon our doorstep."

"Coincidence."

"Bullshit, and you know it."

"There ain't no divine intervention here," his voice rose as he took a step towards her, "and I ain't no savior." She didn't respond, simply looked up at him and when he went for the door she looked down at the floor.

"I'm aware of our moniker," she said as he turned the doorknob.

"Moniker?"

"The nickname. 'The Frog People.' My worry is that it will follow us, follow the children."

"Follow them?" he asked as he stayed focused on the door.

"Yes, wherever we go."

He released his hand from the knob but stayed focused on the wood grain of the door. "How many?"

"How many?" she echoed.

"How many people are there? Here?"

"Right now, 127."

"And how would I evacuate... move... relocate whatever, that many people?"

"It doesn't matter how."

"Well I think it does, kinda important. That time has passed, Valerie, relocation has long passed."

"And you think that they would turn us away? Turn away children?"

"I think that people want to forget, and you showing up at their doorstep would be a shock, to say the least."

"Then, what? We just stay here? We just let people die?"

"How'd you get that coffee we had earlier?" he questioned. "Got some coffee trees up in this climate?"

"No, I-there are some that go and borrow items from other places."

"So you ain't stuck here."

"No, we're not on an island, but one pickup truck that works ain't going to cut it."

"Then it's time for a walk, your exodus through the desert, if I may," he finished, hoping his tone had concluded the interaction.

"It's always these conversations that brings out someone's true nature," her tone grew more direct.

"An' what's my true nature?"

"Selfish. Selfish for not helping when there's truly a need. Condescending for throwing my faith back at me."

"Selfish?" Nate was a step below yelling. "I'm here, aren't I? I'm here to get those kids back home. To their families. I don't need to be, do I?"

"And I'm asking for a favor, a noble one at that."

"Noble? There's no noble down here."

"But there is out there."

"And when do you want to do this? Huh? Tonight?"

"No, it doesn't have to be now, but soon."

Nate walked over to the window to give him the feeling that the room was larger.

"127 people. To where?" he asked aloud for both his and her benefit.

"I was hoping you knew a place."

"To be honest I haven't been anywhere 'cept the camp and Marysville. Been years. I mean I don't know much more about The Normal than you do. I mean, what, we just throw a dart at a map and that's where we go? If this was gonna happen, that is."

"Marysville sounds nice."

"It's not."

"Got to be better than Eden. What's in Marysville? I mean, why do you go there?"

"Prisoners come through on the train, I transfer them to the camps."

"I see." She stood up from the edge of the bed and walked to the door, their distance as far as possible within the room. "How do you get them," she asked in her most sultry, inviting tone, "from the train to the camps?"

"Well I got a big bus," and he stopped. Realized he had divulged information he had not intended. He felt that she had trapped him but there was no way to retract the statement. "But it's got GPS on it," he lied, "won't work except on designated routes."

"That's a pity," she responded, knowing full well from how short he said "bus" to the delay that that wasn't quite so.

40

Eva had the same impulse as Valerie and pulled the lavender drapes open from the window opposite the door. Unlatched the lock atop the lower pane and pulled up until the wind pushed through the opening. The high brush greenery lapped at the window. The branches nearest on the trees that lined the side of the house. The sparrows and robins set upon the branches instinctually in their evening songs.

It was the juxtaposition that struck Michael as he pushed the door further open and set his feet inside the bedroom. Deep-white polished furniture. Dusted, the smell of artificial lemon wafting with the new air. Photographs set in frames on the dresser. A young woman with a baby. At Disneyworld with a child. Friends around a campfire. A small flat screen television. A DVD player.

Opaque, burnt orange pill bottles on the near one, the caps adjacent. Their contents noted in black marker in lieu of the common white labels. A straw angled into a plastic water bottle. A flowery blue box of tissues, and Eva picked up those discarded on the bare floor and placed them softly in the bin adjacent.

The white headboard rose several feet from the bed frame. Vertical slats. Its top resembled a bell curve and at each end there were two rounded pegs. Several pillows, two of which matched the plaid quilt. Hunter greens and cedar browns and merlot reds.

Eva stood over the bed in front of the one piece of furniture that did not match, a mahogany rocking chair with its own plaid adornments hung over the top and attached at the rods where they connected with the seat. Medallion yellows, and pine greens, and khaki browns. The original wood visible through scratches upon the curved rockers.

"Mama," she whispered.

The woman did not stir. Michael kept his distance.

"Mama," she said with a gentle press of her shoulder. The woman's eyelids fluttered, remaining closed.

"C'mere." Eva beckoned to Michael, who didn't move from the doorway. "C'mon, it's okay."

Michael examined her eyes in the soundtrack of the songbirds. Sympathy was still absent, but he felt reassurance and that was at least something. Cautiously he neared. Followed the corner of the quilt up to the center of the bed where her figure was hidden. Blushed and looked away where her baby blue nightgown revealed her cleavage. Held his eyes closed until he sensed the angle of his neck had moved beyond and when he opened them, he glimpsed first her neck. Swollen, protruded, like that of a bullfrog in mid-croak.

"Mama," Eva said louder and with more force applied to her shoulder. Her eyes fluttered again, and this time opened as she turned towards the voice.

"Hey baby," Mama said hoarsely.

"How you feelin'?"

"Oh," she said with a deep inhale, "just tired. Just tired. I was dreaming, I was dreaming there were buildings fallin' all around. Big ones. Skyscrapers and people were screaming. You

were there and Frank was there. I don't know if
Henry was. I can't remember. Anyways."

"You always have crazy dreams."

"Who's this?" she asked when Michael's
weight shifted, caused the floorboards to creak
and she lifted her head from the pillow.

"This is my friend, Michael."

"A new friend?"

"Yes," Eva answered while wondering how
much explaining she was set to do.

"I see. And how long was I asleep for?"

"Just most of the day, just regular."

"Well," Mama said as she pushed herself up
against the headboard. "I must'a slept through
an interesting day. Please," as she motioned to
the nightstand, "please."

Eva handed her the plastic water bottle and
Mama took two large gulps before clearing her
throat. Michael watched her bulbous neck as
she swallowed, its subtle motion.

The frailty of her body contradicted the
strength in her voice. The thinness of a body
weakened yet on the defensive. His eyes
glanced to her cleavage and then darted above
her neck. He tried to rectify her soft, young
features with what had been in his mind for so
long. He had imagined the engorged necks,
sure, but they were complimented with the oily,

bumpy skin of a frog. The wretchedness was missing, the groans and grunts of the mutants imagined. Their bodies bent over, broken from the radiation as they navigated the apocalyptic scenery through a dense layer of visible nuclear smog and the sun invisible. Yet here, bathed in sunlight in the chorus of songbirds was a woman whose beauty made it hard for him to concentrate.

"Michael, I've always liked that name, starts soft, goes hard, then rolls slowly at its end."

"I've never thought too much about it, ma'am."

"Miss, please."

"Miss."

"How old are you, Michael?"

"Twelve."

"Twelve, same as Eva."

"That would put you in what, sixth, seventh grade?"

"Gonna be in seventh in the Fall."

"Do you like your school?"

"Yes, miss," he lied, and Eva looked to him with an understanding.

"That's good. Where's your school?"

"Marysville."

"Marysville. Never heard of it. Or maybe, I have. Anyways, that sounds like a nice place."

The front door creaked open as she was about to ask another question, and they all turned their attention to the bedroom door.

"Sup, bitch?" a new voice, newly deep, asked from the outer room.

"Sup, pussy?" Nick answered.

"We gotta head back, get the boy."

Nick stood from the recliner. "Boy!" he yelled through the house. "Time to go."

Michael stared for a few moments longer, then walked to the doorway while Eva remained at her mother's side.

"Carmen's ma," he said as he turned back to her, "she's a nurse. She's come and seen me when I don't feel right."

"That's nice of her," Mama responded.

"Who comes to see you?"

She cleared her throat and looked away from him, away from the open window and away from Eva. "Eva, is all the comfort I need."

"Do you got nurses here?" She didn't answer. "Doctors?" She didn't answer.

"We have God, and that's all that anyone needs."

"Well we got nurses and doctors. Would you like to come with us?"

She reached her hand out towards Eva who reciprocated. "I wish I could, Michael. I wish I could."

"Why can't you?"

She squeezed her daughter's hand, "I just can't."

"Get your ass out here!" Nick yelled from the living room.

"Miss Victoria is having a big supper for our guests," Eva told her mother.

"Go, Eva dear, have fun with your friends."

"You want anything, Mama?"

"You got five seconds!" yelled the other voice.

Mama released her hand from Eva's and slid back down onto the bed. "No, sweetie. I'm fine. I'm fine."

41

"So," Bobby asked, his long gun still slung over his shoulder, "what's a camp like?"

Main Street, where the kids had first been encircled by over one hundred, was lined down its center with kitchen tables and folding tables and coffee tables. Some sat six, most four, and some two. 33 of them. The chairs, too, were of different shapes and sizes. Some were born of a set, others seemed more comfortable in a den. The town had self-segregated by age—those of Eva's age, including Alice, Carmen, and Michael, had taken seats at one end. Then the teenagers, the young adults, those of middle age, and finally those later in life, of whom there were few. The exceptions were rare. Bobby, Tessa, and Randy had sat with Nate,

Jeremiah, and Valerie. A young boy was absent, in his room in front of computer monitors watching the roads to Eden—his mother had brought him a plate and a lemon-lime soda. Mama, and the others too ill to enjoy the oddity of a town-wide feast and the visitors. They had put out chairs enough for them, out of respect for their existences.

Steam still escaped the metal pots set aside charcoal grills, cooling from their wood-fired heat, tended by stragglers to the tables. Where the potatoes had been boiled. Where the apples had. softened and then been covered in a cinnamon glaze. Grizzled char, the remains of the wild boar and venison that had scarred the metal grates.

The sky threatened on the horizon yet remained distant. A doe and stag appeared, a hundred yards down the street, stared, then walked calmly off into the neighborhood. Mutts sat below those who had shared scraps before, while pups wandered spastically from person to person—too excited to stay in one place. The cats congregated around the grills, too proud to follow.

"To be honest, this place reminds me of the camp," Jeremiah answered after deliberating on the question, "'cept for the guns."

"No guns?" Randy chimed.

"No sir."

"Not even the guards?"

"No one has a gun."

"How?" Tessa asked. "How does it remind you of the camp?"

"The separation. The separation from the rest of the world."

"My mom likes cherry cola," Eva told Alice who watched her set a can between her hip and the chair. "So what do you do for fun?"

"I don't know, hang out I guess," Alice answered the vague question. "Ride our bikes, watch TV. What do you do for fun?"

"Same stuff."

"Where's your school?" Carmen asked.

"It's gone."

"Gone?"

"Collapsed."

Carmen thought about the cracks that ran down the walls at his school.

"You don't go to school?"

"Miss Valerie teaches us."

"You find it weird," Nate asked Jeremiah while using a second helping to close the distance with him, "that there ain't no little ones here? No babies, no toddlers, or the like?

Kind of a family reunion that had gave up on the family."

Jeremiah looked down the line of tables and concurred by not contradicting the notion. "So," Bobby asked Jeremiah, "what'd you do?" He took a large forkful of meat and potatoes and stuffed them in his mouth while he waited for an answer. "I mean," he continued after swallowing after receiving no answer, "had to do something to get sent away, right? Something real bad to go to a camp."

"Think about what you jus' said, the logic of it," Nate interjected. "Would you, tasked with rebuilding, a town, the country, would you want people who done things real bad? Would you want that trouble?"

"Nah, of course not," he took a sip of soda, "but I heard you got rapists and kid touchers in those camps."

"And where did you hear that?"

"Can't recall," and he put another helping to his mouth, chewed and swallowed, then continued, "but I do remember that whoever told me it was real trustworthy."

"Well, be that so, it's incorrect."

"Hmm. He said that you, how'd he put it... that you 'take care' of them."

"Take care of them?"

"'Cleanse the Normal.' I remember he said that exactly 'cause it wasn't something I had heard before. 'The Normal,' you know?"

"I don't."

"You get rid of them, poof. They gone."

"Kinda hard to do that if we ain't got guns."

Bobby's thoughts ran through the alternatives—knives, baseball bats, arrows, the noose, and the bare hands around the throat. "That would be hard, wouldn't it? Rumors, huh?" He laughed disingenuously.

Eva cursed at herself internally. She wanted to ask Michael if he had a girlfriend but was too embarrassed to do it in front of others. There was opportunity earlier, and it was squandered.

"Have you ever had McDonald's?" a boy asked them.

"Of course," Carmen said. "Haven't you?"

"Once. Burger King?"

"Yeah."

"Can you really order pizza on the computer?"

"If you want to."

There was no point to the question, Eva concluded. He was leaving soon, and she had only met him. What good were thoughts upon which actions could not be taken?

"What plans," Valerie asked Nate, "do you have once the children have been returned?"

"Go back to the camp. Finish the job."

"And how far along are you?"

"Hard to say."

"Yeah? Why's that?"

"I don't know, hard to see it when you're in it I guess."

"That's understandable."

He looked up at her from his plate as she had not asked a question, and he wondered if there was more he could deduce from her mannerisms. When he could not, he set his fork to the side of the plate and wiped the corners of his lips with the hand towel that served as a napkin.

"Whatever the consequences of waiting," Nate said cordially, "this meal was worth it."

"Oh, yeah?"

"Best meal I've ever had. I mean that. Wow."

"And you, Jeremiah?" she asked.

"Delicious, miss, just delicious."

"Wonderful."

"But I'm afraid," Nate said as he stood, "that we must be going if we're gonna have enough time before sunrise."

Valerie herself stood, "Tessa, will you please let our other guests know that it is time to go?"

Tessa obliged and made the long walk to the other end of the tables.

"C'mon guys," as she made eye contact with each of the kids, "time to go." Alice and Carmen took the opportunity to chug their sodas before standing up. Michael looked at Tessa. Then Eva. Then down the row to Nate and Jeremiah standing off to the side with Valerie.

"I'm not leaving," Michael avowed as Alice and Carmen stood.

"Excuse me?" Tessa inquired.

"I'm staying."

Eva smiled involuntarily.

"Okay, kid. C'mon."

"No."

"Yeah, you're leaving," and she walked around the end of the table and pulled up on his arm.

"I ain't going!"

"Let him stay!" Eva said, unsure if her place was to intervene and became certain with Tessa's sneer.

Those closest took notice of the commotion, then the heads of those farther. Valerie, furthest from the din, side-stepped to see around Jeremiah and Nate and sighed—slight smile introduced at her lips. Cautious, as she did not know for sure the nature of their conversation, but she had to believe. The boy had told his friends what he had seen. They knew about Eva's mother; they would be the advocates she needed to convince Nate to take them from here. She beckoned Nate and Jeremiah to approach the kids.

"What is going on?" Valerie asked as she set herself next to Tessa.

"This boy doesn't want to go."

"Excuse me?"

"This one," Tessa pulled up on Michael's shirt at the shoulder.

"I see, and why don't you want to go?"

"I just, I just want to stay."

"We don't know that boy," Bobby said angrily as he approached and settled.

"And he is just a boy," Valerie declared empathetically.

"Yeah. So?"

"We should approach him as such."

"What?"

"Without venom, Robert. There is no reason for anger."

Valerie closed the distance and Bobby ceded his position, both physically and argumentatively. "Why don't you want to leave? Don't you want to go home?"

"No, ma'am."

"I see."

"Well what would you do if you stayed?"

"I don't know."

"He is a crafty one," Bobby interjected.

"Is that a good thing or a bad thing?" Valerie questioned.

"Here, it's good."

"I see."

"Can you vouch for him?" Tessa asked to no one, then turned to Nate.

He was caught off-guard by the question. "Who, me?"

"Yeah."

"I mean, he, I mean I've only known him for, shit, it's only been hours."

"More hours than we've known him. How long does it take to know a boy?"

"More than a day that's for sure."

The group turned to Valerie for a determination. Her thoughts, as had gone the entire day, compressed within the tight timeframe she had herself introduced. She had hoped to induce a trust in others that, within the realm of human relations, normally takes months, if not years. She had believed that her stature, her way with words to transfer understanding which had served her well would produce the outcome she desired. She had tested time, for it was constricting, and now she was faced with bringing in a young man who had convinced himself that this place was, if not Eden, better than his home.

"It'd be your job," Nate ordered Alice and Carmen with a pointed finger, "to explain that this was his choice. That we, me and him," he pointed to Jeremiah, "had nothin' to do with this. Hell, we don't want to be included in any of this. You get home, you say you just ran off and explored a bit. That's all."

"Do you know what you'd be getting into?" Valerie asked Michael.

"Yes, ma'am."

They had to leave, Valerie thought, how could she bring him into a new world only to have that world be taken? What if the new world was the one he was choosing not to return to? Could she control that? Could she say, anywhere but Marysville? Would that work? With Nathaniel? With NME, if they do come in as she was told?

"No!" followed by hard fists against the table. "No," Carmen repeated when all eyes were upon him, "we ain't leaving without him."

"This is my choice, Carmen."

"We came down here together. We got here together. We survived this together. We all go back or none of us go back."

"Aw, shit," Nate muttered.

"I'm not going back!"

"You have to," Alice said softly, "we have to."

"Why? What's back there for me? A shit home I get to come home to from a shit school. Ain't got no friends, what's the point?" He sunk back into the chair. "What's the point?"

"I'm your friend, Michael," Alice implored.

"Now you are, but when we get home, you'll be with your friends—your real friends—makin' fun of me." He looked over to Carmen, "what about you Carmen, are you going to say you're my friend too?"

"No," he said and sat in the chair nearest Michael, "no I'm not. We brothers. Brothers go through shit like this, and I ain't leaving without a brother, my brother."

"Sure," Michael said half-heartedly and looked away.

"Hey, look at me." Michael disobeyed. "Look at me." Slowly he turned. "We're not out of it yet, we still have to get home. I can't, we can't, do this without you. And once we get home, if anyone fucks with you. At school. At the field.

Anywhere, I promise you, I will make them pay."

"Me too," Alice added with conviction.

"Do I have to go to my house?"

That consideration had not occurred to Carmen. "Not tonight," he answered, "and not tomorrow," as that was all he could promise.

Michael stood up from his chair and took notice of the crowd who had heard every word. His vulnerabilities, his fears, and his sensitivity that contradicted his belief that he was a man. Valerie was relieved with his choice. Eva rued the loss of whom she felt a soulmate, and upon the calculation of another one despaired. She thought about standing up and declaring her intention to go with them, but she could not leave her mother. Nate ticked with the waning sunlight. Jeremiah was comfortable in his role as spectator, finding no right or wrong as it just was. Bobby rolled a small piece of pavement under his shoe, upset that he had come so close to having a protégé only for it to slip away. Tessa kept her worry for Alice, and Randy belched under his breath.

42

"I saw one," Michael said faintly in the quiet, positioned between Alice and Carmen in the backseat of the cab.

"Saw one what?" Alice asked.

"A Frog People. A Frog Person."

'Eden,' read the broad side of the semi. The rainbow and the apple tree. Protocol dictated that at least two armed citizens be involved with any intruders, especially at the borders. Tessa had taken position several feet from Valerie, while Bobby, with the radio microphone embedded in his ear, tossed the black duffel into the truck bed then took his position near Nate and Jeremiah.

"These children," Valerie said, holding a flower-patterned tote bag close enough to the truck that she could reach out and touch it if she wished, "they are now in your charge. I expect great care to be taken." Nate nodded his understanding.

Alice rested her feet on ammunition boxes as Carmen and Michael rested theirs on barrels and stocks—too exhausted having not truly slept in two days to wonder or hypothesize their need.

"She was very nice," Michael continued. "And very pretty."

"Pretty?" Carmen asked, for the adjective did not fit with his imagination.

"Yes."

"But did she..." Alice started to ask.

"Yeah."

"It's true, though?" Carmen asked.

"Yeah, I seen it with my own eyes."

"I wish I had seen it."

Michael's breath pulled in, deep and held before he allowed it to exit. "No, you don't."

Valerie took a step towards Nate, "have you given any thought, or come to a conclusion, about what we discussed?"

"I have not. I mean I have given it thought, jus' have not come to a conclusion. The logistics of the thing an' all."

"Well, I hope to see you again."

Michael's eyes began to waver, and he set his head against the hard rubber door frame. "It was more sad than anything." He yawned.

"Would you really have stayed if you could've?" Alice asked him.

"Yeah, yeah I would've."

"I couldn't do it, couldn't leave everything."

"Are you worried about what your dad will say?" Carmen asked Alice. "About your cheek?"

"Nah, but my mom's going to kill me." She turned and looked out the window. "Maybe I should stay, just gonna be dead tomorrow anyways."

More time, Valerie thought, would have allowed her more opportunities to persuade him to return. Perhaps the bible, its allegories pertinent to their situation. More stories of those who had perished or were about to. She envisioned letting him enter her, of womanly seduction and consummation—the thought of which made her blush. She did not press the issue further, as uncertainty was more palatable than denial. "Well, you should be going."

"Yes, we should be getting on."

"Here," she extended her hand, "for your travels."

"Thank you kindly," as he took the handles of the tote. He stood in awkward silence as she stared at him, for he was unsure if she would say more. The silence caused Bobby and Tessa to look back over their shoulders. They watched as Nate turned to the truck, pulled open the door and slid into the cab.

"Goodbye, Jeremiah," and she walked to where he had been standing quietly and enveloped his large frame in embrace. He reciprocated, as he felt there was no other choice, his arms around her and he squeezed once, then released and got into the truck. Nate pushed the 'start' button and the engine cranked. He turned the steering wheel hard left, then reversed and repeated the process until the truck faced opposite within the confined space between the rows of cars. Michael thought of his life in Eden with Eva. Carmen wondered if his mother would slap him or hug him, or both. Alice had exhausted her thoughts and stared out the window as the idle cars hypnotized her.

Nate set the GPS for Marysville, which gave him a question mark in lieu of an estimated time of arrival. A warning of unmanaged roads and unknown traffic conditions. With deftness opposite the warnings he maneuvered the truck out from the slender entry to Eden, through the suburban remnants overgrown and back out onto the country roads that led north.

"Why didn't you ask to stay?" Nate asked Jeremiah.

Jeremiah was at first taken off-guard by the question, and it took him some time to find a suitable response. "It wasn't my decision to make."

"I guess, but there's no decision if you don't ask."

"Maybe I just didn't want to hear an answer."

"I guess. I guess. Would you have wanted to stay, if they had offered?"

"Yes."

"Then you should have asked!"

"It's not that simple."

"Sure it is, you ask, if they say yes, you just stay."

Jeremiah turned to look at him and judged whether his line of thought should be vocalized.

"And do what? Be what?"

"I don't know. Live? Be free?"

"Free within the confines of how they live, how they want me to live."

"That don't make no sense."

"Ask the black boy in the back in a few years if it makes sense. Hell, ask him now." Jeremiah craned his neck to the rear and started to speak but stopped himself before any vocalization. Carmen was asleep, his head rested against Alice who was, herself, sleeping. He could hear Michael's snores without having to turn his neck further, but he did anyway.

He thought about what the boy had told his friend. About being brothers, about how he wasn't leaving without him. If he was going to live anywhere, it'd be where these kids lived. At least, Jeremiah thought, there was hope, and hope would push him to overcome the comfort of the camp, of its logical extension of the prisons he had become accustomed to. He was someone in the camp, but not the someone he wanted to be, and a purported paradise was something to be wary of when the promise to people like him had been broken ad nauseam.

Yet here, next to him, was a man who knew his secrets. Knew what he had not done to get to the camp and what he had done once inside. A leader of faux justice thrust upon him without choice. In the bright, fluorescent room where it was decided. Handed down by white men in polo shirts and khakis—more approachable than suit jackets.

Without choice they made him choose, let the dregs of society, determined rightly or wrongly, breathe free and exist in the same "freedom" of the camp as you, you who have earned your way, or take them to the trees for their perverse wickedness. Be righteous, be swift, and be decisive. Be these things and be a leader of men, eat your meals at the captain's table. Be someone of consequence in this world, be a man that is close to God and that man matters.

The time had passed to do right in a normal world, or had it? Help us, and help the woman and children sleep soundly at night. Without the worry of vile men stalking innocence and we, we men in polos and khakis, will see that you are compensated for your righteous actions, that you will be set free and can return to your home. To your woman and your children. The choice is yours, to stay here *indefinitely*, you three-strike insignificant, or know that once your quota has been met, we will come for you, you righteous man, and set you free.

The sun fell behind the trees, and its pointed brilliance seemed to melt into the purples and reds and oranges spread out against the horizon. Jeremiah rolled the passenger window down several inches to shake the memories from his mind and asked, "Do you think that food was, you know..."

"Irradiated?"

"Yeah, I mean it comes from the ground."

"Yeah, but it was good, huh?"

Jeremiah laughed, "Yeah, it was damn good."

"Fast-food ain't good for you either, but it's good too, right?"

"That ain't the same thing."

"Yeah, but it makes me feel better about it to think it is." Nate turned the wheel and headed into the brush to avoid a fallen tree. The tires fell into hidden ruts then caught a grip and he returned to the road to continue on more suitable ground. "Thanks for not sayin' nothin', you know, when I was fibbing about the camps."

"Well, you were doing such a good job of it."

"Yeah, it wasn't my first time doing it. What's in that bag?"

Jeremiah reached down, took the bag from between his legs and set it on his lap. "Got water, looks like brownies or something, and a bunch of leftovers."

"That it?"

He slid his hand around the inner sides of the tote, "Yeah."

"No note or nothin'?"

"Nope, just water, sweets, and food."

Nate cursed to himself. He had hoped for a note, a letter, something, no matter what it had said. Anything, anything at all to show desperation, a last plea. The lack thereof put the decision, its hypotheticals, and its morality on him. She had somehow asked for help while seemingly not asking. A directive given from a place of strength, and he could not figure out how she did it.

This, more than the actual decision, bothered him greatly. Stay, and feel the weight of death, innocent death. Return, and he would feel as a servant rather than a savior. He drove onward. Dusk set in. The automatic headlamps turned on but were still balanced with the outside light. It was the dials, the tachometer and the speedometer coming alive that the driver and passenger noticed. Realized the darkness was upon them and Nate only knew the road ahead in daylight. He knew the importance of returning the children safely, and soon. He was nervous.

43

Nate unscrewed the gas cap, lifted the first plastic can to the opening and angled the funnel until he heard the gulp. He could feel the presence of Reactor 3 even though it was hidden in the natural darkness. Far from the truck's high beams. Steeped in the semi-clouded starlight and waning moon. Stopped at the edge of the bridge. The idle of the engine, the water below, the *yip* of coyotes. He lifted the can to remove the remaining gas then set it on the ground and repeated the process with the second. Gulp. Lift. The empty vessels returned to the bed. He set the cap flush and turned it until the click. Pressed the cover until the snap. Walked with his feet over scattered gravel and swore, but did not believe. He saw something in the wilderness across the bridge as he froze next to the driver's door.

He opened the door and stood behind it. Watched. The strobe of lights in motion within the trees. "You see that?"

"Yeah," Jeremiah said, only loud enough to rise above the engine. "I see that." It was a speck still. A flicker. "Should we go back?"

"Gotta be them looking for the kids. Shit, I thought we had more time."

"Should we turn around?"

"'Have supper, I insist.' Shit. Running ain't a good idea."

"Why's that?"

"Well, we seen them, chances are they seen us. If we turn around that implies guilt. And even if they don't, they're already out here lookin' so it doesn't matter much anyways. And is there even a different way? I don't know."

"What does this mean? I mean, for us?"

"It means there's gonna be a lot of men in suits at the camp soon. Shit."

"So we don't move?"

"Nope, just wait here and take our licks."

The road running south towards the bridge bent slowly and the overgrowth made movement slow. Nate stayed behind the open door as the minutes elapsed, the low beams curving as the vehicle made the turn, the lights almost upon the structure. Cautious as it approached the southern side of the bridge and rolled to a stop. The driver flicked on the high beams, edged forward, then reversed and reset in front of the northern lanes. Slowly he went, stopped at the apex and did—nothing.

"Hello there!" Nate yelled towards the idling pickup truck at the bridge's precipice.

Michael was the first to wake up, relieved he was still in a strange land. He shook Carmen's shoulder, and his movement from Alice's body woke her.

"Nate Jones! Operations Manager! Federal Bureau of Prisons!" He waited for a response and heard only a wayward coyote. The headlights blinded his view into the cab, "I have the kids, they're fine!"

There was again no response, no movement. "Something ain't right," he said to his travel companions.

"What's not right?" Alice asked.

"This. These people, these people do not do subtle."

"What do we do?" Michael asked.

"Hand me a gun."

Michael looked on the floor. "Which one?"

"A long one."

Alice, closest to the stocks, reached down and picked up a gun at random. Jeremiah pulled the barrel through the opening between the two front seats. With limited movement Nate took the weapon. "Hello there!" he yelled again as he checked the chamber. "Are you with B.O.P.?"

The door opened and a figure gradually emerged, shadowy behind the headlights and mirrored Nate's position. "What's your business here?"

"Just heading to another camp," the man said, his voice raised to cover the distance.

"Ain't no camp this way."

"I knew this didn't look right. Musta got turned around, GPS on the fritz in my truck."

"What camp you comin' from?"

"Douglas."

"Why you traveling at night?"

"Was about to ask you the same thing."

"What's your name?"

The man hesitated, "Mason, yours?"

"Jones. Which camp you heading to?"

"Lawton."

"Well Lawton ain't this way."

"Well what is this way? Seems like you're coming from somewhere?"

"Got lost myself. Ain't nothin' back that way." Nate looked inside the truck, the kids' heads straining to see out the windshield. "Get your asses down." Three heads turned towards him from the backseat. "Now," he commanded harshly. "You too, Jeremiah." He returned to his position once they had complied. "You know, this is kinda silly, yellin' across a bridge like this. Let's talk up between the pickups."

"It is silly. You first," Mason requested as he leveled the AR-15 and pointed it in the direction of Nate's voice and neither moved.

"How's Douglas?" Nate asked during the stalemate. "Haven't been there in a while." Ten seconds, then twenty.

"It's fine, just fine," Mason broke into the silence and when he did Nate slunk down. Sidled around the back of the truck until he emerged on the passenger side and set a new position in the muddy dark near the bridge's beginning. "You there, Jones?" Nate didn't answer. "Jones?" Mason repeated, and the silence agitated. "This is the way to Eden, isn't it? Isn't it?!" His patience extinguished and was replaced with the pull of a trigger. The bullets pelted the open door and shattered the window. One wayward shot through the windshield and out the back window. The kids held each other, pushed each other down further into the floor, hoping that it would envelop them. Jeremiah slumped down as well, but his size kept him exposed.

Nate relaxed in the cacophony, his breaths calm, the gun an extension of himself—it breathed with him. There was nothing but the muzzle flash, the curvature of the bridge, and the estimation of body size who's only clue was the voice. He pulled the trigger. A millimeter adjustment and again. An adjustment and again. And again.

He walked backwards and sideways to the rear of the truck and up towards the driver's door of broken glass. "Stay down!" he directed as three heads raised up from the backseat then disappeared. He climbed into the truck and inched it forward onto the bridge, the door still open and his left shoe dragging. He turned the wheel to fully illuminate Mason's lifeless body. Shift into park, out with the gun and knelt to inspect—two bullet wounds, one through the chest which left a hole in the purple D.O.C. shirt. One above his eye. He set the gun on the pavement, lifted Mason from under his armpits and dragged him to the concrete barrier that separated the height from the river. He strained his ears to hear the body hit the water, but the rush of the rapids made it impossible. "God's will," Nate muttered to himself, half sarcastic and half reflective. He looked up from his contemplation to see the three heads once again straining from the backseat. Jeremiah, too, was watching. He walked over to Mason's truck to cut the engine and the headlights shut off.

"When you tell them what happened," Nate said after he closed the truck door, and as he carefully picked away the remaining shards left in the window opening, "the police, your parents, let's leave this part out."

"Have you ever killed someone?" Carmen asked slowly, "I mean, before today."

Nate's breaths were quick. Elongated. The aftermath of anxiety followed by false calm followed by chaos. It took him some time to respond, to settle his heart. "Yes."

"What's it feel like?"

"Not good." He set the gun between the seat and the center console. Douglas had been compromised, and there was no telling how many more were out there. "It doesn't feel good." He shifted into drive, cut around the vacant truck and left the bridge.

44

Sleep was impossible. Alice looked out her window, Michael out his. Carmen looked between the two but mostly focused through the windshield. Nate kept steady, fixated on the terrain and the GPS until it became unnecessary as they passed the sign that read "Welcome to Andersonville." The roads were still cracked, there was still debris scattered, but this was now the route he had traveled a hundred times. Perhaps more.

Each looked out from the backseat and remembered. Michael, fondly of Andersonville where they had escaped. Alice, a shudder on Main Street where the boars had trampled. Carmen, solemn at the marquee where the dead family huddled under blankets, skeletal in theater number four. The bridge where Carmen had frozen aloft, and now the gate swung open for the truck and there was no need for acrobatics.

Nate entered the highway at the first feel of dawn, the last stretch home. Mile markers descended. 107. 101. 98. "Wait!" Carmen exclaimed. "I mean, slow down."

"Why?" Nate asked.

"Just do it, please." Nate reluctantly lowered the speed. "It's coming up."

"What's comin' up?"

"Just wait." A half-mile elapsed. "Here, stop here."

"Oh shit," Alice said, propping herself up to see out the windshield, "our bikes."

They slipped out of the cab and each took the handlebars.

"You know you can't go past the barrier," Nate said, almost apologetic.

"I thought you said they don't track," Jeremiah said while turning the red bracelet around his wrist.

"Yeah, well, they might not care where you go inside, but I'm not sure about out there. Don't want to risk it and that means I gotta leave you here."

"Yeah."

"Yeah. You should let the boy drive." Jeremiah said to Nate.

"What?"

"The boy that got them here, Michael, let him drive."

"Why?"

"Let him finish what he started."

"Can't risk that neither."

The truck bounced, and they both turned towards the perceived source. Michael stood in the bed, reached down, took the duffel bag over his shoulder, and leapt down. "What you doin?" Nate asked him.

"Getting' my bag."

"Nah, put it back and put your bikes up."

"Why?"

"Why? Cause it's my job to get you home and I intend on doing just that."

"Why, we got our bikes?"

"You think I'm gonna let you ride your bikes in the dark? No, I'm taking you home."

"We can do it," Alice added.

"It's so close," said Carmen.

"Exactly," Nate scolded, "what does it matter? Ain't no difference between me dropping you off and you riding your bikes, 'cept longer."

"What if we drive behind them?" Jeremiah asked Nate.

"There's no point to that."

"Let them finish it."

"This is finished. Over." To the kids, "get in the truck!"

"No," Alice responded, "no disrespect or nothing, but we have to ride our bikes back."

"You don't have to do nothin'."

They had lined their bikes next to each other in a united front, Alice's a half-foot forward. "Then let me drive," Michael bargained, and Carmen and Alice felt it was an agreeable compromise.

"Ain't no way."

"Then we're riding our bikes," Alice decided.

"Why? Why does it matter?"

"Because we did this," Carmen said as he inched his bicycle forward, "we started this, and we have to finish this. Together."

"Shit."

"I told you to let the boy drive," Jeremiah said smugly, respectfully.

"Shit."

"Do you promise not to die?" Nate asked in all seriousness.

"What?" all three responded, having felt they had not heard correctly.

"Between here and home, do you promise not to die?"

"Yes," Michael answered, "yes we do," as the precondition was acceptable.

"No fallin' off your bike, no scrapes, no broken bones, no nothin'."

"That ain't dying," Alice clapped and received stern looks from both sides of her bike. Nate, too, threw a look her way from the truck cab.

He inhaled. Held. Exhaled. "Go quick and go safe."

The kids turned the handlebars north and pushed with their feet against the pavement. "Hey," Alice said, turning her head back, "Mr. Jones? Mr. Jeremiah?"

"Yeah?" Nate answered and Jeremiah looked.

"Thank you. For everything."

Nate saw the sincerity on each young face and nodded. They pushed off, caught the balance and pedaled forward in the light of the high beams behind them.

"Think there's more out there?" Jeremiah asked Nate. "From Douglas?"

"I've thought on that. Seems unlikely and besides, they come this way we'll see them." The dawn peeked. "Might have a bunch of new ones to bring in soon, depending on what happened there."

"Think we'll shit green from that food?" Carmen asked. "Radioactive green?"

"Gross," Alice responded. "Why does your shirt say, 'it's all apples, baby!'?"

"What?"

"That shirt they gave you, in Eden. 'Smith family reunion, it's all apples, baby!'."

"I don't know. Didn't really think about it."

"It bothers the hell outta me."

"Why?"

"I don't know, but it has since you got it."

"Does it really bother you?"

"So much."

They rode as instructed. Quickly. Safely. Their shadows produced by the truck's lights fell away until they were imperceptible.

"How many people did we see dead?" Carmen asked.

"Four," Alice answered quickly, "but one was alive first."

"Five if you count Eva's momma," Michael offered, "she's about to die, probably."

"Think those guys at the camp were gonna get killed?" Alice wondered aloud.

Carmen thought about it, "So more than five."

As the eastern hue grew lighter, they could see the blurry signs alit in civilization. McDonald's yellow. Taco Bell purples. Green sun over white BP. The cars against the highway barriers, whose frames had been shadows become more defined. They pedaled at a steady pace and spoke no words as there were none.

Michael thought about Eva. How he regretted his harsh words. How the reality of his return was now real and how his life would be had he stayed. Where he would have slept. Breakfast in that kitchen, for he had not been in another in Eden and could not imagine another. What she would be wearing this morning. How she would smell and what she would say.

Carmen prepared himself for the beating of a lifetime. Not literally, but the verbal storm that awaited him made him pine for the preciseness and quickness of a switch across his bare ass. He had apologized to his mother for his transgression a hundred times as it was happening. As a passenger. In the cars, in the trucks, and he could not wait to be past its reality. He found it odd how much he missed his brother, the visceral emotion he felt.

Alice, too, had apologized. She had explained the slice in her cheek in different tones and in different ways. She thought about kissing Carmen and how long ago it felt. How insignificant it felt now, where at the time it felt momentous. Death, she thought, makes everything inconsequential. Makes everything small and petty, but in those moments, with death hidden in the shadows, those things feel extremely important.

'Next Exit—Marysville.' They saw headlights on the bridge ahead and pedaled faster. Their taste for adventure was exhausted, replaced with the comfort of home. Familiar streets and established faces. The water trucks and the minor tremors that soothed them to sleep like the distant train whistle or summer rain. The curvature of pillows and the firmness of a mattress. Known. Reassuring.

Alice led them up the embankment and was the first through the hole in the fence and into the tall grass. Then Carmen, and finally Michael. They set their feet again on the pedals and rode down the sidewalk. Past the fast-food chains with breakfast menus, stopped as a car exited the drive-thru lane and turned right then continued. Past Wu's Army Surplus and Pawn Shop, the doors and windows protected by a diamond patterned metal fence. Across Main Street and the train tracks and into a neighborhood—their neighborhood.

They stopped at an intersection; it was time for one to leave the trio. The sun had just about made its first appearance, its first true mark on the day. They stayed silent where the sidewalks intersected and dipped to the street. There wasn't time yet to unpack what they had done, what they had seen. They didn't want to let it go and at the same time wanted it to end.

It was Michael who dropped his bike first and embraced her. There was no hesitation as she wrapped her arms around him and pulled him tight. Carmen joined, wrapping his arms around both of them and they held each other tightly until a passing car made them aware of the oddity for any passerby. The two boys stepped back and she took her bike by the handlebars. She lingered on them for a moment, then turned and rode down the street.

A man stood on his front porch in a bathrobe and watched Carmen and Michael pedal down the sidewalk. A dog barked from beyond a fence. A car drove by, then another. "Did you mean what you said?" Michael asked as they turned down Carmen's street, "about being brothers?"

"Fuck yes I did."

"I mean, cause you said it when we were there and now, we're here."

"I meant it no matter where we are. Here, there, wherever."

They pulled on the brakes and settled the bikes on Carmen's lawn. "If my mom kills me, you can have my bike." He led Michael to the front door, turned the knob and thought about climbing through a window as he had done many times before and at the camp. "It's a nice bike," he added, and then knocked.

She pulled back the curtain from the windowpanes and before she could unlock the door and swing it open her eyes swelled. "My baby!" and she yanked him from the ground and squeezed him. "My baby," as tears fell from her cheeks. "Dorian! Wake up! Dorian!"

"I can't breathe!" Carmen let out from his compressed lungs. "Ma!" She released him reluctantly and ran her hands over his head and down the sides of his face. Dorian appeared in the door frame and reacted as she had. If this is how I die, Carmen thought as his brother squeezed him, then that would be alright.

In giving Dorian his turn at embrace she noticed Michael standing a few feet back. "Come here, child," she said. "I'm so glad you're alright," as she hugged him. "We were so worried about all y'all." Michael reached around her waist and felt warmth. Felt comfort naturally and guilt that perplexed him. That she should be the first to pull him tight, and that what he had run from was the same that, at this moment, drew him back.

"I have to go home," he said as he released from her. "I have to go home."

"But you said…" Carmen started.

"I have to go home," and the duffel bag separated then returned to his back as he lifted his leg over the crossbar. Pushed against the grass until the momentum allowed him to set his feet on the pedals. He passed two houses, and without words, Carmen was pulled back into his mother's clutch.

The coffee mug shattered on the kitchen floor. Linoleum sheen. Faux marble tile. "Robbie!" she screamed. "Robbie!" Alice's mother dropped to her knees and beckoned her to open arms. Their ears touched and Maggie's hand pulled against the back of her head. She released her grip and her hands rounded Alice's head until they were against her cheek. She had not noticed the bandage until she felt it, for the light in her daughter's eyes was all that mattered at that first glimpse of her breathing soul. Alice had chosen, before opening the door, to show strength, to show she had grown—before any apology. Yet as she stared into her mother's watery eyes, she had no control over her own.

Michael imagined the empty beer cans strewn about the living room. On the coffee table. The end table. Balanced on the arm of the sofa. The stale smell of dust and dirty clothes piled and decaying food next to the full sink.

He pulled the screen door then pushed the wooden door. "It's clean," Michael said, still near the door. The aroma remained, but there were no cans, no fast-food wrappers, nothing except the furniture, the television, and a pile of clothes neatly folded on the couch.

"Water comin' next week, good water," his father said from the couch, centered with his back straight. "Got an appointment between one and four. Tuesday."

"Okay."

"These are all clean for you," he looked to the pile of clothes next to him. "Went to the laundromat."

"Okay."

"I thought I lost you."

"Well, I'm back."

"You hungry?"

"Nah. Just tired."

"Bed's made up."

"Think I'll sleep out back."

"Okay."

"For now."

"You thirsty?"

"I got water in my bag."

"Alright."

Michael stood for a few seconds before walking through the room. Through the kitchen. Unlatched the hook on the screen door that led to the backyard and made his way to the metal shed with warning to trespassers written on the doors.

45

Up the wooded hill. The crunch of footsteps among the twigs. Decaying leaves. Neon green lights intermittent on wrists. Flashlights. They caught glimpses. Footfalls. Scraped bark. The undersides of leaves among branches still vibrant aloft. Coiled rope flung over them. Soft sobs. Coiled rope returning to the earth. "D.O.C." A man. "Camp A." Another. Wrists bound with zip ties. The third man squirmed out of his captor's grasp and started down the hill only to trip over a tree root hidden among the plants and in the darkness. The captor gauged his steps, as did two others unbound as they reached the man slithering, digging his feet into the dirt to propel himself down. The captor reached him and set his boot against the back of the man's neck, pushing his face into the earth. All else becomes secondary when the air, which has not disappeared, becomes trapped before one's lungs. The two others took a leg and dragged him back up the hill. What were muffled screams into soil shrieked. Begged. Threatened.

It was understood he would be first. They held him against the tree. At his shoulders. At his chin, yet the man would not be placated so they returned him to the earth where the rope could be applied. Face down. Suffocated. Released. Suffocated. Released, and Jeremiah slid the rope over the top of his head. The friction burned over his eyes. Wayward fibers bristled his nostrils, that odd sensation of life that he felt through the precarious moment. Stuck upon his chin then freed to broach his neck.

Jeremiah adjusted the noose until it was tight, pushed himself up with fists in the ground and the assistance of a low branch nearest the trunk. He took the rope that was handed to him and to his left the other two men had been prepared. He, an anomaly of strength, of size, held his rope without assistance, whereas two prisoners were assigned the other ropes. Those with flashlights focused on the condemned. The wolves did not howl. The coyotes forbade their young from yipping, and the boars dared not grunt—they sensed the death before it was.

The escapee ceased his protest. Societal norms, in this instance, the quiet, made him uncomfortable to be speaking out of turn. Had he been the only one with a rope around his neck, perhaps his reaction would have been different. The longing for action grew, that desire to complete morally ambiguous tasks as quickly as possible, without of course, depreciating the rite. A flashlight turned from the condemned to Jeremiah's face. Seven seconds of quiet reflection and he nodded. With that, the men pulled hard on the ropes which made the bark fall from the branches until they slid into the grooves made by previous events.

The flashlights followed the figures into the air. How their legs kicked. How their veins pulsed, and their faces contorted. There were some who watched intently. Others looked away, kicked the leaves, and imagined being somewhere else. One put his hands over his crotch to hide his growing erection. Jeremiah held the rope with ease which allowed his mind to retract. There was no reaction as there was no thought, at least none of consequence. He held tight, feeling through it the violence, the realization, and finally, the acceptance. Protocol dictated that they hold for two minutes once the last movement had been felt. Explicitly felt, not seen.

They did not slit the necks to insure death. No, they slit them as a signal. A signal to the wolves and coyotes and boars that the deed was done. Men coiled the ropes. Men with flashlights led them down the hill and as they crossed the abandoned football field the animals sounded their intent to ravage the meat left behind.

Men passed Nate as he stood under the 'Welcome to Bison Country' sign at the entrance to the field. "You met your quota," he said to Jeremiah, who wanted to walk past him instead of engaging. "You know what that means." However stoic Jeremiah seemed, the events had, as they always had, affected him deeply. "It means you get to leave. It means you get to go home."

He nodded slightly as he left Nate standing under the sign and walked to his trailer. He pushed the door open and it squeaked. By memory in the darkness he grabbed the LED lantern that was on the kitchenette counter and brought it into a bedroom. He clicked the button, it set light across the room and he placed it on the floor between the bunks. With a thump he fell into the lower bed along the near wall and exhaled. Stared.

"I heard you make speeches on the football field," a voice said from the top bunk opposite his. Jeremiah did not expect the voice, but it did not startle him. "Make us feel right about it, get us in the right mindset." Jeremiah turned his head, but the voice's origin was unseen in the angle. "I feel sick, a little, being my first time and all, but I guess you get used to it."

"There's no getting used to it," Jeremiah said quietly. Murmurs of men grew louder, peaked near the window, then receded.

"But you do it to get your freedom."

"Nah, it makes you more of a slave."

"How? It gets you outta here. You're getting out of here, hit your quota I heard."

"That doesn't make me free."

"Yeah," the voice agreed, then swung its legs over and they dangled below the top bunk. Jeremiah looked again. A boy, maybe 18 but looked younger. Black, like himself, yet the opposite in all other respects. Thin, and one would consider him sickly if his voice had not been strong, coherent. Eyes unsettled, as a child on his first day of school, which the situation mostly resembled. The camp uniform loose about his frame. "I don't understand."

"You're a passenger now, probably been for a while, maybe all your life. Someone took you, from your home, from your street, from your car."

"Who?"

"The police."

"Got me in my car."

"Got you in your car. Then they put you in their car. Drove you to their house. Put you in their cell. See, you were a passenger then, to your lawyer, to your judge, to the cops that brought you back to that cell. How'd you get here?"

"A train."

"Were you the conductor?"

"Huh?"

"Did you drive that train?"

"No."

"Did you take the wheel when they put you on that bus?"

"Course not."

"Did you want to go up that hill tonight?"

"I want my freedom."

"That's not what I asked."

"These are evil people."

"So you righteous now? Doing God's work?"

"In a way, yeah."

"Did God come down from the heavens and tell you? Tell you to do this?"

"Course not."

"Then who did?"

"They..."

"They did. And what did they say was in it for you?"

"My freedom."

"Your freedom. Do you feel free right now?"

"Well, no, cause I ain't hit my quota yet."

Jeremiah left the conversation to consider his impending exit through the grated underbelly of the bunk above. He thought about seeing his mother, what she would say and how, upon his appearance, she would realize he was no longer her "baby boy." There was a part of him that didn't believe it would be real. That there would be a hiccup, a complication that would keep him here. "Why didn't you make a speech tonight?" the voice questioned.

Jeremiah rolled towards the wall and pulled lightly on the peeling wallpaper. The faded flower imprinted. The decaying green dye. The glisten of the dried glue exposed. He considered not returning home. To start a new life with an imaginary wife. Playing catch in a front yard in some generalized suburban landscape. Waving to the neighbors as they drove by in their minivan, the children shaded within the tinted glass. A playful tackle as they fell to the freshly mown grass. No alarms, and no surprises. No more a passenger, and as his eyes closed, he fended off the reality that would hinder this daydream at every turn. No more a passenger, at least not tonight.

46

A leaf fell from the elm. A deep orange that transitioned to a potent red and it nestled between blades of grass that ran between the train station parking lot and Main Street. Another alit from the tree, then another from its arbor neighbor. Four children straddled their bicycles upon the grass patterned sparsely with the Fall canvas.

"Down the stairs! Single file!" an officer in olive green barked over the din of the Texas Eagle's engine. The men did as they were told, one by one exiting the dark interior of the train car in purple shirts and matching pants. 'D.O.C.' and 'Camp D' imprinted. White zip handcuffs and red bracelets. This was new to them. Marysville, its signature aroma like that of any town, ventured for the first time. The amalgam of foliage and food and location.

They lined up where they were told, twenty feet from the train and facing away. Near the simple sign that read "Marysville." Facing Main Street, their last glimpse of The Normal. The abandoned strip mall with its diner. The liquor store with its neon. Each had their own feelings about the setting. Regret. Indifference. Failure. Hatred. Each had their own reaction to the kids on bikes idled on the grassy lawn. Jealousy. Regret. Arousal. Some remembered themselves at that age. The innocence that bordered on true consequences. What paths were laid before them and what paths were chosen. Fatalism, free will, and the gray area between.

The sun arced towards its destination. Three patrol cars with lights but no sirens came from the West. Two from the east. Fast on the brakes and out with guns prepared. They waited in blue with the guards in green. A prisoner coughed, then spit. The train waited.

In the sporadic traffic of Saturday pre-dusk appeared the white charter bus with its coat of dirt that splatted within the wheel wells. Up onto the paint. "New Madrid Energy." Its blue flame logo. Nate turned the bus into the parking lot, and through the tinted windows, he glimpsed the kids looking up at him.

The air brakes hissed, and the doors opened. Jeremiah stepped down, his frame filling the exit. Protocol dictated that he be zip tied. Dictated that his hands be behind his back from the moment he left the camp through to his release. The danger of prisoners, protocol told, is that they are unpredictable, even when the situation cannot conceive of such behavior.

Nate exited after him, the limp from the prosthetic noticeable to the prisoners aligned. Protocol had informed them to look for weakness and perceive it immediately for an advantageous position.

"Stop here," he told Jeremiah as they were several feet from one of the guards. Another guard positioned himself behind the large man. Zip tied. Compliant. He took a tool from his belt that resembled two small Allen wrenches side by side but cut intricately at the ends. He held Jeremiah's wrist steady as he set the tool into the two holes barely perceptible near the digital readout on his red bracelet. He turned the device, the bracelet separated, and he stepped back with the band in his grip.

"Let's go," the guard in front ordered, and Jeremiah lumbered up the steps and disappeared inside The Texas Eagle.

"Get in line!" an officer in blue yelled as he took up position in front of the bus. "Here!" The prisoners complied, maintained their racial self-segregation.

"Welcome to Missouri!" Nate barked over the Texas Eagle's engine as he stood between the bus and the prisoners. "Gentlemen," he continued as he started to pace, "we all know what the alternative is to be standin' here right now, so consider yourselves lucky." He raised the tablet that he held in his grip and turned it on. Pressed. Swiped. Pressed. "You are about to transition," he read aloud, "from the custody of the Federal Department of Corrections, from here on known as D.O.C., to the custody of New Madrid Energy, Incorporated, from here on known as NME. However, you will remain under the jurisdiction of D.O.C. and are bound by their rules. D.O.C. regulations supersede..."

"I'm hungry," Michael said over the train's engine.

"You're always hungry," Alice responded plainly, the long scar formed and settled down her cheek.

"He's a growing boy!" Carmen yelled and grabbed his crotch.

"Gross!"

"I want tacos," Michael petitioned.

"You always want tacos," Carmen countered.

"They're cheap."

"Fuck tacos."

"I want tacos," Alice said, and Michael knew he had won. Carmen shot her a look with squinted eyes, to which she responded by sticking out her tongue and blowing. He reluctantly put his foot on a pedal and pushed off towards the fast-food sirens that rose above the street in the distance. Alice ran next to her bike to gain speed, then threw herself onto the seat.

"You know that's not real meat, right? In those tacos?" Carmen told Alice as they rode next to each other.

"It sure tastes like it."

"Well," Michael said as he watched Nate continue reading from the tablet, "this is where it all starts. Now you seen it."

"Yeah," Eva said softly.

"C'mon," he implored and turned his bicycle. For a few moments she kept her position, eyes fixed on Nate as he read aloud to the prisoners. The charter bus and the deep roar of The Texas

Eagle. Michael didn't rush her, as he remembered all the times he watched the scene unfold and wondered what lay beyond. For her, he assumed, it was about what had come before—and he would not be the one to stop short her thoughts. On her own time, she walked her bike to the sidewalk, and he followed. A last glance, and she pushed off and pedaled down the sidewalk with Michael next to her, a leisurely pace towards the orange spread of the setting sun as the cars rushed down Main Street.

Other books by Steven W. Simon

Red as Apple

It has been years since Keenan had been to the farm. He had vowed to move on, to move up, but this has brought him back. To his introverted older brother and confident sister. After this, their lives will never be the same.

Out Pondered the Hare
Poetry

A collection of poems written in sobriety. Or a Lorazepam fog. A whiskey-infused detour and lysergic-stamped synapses. All in the hopes that some of this makes sense to those who were not there in those specific instances where there is truth.

1200 Miles from Los Angeles

When his car breaks down on his way to Los Angeles, Sanford takes a job at a small-town diner along the interstate to earn the money he needs to keep going west. He learns that his religion means something different there - for better or worse.

stevensimonbooks.com
boundharepress.com